Billionaire

Peter James

W F HOWES LTD

This large print edition published in 2017 by
W F Howes Ltd
Unit 5, St George's House, Rearsby Business Park,
Gaddesby Lane, Rearsby, Leicester LE7 4YH

1 3 5 7 9 10 8 6 4 2

First published in the United Kingdom in 1983
by W. H. Allen

A CIP catalogue record for this book is available
from the British Library

ISBN 978 1 51004 656 6

Typeset by Palimpsest Book Production Limited,
Falkirk, Stirlingshire

Printed and bound by
Printforce Nederland b.v., Alphen aan den Rijn,
The Netherlands

FOR ALEX, DEBBIE AND KATEY

FOREWORD

They say timing is everything in life. Being in the right place at the right time. I've certainly come to believe that. I met my wife, Lara, on a ski-lift in France, one of those 'bubbles' – a gondola contraption like a mini-cable car. If she or I had taken the one after or the one before – they were separated by thirty seconds – we'd have probably never met.

I've often wondered if timing was the reason why *Billionaire* and my two novels before it – *Dead Letter Drop* and *Atom Bomb Angel* – failed to set the literary world alight when they were first published back in the early 1980s. Either that or they – erm – weren't that great! Taking the latter view, I kept the books out of print for three decades, and it was only after numerous requests from many of you, my lovely readers, complaining that the prices for the originals on eBay and such put them out of reach, that I relented and allowed them to be republished.

But let me try to defend myself, first, with the timing. From as far back as I can remember I wanted, above all else, to be a published novelist.

From around the age of eight I began writing my thoughts into a red notebook I kept beside my bed. I found it a while ago in the bottom of a trunk and it was full of such great pearls of wisdom as, 'Life is a bowl of custard. It's all right until you fall in.' I returned it to the bottom of the trunk!

I wrote three novels in my late teens and early twenties, including one I was convinced was the Great British Novel. All three are at the bottom of that same trunk, where they will remain until the mice have digested them. But the Great British Novel got me an agent in New York, who signed me up at the age of twenty. That was a huge moment for me – to realize that someone out in that real publishing world actually believed in me.

I then spent the best part of a decade writing and producing film and television, including being almost entirely responsible for a comedy movie called *Spanish Fly*, starring Terry Thomas and Leslie Philips, which the eminent film critic Barry Norman reviewed on his BBC *Film Night* programme, calling it, 'Probably the least funny British funny film ever made, and without doubt the worst British film since the Second World War.' The review prompted my then wife to say to me, 'When are you going to write that novel you've always been dreaming about and talking about?'

That very week there was an article in *The Times* that said there was a shortage of spy thrillers being written. So I had a go at writing one, *Dead Letter*

Drop, and to my absolute amazement it was accepted for publication by the eminent British publishing house WH Allen. To my even bigger amazement, the book totally didn't sell! They had given me a two-book contract, and I wrote a second spy thriller, *Atom Bomb Angel.* That did equally badly!

My publishers were quick to assure me it was not the quality of the writing that held the books back; rather it was all down to unfortunate timing. It was Mikhail Gorbachev's fault for bringing in *perestroika* and *glasnost.* The writing was on the wall for the Soviet Union, and in just a few years that Big Wall in Berlin would be coming down. The era of the Russians as the bad guys was coming to an end, so nobody really cared about spy thrillers anymore. That was what my publishers told me.

I needed to find something else to write about, something that might capture the zeitgeist of the 1980s, and something that might appeal to a wide spread of readers. Money was the topic, I decided – everyone was fascinated by money back then. It was the era of the Porsche-driving, champagne-swilling yuppies, the era of consumption more conspicuous than ever before. One of the defining phrases of the 1980s came from Gordon Gekko (Michael Douglas) in the film *Wall Street* – 'Greed is good.' So I wrote my third novel, *Billionaire,* a thriller about greed, ambition, money and success – with a fair smattering of sex and action. But it didn't sell any better than the first two. Maybe the world was becoming saturated with books and films about money and greed. Or maybe, as I suspect is closer to the truth, this was a book on which I was still cutting my teeth, still learning my craft. So, dear reader, please read it with that in mind and forgive me its deficiencies!

But there is a postscript that perhaps vindicates me – even if just a little. In 2014 *Dead Letter Drop* came back into print, and to my astonishment went to number four on the *Sunday Times* best-seller list. But even more incredibly, in May 2015 it went to number one in Russia!

See, timing is everything!

Peter James
Sussex

I would like to acknowledge the enormous help given to me by my wife, Georgina; and by Alex Heath, Gary Monnickendam, Lyn Colman, Jackie Edwards, Sue Ansell, Renée-Jean Wilkin, Paul Longmore, and Jesse (for once again not eating all the manuscript).

'How pleasant it is to have money, heigh-ho!
How pleasant it is to have money.'

ARTHUR HUGH CLOUGH
(1819–1861)

CHAPTER 1

Two of the men driving eastwards down the M4 Motorway, near London's Heathrow Airport, were driving particularly badly. One drove badly because he was a rotten driver. The other, who was normally a good driver, was distracted by the blonde girl in the seat beside him who was trying to remove his trousers.

It was five past one on a blazing hot early June afternoon. Both men were late. One was on his way to his office in the City of London. The other was on his way to kill someone not very important.

'Move over, you bastard, move over!' Baenhaker pushed down on the horn rim with the palm of his right hand. 'Oh move over, why can't you just move over?' He pushed the horn rim twice more, holding it down each time for several seconds, holding it down so hard that the thin metal cut into his hand.

'You pig,' declared Baenhaker. 'You bloody pig!' He pulled the head-lamp switch on the dashboard full out, pushed it back in, then pulled it out again. In the bright sun, there was only the faintest gleam from the lights that reflected on the gun metal grey paintwork of the Porsche in front of him. He pushed the light switch back in. 'Fucker!' he shouted uselessly through his windscreen, and yanked the switch back out. It came away in his hand; he tried to replace it, dropped it, and it rolled away somewhere underneath his feet.

Baenhaker glanced at his watch: one-five; over half an hour late already, not yet past Heathrow Airport, and stuck behind this bastard in his Porsche crawling along in the fast lane. He banged the horn rim down hard and held it there for several more seconds before releasing it. He was now convinced that the driver in front was blocking his path deliberately. His rage caused him to start breathing in short sharp bursts; he looked at the red ribbon on his speedometer, flickering between forty and forty-five miles per hour, and wondered whether to risk getting booked by passing on the inside. He decided not to; he knew this motorway was always crawling with police.

Baenhaker's Volvo, with its faded red paintwork and worn upholstery, was living testament to the car company's claims about the longevity of its products; this particular one had survived one hundred and thirty-seven thousand miles and six owners since it had first rolled out of the Cardiff dealer's showroom. Baenhaker had bought it neither for its looks nor its durability nor its history; he had bought it because it had been all that he could afford. Whenever he saw any young man of similar age to himself driving a smart car, he became eaten up with jealousy. He had not yet seen the driver of the Porsche, but he had already decided that he was young. He had also decided that, whoever he was, he hated him more than he had ever hated anyone before in his life. He was not yet to know it, but in a few moments he was going to have good reason to magnify that hatred by several hundred per cent.

'You shmuk!' he yelled. He pushed the horn down hard, and held it there. This time, he decided, he was going to keep it pressed down until the Porsche moved over.

Alex Rocq gripped the small three-spoked wheel tightly. The refrigerated air in the cockpit of the Porsche 911 Turbo had a rarefied smell of new leather and expensive perfume. Four Blaupunkt speakers delivered the crystal-clear, graphite-equalized, DBX expanded rendering of Elton John's solemn farewells to a Yellow Brick Road.

'Not here!' said Rocq, wriggling and trying to move upright in his seat. He took his right hand off the steering wheel, and tried to refasten his fly zipper. He put his hand back on the wheel, and her hand pulled the zipper down again. At the same time, her tongue burrowed into his left ear.

'Winkie wants to come out,' she said.

'Amanda, I can't drive.'

'Why don't you pull over?'

'I have to get to the office. Ouch!' A very cold hand slid down inside the front of his trousers.

He was vaguely aware, a mile or so down the motorway ahead, of some obstruction in the fast lane: an orange hazard light was flashing. Above the music was another noise, something persistent. Her mane of expensively highlighted blonde hair descended onto his lap. 'Come on, stop it!' He tried to push her off with his elbow; that noise persisted. He glanced at the speedometer. 'Christ!' Forty miles per hour in the fast lane. A sharp pain: 'Owww!' he yelled. 'You're hurting!'

Rocq looked in the mirror; there was on old Volvo with its lights blazing, right on his tail. He pressed the accelerator down and as the Porsche surged forward, it began to move over into the middle lane. 'Sit up, Amanda, for God's sake – someone's passing us.'

'Mesugener!' shouted Baenhaker, as the Porsche suddenly pulled away from him, as if taunting him, and then moved over into the middle lane, as if to really rub it in. 'What the hell do you think you're bloody playing at?' he yelled. He changed down into third gear, and flattened the accelerator. The steady ticking of his engine turned into a hard-working roar, but for some moments he made no headway against the Porsche. Then the Porsche suddenly slowed down, and Baenhaker began to draw level. As he did so, he removed his left arm from the steering wheel, opened up his index finger and middle finger, and began to flick V-signs at the driver of the Porsche for all he was worth. But the driver did not notice him; he appeared to Baenhaker to be in a trance.

'Bloody well concentrate on your driving!' yelled Baenhaker. Then he saw a mane of blonde hair rise up from the driver's lap, and the smiling face of a beautiful girl look up at the driver, and say something.

Baenhaker's eyes became transfixed on the girl's face. Already contorted with anger, his own face now assumed an expression that would have opened the bowels of a rabid vampire bat. The girl he was staring at was the girl whom he had been planning to propose to this past weekend. They should have spent the weekend together in the country. Today was Monday; on the Thursday, she had telephoned him to say that the weekend was off because she had suddenly been called to an international architects' conference in Cologne. He had never been to an architects' conference, but what he was looking at didn't look much like an international architects' conference to him.

He sat, stunned. He mouthed, 'Bitch,' but no words came out. She didn't even notice him. Suddenly, the Porsche accelerated off again. He turned his eyes back to the road. Less than fifty feet in front of him, and completely stationary, was a tarmac-spreading lorry; along its back was a massive flashing arrow that pointed to the left. At seventy miles per hour, fifty feet wasn't very far.

Baenhaker stood on the brake pedal, and froze.

5

The Volvo slewed to the right, ripping into the central reservation barrier; the front left of the car slammed into the rear of the lorry. As if on some nightmare ride at a fairground, Baenhaker felt the rear of the car rise up, and keep rising, and then over, slowly, very slowly, everything suddenly went into slow motion, and he knew he was going to die.

Then everything speeded up again. The roof smashed into the tarmac, and the windscreen exploded in front of his eyes; fragments of glass rushed in, lashing him like winter rain. Then up again, and over. He was aware of lorries, cars, screechings, roarings, silence for a moment, followed by the bang of a thousand dustbin lids; all four doors flew open and there was rushing wind, then over again, then sliding, sliding like a mad thing, now downwards, down a dip, then stopping dead. Baenhaker carried on travelling forwards; his chest snapped the steering wheel in half; his forehead ripped open on the windscreen trim.

He hung, upside down, half-impaled on the steering column, with his head out through where the windscreen had been, supported by several inches of wet mud, his eyes staring at a grassy bank. He was still alive somehow, he knew; but the pain was terrible; and then, he realized, there were more pains, so many pains, one after the other, all getting worse, and he began to panic, for he knew, again, that he was going to die. He could feel his life ebbing away and he raged silently at himself, and then began to feel sad, and then raged again. He didn't want to die, not here, not alone in this ditch, not with Amanda with that creep in his Porsche, whoever he was, and her not even knowing that he was here, not even caring a damn. It was ebbing away; he tried to stop it, but he knew it was no use. He lapsed into unconsciousness.

Baenhaker might have felt a great deal better had he known that in a few weeks' time instructions would be issued, by the highest authority he knew, for the driver of that Porsche to be tracked down and killed.

CHAPTER 2

The gunboat cut through the ink-black water of the Strait of Hormuz, at the mouth of the Persian Gulf. The water was flat now, with just a slight swell; the storm that had raged for the past two days had finally died at dusk.

The commander of the gunboat, Nasir Hoos, stood beside the pilot on the bridge and looked at his watch. It was 1.30 a.m. At 5.00 the sun would appear and within an hour, the sea would become a glorious cobalt blue. But right now it was darker than the oil in the supertankers they were out here to protect: an average of three supertankers an hour, twenty-four hours a day, seven days a week, churned down through the Strait and turned right for the Western World. There was one now; he could see its lights. It was about five miles off, and coming across behind them.

The radar operator looked up from the screen. 'I'm picking up something three miles to starboard, coming this way very slowly.'

Hoos nodded. Probably a fishing dhow; the night

seas were sprinkled with them, badly lit and badly sailed. He looked out of the window, squinting his eyes to cut out the cabin light. 'Three miles did you say, Hamoud?'

'Yes.'

'Can't see anything. Probably a damned dhow without lights. Better take a look.' He turned to the pilot. 'Starboard thirty.'

'Starboard thirty, Sir,' the pilot repeated, turning the wheel. 'Thirty of the starboard wheel on, Sir.'

The fast boat swung round quickly. Hoos waited a few moments and then gave the command to straighten out: 'Steady.'

'Steady, Sir. Course zero five degrees.'

'Steer zero five.'

Hoos took his night-vision field-glasses and went out onto the deck; he put the glasses to his eyes and stared ahead, but could see nothing. The warm breeze gently whipped his face. He waited for five minutes, then raised his field-glasses again. He could make out the shape of a dhow, a fairly large one, about two miles dead ahead, and carrying no lights.

'Gun posts,' commanded Hoos. He never took chances on night patrol. The boat had four gun posts – twin MG machine guns mounted fore and aft, and twenty-millimetre cannon also fore and aft. 'Slow ahead. Search lights,' he said, after another eight minutes.

Five hundred yards of ocean in front of them

erupted into a bright glare under the beams of the eight halogen search lights. Seconds later, the dark hull of the dhow rocked into the centre like an eerie stage prop in a pantomime. The forward guns swivelled and trained on the dhow and, with its speed cut to five knots, the gunboat cautiously began to circle the dhow in a large arc.

Hoos switched on the loud-hailer. 'This is the Sultan of Oman's Navy. Come up on deck and identify yourselves.' The voice cracked out over the water; the dhow remained silent. As they closed in, they saw that the sail was in tatters and the mast was broken and tilting crazily; there was no sign of any movement. As they came around the stern of the dhow, they saw two figures slumped on the rear deck. 'This is the Sultan of Oman's Navy. You are in territorial waters of Oman. Anyone who is below deck is to come up immediately and identify himself.'

The silence persisted. 'Take her alongside,' said Hoos. 'Stand by to board.'

The pilot brought the gunboat beam-to-beam with the dhow, and six naval ratings and a Petty Officer jumped aboard. Two secured the two vessels together and the other five went below, Webley revolvers drawn. After a few minutes, the Petty Officer came back up on deck and addressed Hoos, who remained standing on the gunboat.

'Two below, Sir, two on deck; all dead. They are all in the uniform of the Israeli Navy, Sir.'

'What?'

'They're Israeli sailors, Sir.'

Israeli sailors? Hoos felt a cold shiver run through him. What, he wondered, were Israeli sailors doing on a fishing dhow in the middle of the Persian Gulf? Something was wrong here, very wrong indeed. Piracy in the Gulf was not uncommon; boats with murdered crews he had seen before, several times. But this was different. He jumped onto the dhow, examined each dead sailor carefully, and then looked all around the deck and the squalid cabin area. There was no sign of violence, only the remains of an unfinished meal on four plates – an extremely nasty-looking dried-up stew.

'Food poisoning?' said Hoos.

'Could be,' said the Petty Officer. 'Looks like it. I'm no expert on corpses, but I'd say they've been dead for a good day or so.'

'Where's this boat registered?' said Hoos.

'There's a sea-worthiness certificate and fishing licence in the cabin – issued in Umm Al Amnah.'

'Umm Al Amnah?' said Hoos, with surprise. 'They've drifted one hell of a way to be down here.'

'Storm probably blew them down.'

'Umm Al Amnah,' repeated Hoos, to himself. 'Search the boat from top to bottom; turn it inside out.'

'Yes, Sir.'

Hoos began to walk around the boat, carefully,

11

slowly, methodically; he felt uneasy. Umm Al Amnah had been a province within one of the Trucial states which comprised the United Arab Emirates; although, many years before the formation of the UAE, it had been a state in its own right. Umm Al Amnah was ruled by an eccentric despot, Sheik Hyyad bin Bakkrah al Quozzohok, who had been at loggerheads with the Government of the United Arab Emirates ever since their formation, in 1971. It was Quozzohok's view that the United Arab Emirates had been formed for the sole purpose of squeezing Umm Al Amnah into oblivion, and he wasn't having any of it. Anti-British, anti-American, anti-Israeli and apparently pro-Libya, his tiny province of one thousand, five hundred square miles and a population of seventeen thousand had been a continuing embarrassment to the United Arab Emirates. When, finally, in a bloodless military coup in 1975, he had declared Umm Al Amnah's independence, he found he met with no resistance from the UAE at all and – if anything – a hint of relief.

The Western World, however, viewed Amnah's independence less happily: over half of the West's entire oil supply had to pass down the Persian Gulf and through the Strait of Hormuz. With an unstable Iran, and a Russian-occupied Afghanistan controlling one whole side of the Gulf, the West needed all the friends it could get down the other side. Oman, which occupied the land one side of the narrow Strait of Hormuz, was openly friendly to the West, allowing both British and US forces to maintain bases in the country. The United Arab Emirates, which covered the area of coast on one side of the Gulf that ran up to the narrow Strait of Hormuz, was also friendly with the West, if less openly. Umm Al Amnah occupied forty miles of that coast within the UAE.

Nasir Hoos knew that if anyone blocked the Strait of Hormuz, they would be turning off half the world's oil supply. It was for that reason that the West poured all the aid into the Oman that it would accept. In return for the aid, the Oman policed the Strait. In eight years of gunboat patrol, Hoos had developed a policeman's nose for what was right and wrong: for the lights of a friendly tanker, or a local fishing dhow; the occasional dark hulk of a Soviet sub coming up for a sniff of air. Some vessels smelt fine, others stank. Right now, he was standing in a fishing dhow; it had been at sea for several days. The stink of putrefying fish should have been overpowering, but there was no smell of fish at all.

'Commander, Commander, come here!' a voice shouted from the stern. He walked quickly down the boat. The Petty Officer was standing beside the open fish hatch. 'Look down there,' he said, shining his torch.

Hoos looked, and a cold prickle began to run the length of his back: the beam of the torch lit

13

up one oval metal object after the next: the hatch was packed full of mines.

Three hours later they were berthed at the naval base on Goat Island, and the US bomb disposal experts were opening up the first mine. Hoos, some distance away, paced up and down the quay. Dawn was breaking now, but he did not feel tired. He saw one of the Americans climb out of the hatch, get off the boat, and walk up towards him. The American pulled a packet of Chesterfield cigarettes out of his pocket, and pulled a cigarette out of the pack.

'Reckon you've got yourself a nice can of worms there, Commander.'

Hoos nodded.

The American lit the cigarette and blew the smoke out of his mouth; the breeze carried it away. 'They're not ordinary mines, Commander. Fact is, they're the first I ever came across. I've heard about them – but never seen one before. He dragged hard on the cigarette, then pulled some tobacco strands off his tongue. He stared out towards the Gulf, and pursed his lips.

'What precisely are they?'

'I'll tell you what they ain't, Commander: they ain't just your old Second World War surplus flogged off by some two-bit back-street arms dealer. Those are nuclear mines; they're stuffed damned full of uranium. First damned nuke mines I ever saw.'

There was a long pause before the American continued. 'Whole new breed, those, Commander; must be Russian-made. One of those would take a supertanker out, and you wouldn't be able to find any bits left over big enough to cover the end of a matchstick.'

Hoos looked at the sky; it was going to be a fine, blistering-hot day. He looked out across the Strait at the shadow of Iran, at the red tip of the sun that was rising above it; he was filled with a deep sense of foreboding. After thirty years of waiting, he had a hideous feeling that the worst fears of the Western World might be coming true.

One of the first men outside Umm Al Amnah to learn of the discovery was General Isser Aaron Ephraim, head of the Mossad, Israel's overseas secret intelligence service. He sat up with a start as one of the two telephones beside his bed in his Tel Aviv apartment began to ring, and answered it in a quiet voice so as not to wake his wife. It was Chaim Weiszman, Director of Israeli Military Intelligence; he explained what had happened. 'This anything to do with you, Isser?'

'No, Chaim.' Ephraim thought hard for some moments. 'Four sailors disappeared off Haifa last week – Monday, I think. Patrol boat vanished; no one's found any wreckage or any bodies so far.'

'The Prime Minister's going crazy. Do you have

any idea how embarrassing this is going to be to the Government if this gets out?'

'I can imagine. It doesn't make any sense, Chaim – I'm stunned. Who knows about this so far?'

'So far, the Commander of the gunboat, the US military in the Oman, and ourselves. They need to find out fast if any other dhows have been out there dropping mines into the Strait. If there have been, then they have to stop all shipping, at once. But equally, if this is some weird hoax, they don't want to cause a panic; once any shipping crews get word someone may have been dumping nuclear mines in their path, the Persian Gulf – and half the world's oceans and ports – are going to be knee-deep in abandoned tankers.'

'Four dead sailors and fifteen nuclear mines doesn't sound like a hoax to me, Chaim,' said Ephraim.

'Nor to me. I think we'd better have an early start; meet me in my office at eight.'

'Eight o'clock,' agreed Ephraim. He replaced the receiver, sat up in his bed in the warm dark room, and thought for a long time. He had a sick feeling that ran from the pit of his stomach to the top of his throat, and a sweat began to break out over his body, increasing in intensity, until he felt he was engulfed in a flowing river. After a while it subsided and as it slowly dried, he began to feel very cold. He had a sense of apprehension deeper than he had ever felt before. All his life he had faced trouble; when it hadn't come to him, he had gone to search it out and, if not always conquer it, at least somehow come to terms with it. Something in the night air carried vibrations of a new kind of trouble through him; his brain turned itself inside out trying to make sense of it, and failed. The General lapsed into an exhausted doze.

CHAPTER 3

From the time Baenhaker's Volvo had slewed into the deep ditch beside the motorway to the time the ambulance arrived, a mere thirty minutes had elapsed. During that time, the police had halted all traffic, put up accident warning signs, cleared glass and metal off the carriageway, re-started the traffic, and given Baenhaker, who appeared to have stopped breathing, the kiss of life.

'Forget it, he's a goner.'

Police Constable Harris looked up at the ambulanceman despairingly; it was the second bad smash he'd been to this morning. 'He's got a pulse!'

The ambulanceman took Baenhaker's wrist; after a couple of moments he nodded, and the team went into action. Twice, during the process of separating the wreckage of Baenhaker from the wreckage of his car, his heart stopped. Twice, the team restarted it.

'Don't know why we're bothering,' said Jim Connelly, the ambulance driver. 'There's no way he's going to make it through.'

The rest of the crew agreed with him. Probable fractured skull, femur and ribs, probable ruptured spleen, possible fractured spine, massive blood loss from internal haemorrhage, punctured lung and massive lacerations; and that was without looking too closely. But they kept on trying; less bits than were left of Baenhaker had been reassembled into perfectly acceptable human beings in the past; not often, perhaps, but enough times to make their efforts with every accident victim worthwhile. Eventually, they hoisted him into the ambulance and, with fluid pouring into his veins, pumping oxygen via a breathing machine and giving him a cardiac massage every time his pulse faded, raced him, with little optimism, to the West Middlesex Hospital.

Three years earlier, Alex Rocq had also been smashed to pieces, when his life had collapsed. Although his wounds had not required the surgeon's knife, the scars that remained were deeper than any surgeon's knife could have inflicted. The first disaster had been when his wife of less than two years had walked out, accusing him, not entirely inaccurately, of being more in love with his work than with her; the second disaster, within weeks of her leaving, was when the stockbroking firm, for which he had slaved for five years, and which had just made him their youngest-ever partner, went to the wall.

As the partners themselves were personally liable

19

for the debts of the firm, Rocq lost everything he owned: his Paddington mews house, his car, and all his savings. He also lost his Membership of the London Stock Exchange, with little chance of regaining it for a long while, if ever.

So at the age of twenty-eight, after ten years of training, experience and dedication, he was out of a job, out of a marriage, out of a home, out of money and fresh out of prospects. As Amanda pulled his fly zipper back up, he thought back about all the turbulence, all the knocks and blows, and the despair; Amanda looked up at him and smiled, and he smiled back. He thought about how, now, three years on, the pieces all seemed to be slotting back together very nicely.

She leaned up and kissed him; he kissed her back, looking over the bridge of her nose at the road ahead. The Volvo that had been on his tail seemed to have vanished. He wondered idly for a brief second where it had gone, because he hadn't seen any turn-offs; then it went completely from his mind. He slid his hand up inside her skirt, pushed his fingers down inside the top of her tights, and slid them deep down into her silk panties; she breathed in sharply, and ran her tongue over his nose.

He was already starting to feel horny again; it was a long time, he reflected, since he had felt horny so often, a long time since he could remember feeling almost permanently horny, the way he did now. Too damned long. He didn't ever want to have bad times again, didn't ever want to be poor again, didn't ever again want to go through the hell of the last three years.

Amanda began to blow a sweet warm hurricane into his ear. He saw a patrol car racing up the westbound carriageway, blue lights flashing, headlights on. A couple of minutes later, an ambulance, siren screaming, was tearing up the road; somewhere back there there must have been an accident, he figured.

Rocq pulled the Porsche up at the high kerb in Knights-bridge, and Amanda opened her door. He looked at her. 'Would you consider me forward if I asked if you'd like to come out and have a drink tonight?'

She grinned. 'I don't know,' she said. 'My mother always warned me about strange men.' She hoisted her soft Enny overnight bag from the rear seat.

'Maybe if I write and ask nicely?'

'Maybe!' She grinned again, blew him a kiss, shut the door and stepped, with the careless abandon that only a very pretty girl can get away with, out into the thick lunch-time traffic.

Rocq turned to watch her; she had already reached the safety of the traffic island in the middle of the road. She turned, saw he was still there, and smiled again.

Rocq put the Porsche into gear and pulled back out into the traffic. He drove slowly, in a contemplative mood. He went around Hyde Park Corner, down Constitution Hill, the Mall, then along the Embankment, heading towards the City. At the end of Lower Thames Street, he cut through Mark Lane, into Fenchurch Street, and turned left into Mincing Lane. For the first time in two years, there was an empty parking bay in the street; not only that, it was slap outside the front entrance to Number 88. Right now, he decided, he really did not have a lot to grumble about.

The man standing on guard outside the front door was wearing a uniform that would have made the full battledress of a Brigadier look like a boiler suit. It was a tribute to his physical strength that under the full weight of the several yards of braid, the tonnage of glistening brass buttons, the acreage of immaculately blancoed webbing and the battery of medals, he was able to remain upright.

'Good afternoon, Sarge,' said Rocq to Retired Sergeant-Major Horace Bantram, the security guard and live-in caretaker.

'Good afternoon, Sir, nice one today, Sir,' he said to Rocq. Then, as he always did, with the knuckle of his index finger he pushed his nostrils sideways and sniffed loudly. 'Smells like rain later, though, Sir,' he said.

'Let's hope it doesn't,' said Rocq, walking swiftly past him. He had learned, a long time ago, the folly of engaging Sarge in a conversation about the weather: it had cost him an entire morning. He walked past the discreet sign, in the shape of a gold ingot, with the words GLOBALEX LTD engraved on it in small block capitals, through the revolving door, and down the white marble corridor, past the receptionist, Mrs Deale, a smart woman in her early forties. She gave him a brief smile of recognition whilst struggling hard, with considerable dignity, to hold her grip on a switchboard which sounded as if it had gone berserk.

He took one of the four elevators up to the fourth floor, and stepped out into a carpeted corridor. Opposite was another sign on the wall, again in the shape of an ingot; it read: GLOBALEX METALS DIVISION. Rocq looked at his watch; it was just on two o'clock.

He walked down the corridor and turned left into his office. It was an extremely large room, in the centre of which was a massive oval console around which sat twenty people, each with two telephones, an intercom, a computer terminal and a small flat work-top containing a switchboard with one hundred telephone lines, known as a Dealer Board.

Globalex Limited was one of the largest commodity broking firms in Britain, with additional branch offices in Zurich, Hong Kong, Tokyo, Chicago and New York. The company dealt in all types of commodities, from foods, such as soyabean, grain, barley, sugar, cocoa, coffee and frozen pork bellies to materials, such as plywood, rubber, cotton and wool; to minerals, such as tin, copper, lead, zinc and precious metals, such as silver and gold.

23

Commodities are basically just raw materials, and the world commodity markets began life simply as places where raw materials in wholesale quantities could be bought and sold. From these, developed futures markets. With massive price fluctuations in raw materials – depending on supply and demand in any given year, or part of a year – and international currency swings, users of commodities, in planning their end products, need to insure against massive rises in the price of their raw materials; similarly, producers of commodities need to insure against massive price drops. Out of these two needs came the practice of 'buying long' – agreeing to buy a commodity on a specific date in the future, often three months, for a specific price. If the commodity then rose in price, the vendor would still be obliged to sell the product at the price agreed upon three months before. The purchaser is protected against a price rise, but loses out if the price has in fact dropped in the meantime. Also out of the two needs came the practice of 'selling short' – agreeing to sell a commodity on a specific date in the future, for a specific price. This protects the producer against a drop in price; however much the price of the commodity may have dropped by the delivery date, he is covered by having sold it at a prearranged price.

Whilst the producers of raw materials and the manufacturers who use the raw materials make up an important part of the world commodity markets' clientele, there are also numerous speculators, who invest in commodity futures but have no interest whatsoever in the end products themselves. They trade purely in paper, and have almost always sold on the paper before the delivery dates are due. Not many punters want to have twenty thousand tons of soyabean meal delivered to their back yards.

The attraction of the commodity market to the speculator, both institutional and private, is the ability to make far higher profits in a short space of time than are usually attainable on the stock exchanges. This is for two reasons. The first is the high rate of fluctuation of the price of commodities. The second, and more important, reason is the gearing: in buying commodities, the purchaser is only required to pay a deposit, normally ten per cent of the total price; if the purchaser does not take delivery of the goods, but sells them on or prior to the delivery date, he is not required to pay up the balance of the price. In effect, this means that he is able to gamble with ten times more money than he actually has. If the commodity rises in value ten per cent, he ends up doubling his money; but the risk is in proportion. If the commodity drops ten per cent, he will have to find and put up ten times his original stake. Fortunes are made every day in the world's commodity markets; equally, many men are bankrupted every day.

Most of the twenty people in Rocq's office were,

like Rocq, account executives; their job was to act for the clients of Globalex, buying and selling for them according to their clients' instructions and, equally, advising and keeping their clients up to date on all conditions which might affect the commodities that interested them. Six of the brokers were girls, two of them Japanese. At the head of the oval console was a fiery red-headed girl order clerk who was firing questions out across the console in a broad cockney accent and firing answers back down the telephone receiver that she brandished about as if it were a dagger.

There was a hub of activity, the likes of which Rocq couldn't remember seeing for a very long time. After-lunch lethargy, combined with the generally quiet state of trade at the present time, normally made early afternoons the dullest of times, but today was different. Every desk except his own was attended, and all the brokers were talking earnestly into both their telephones at once, taking new calls and writing down instructions and orders furiously.

Lester Barrow, a short fat man in his late forties – an old age for this high-pressure job – immensely cheerful in spite of two near-fatal heart attacks in the last three years, turned to Rocq as he entered. 'Here comes Early Bird.'

Rocq grinned a short, rather pained grin.

'Been carving yourself some fat worms?' Barrow's chirpy voice cut through the general hum of action.

'I've been to the dentist all morning,' lied Rocq.

It was an old trick he had learned many years before: if you have to make up an excuse, make up one that evokes sympathy. Not, he knew, that it would cut much ice in here. He was well aware that none of the people in here knew the meaning of the word 'sympathy'; they didn't know the meaning of any word that wasn't in the Dow Jones Index. The pressure of the work gave them little time to know anything else. In spite of the activity there was a feeling in the office of a lull before a storm. It happened frequently at this time in the afternoon, with many of the large exchanges in the world closed, and everyone waiting for the New York markets to open.

Communications play a vital part in an international broker's job. The London offices of Globalex were the central hub in a highly sophisticated network of telephones, telex and computer links, that cost Globalex over £100,000 a month in electricity and call charges alone. There were direct links to the offices in Zurich, Hong Kong, Tokyo, Chicago and New York, as well as direct telephone lines to every major client throughout the world. Modern communications had reduced the entire world to one large trading floor and, with changes in technology occurring almost daily, international commodity broking was a fiendishly expensive game to stay in.

In order to keep overheads in line with the volume of trading, the account executives received a modest basic income of £10,000, with their

27

opportunity to earn large sums coming from a direct percentage of the brokerage fees Globalex charged its clients for every order, whether it was buy or sell. It was not uncommon for a Globalex account executive to earn two to three times his basic salary in a good trading year.

All commodities are traded in minimum units called 'lots'. A 'lot' of gold is one hundred ounces, for example. At $498 an ounce, one 'lot' of gold was worth $49,800. The brokerage Globalex charged on one lot of gold was $25.00 and the account executive's share of that was $6.25. It needed a great many lots to pay the phone bills for the office and the American Express bills of the account executives, but at $833 a ton for copper, $7,856 a ton for tin, $404 a ton for lead, $526 a ton for zinc, $653 a ton for aluminium, $2,880 a ton for nickel, $197 an ounce for platinum, $4.23 an ounce for silver, and $498 an ounce for gold, it did not take many lots for a deal to get up into the one hundred thousands – or Long Ones, as Gary Slivitz, who sat next to Rocq, called them – the millions, or Big Ones as Slivitz called them, and even, on occasions, the Wide Ones, which were billions.

'What did you say?'

Rocq wasn't quite sure whether Barrow was talking to him or to whoever was at the end of the telephone receiver he was holding in his left hand. Reading Rocq's mind, Barrow lifted the telephone away from his ear.

'Been to the dentist.'

'How much did you sell him?'

Rocq decided Barrow probably wasn't joking: Barrow, like most here, lived, ate and breathed metals. Anything that existed beyond the revolving door of 88 Mincing Lane and outside of the portals of Plantation House, just across the road, which housed the London Metal Exchange and the Gold Futures Market, as far as Lester Barrow was concerned existed for the sole purpose of buying and selling metals through Globalex and, where possible, through the able personage of Lester Barrow himself. The New York light lit up on Barrow's Dealer Board; he hit a button and grabbed the second receiver. Almost immediately, now holding telephones to both ears with one hand, he began to write with the other hand.

Rocq took his seat, between Gary Slivitz, who appeared to be playing his Dealer Board as if it were a space invaders machine, and the permanently miserable Henry Mozer, who was performing the deft art of writing with one end of a pencil whilst picking his ear with the other end. 'What the heck's going on, Henry?' Rocq asked.

Mozer pulled the pencil out and turned to him: 'Where the hell have you been – down a hole in the ground?'

'I've been to the dentist.' Rocq deliberately grimaced as he spoke.

Almost every light was flashing on Rocq's Dealer Board.

'What did you say?'

'I've got a frozen mouth – can't talk properly.'

'What you been doing?' shouted Slivitz. 'Kissing polar bears?'

Rocq decided to abandon his excuse for not turning up to the office until two. He was unpopular enough as it was. The past two years had been lean years for most metal brokers, but he, completely by luck, had tumbled into half a dozen of the best accounts Globalex had ever had: Sa'ad Al Rahir, a bored, thirty-seven-year-old Kuwaiti who played the metal exchange through Alex the way most people play a roulette wheel, and who would think nothing of buying and selling three or four hundred thousand pounds worth of whatever metal particularly took his fancy in a single week. Louis Khylji, the immaculate Iranian food snob and wine connoisseur, who daily gambled with more than just petty cash from the many hundreds of millions his late father had removed from the Ayatollah's claws. Prince Abr Qu'Ih Missh, the playboy son of Sheik Quozzohok, Emir of Amnah, the tiny oil-rich state which had seized independence from the United Arab Emirates. Baron Harry Mellic, the Canadian son of an immigrant Hungarian lumberjack, who had arrived in Canada in 1938, prospered, and bought a thousand acre lumberyard in the Yukon. It wasn't a bad investment in its own right, but Baron Harry Mellic's father, Joseph Zgdwimellik never did rue the day he allowed Rio Tinto Zinc to come and

30

do a spot of test drilling; it turned out his lumber-yard was perched slap on top of the then third-largest uranium bed ever discovered. When the old man died, his son, Harry, decided that a shorter name and a smart title would befit the inheritor of one and a half billion Canadian dollars very nicely. There was Joel Syme of the Country and Provincial Investment Trust, who had a portfolio in his charge of some £160 million and turned a good percentage over, annually, in metals, through Alex Rocq. And there was Dunstan Ngwan, the Nigerian who had made vast fortunes out of buying up out-of-date drugs and selling them to the hospitals of emergent Third-World nations. Ngwan rarely turned over less than £1 million a month through Globalex, via Alex Rocq.

The picking up of all these clients had, in the first instance, been just luck. There was a rotation system among the brokers for new enquiries, and each of the above had arrived on Rocq's due dates. This had been assisted not a little by Rocq's generous gifts to the switchboard operator. His skill, however, had been to hang on to them. He had done so not so much by his ability to produce results, which were only just above average, but far more by his ability at getting them laid, which apart from money was the only interest they all had in common. Sa'ad Al Rahir liked seventeen-year-old schoolgirls. Louis Khylji liked black men and yellow women. Prince Abr Qu'Ih Missh liked blonde women; whilst looks mattered, his main interest was quantity. On his, fortunately for Alex, infrequent trips to London, he liked to have at least ten girls fixed up, all together. His favourite passion was his own particular version of Blindman's-buff: he would be led, blindfolded, into a room full of naked blondes, grope his way around them, seize one and make passionate love to her then and there. Afterwards, he would try to guess her name. If he got it wrong, he would be led out, and play the game again. This would go on until either he got the right girl or he collapsed with exhaustion. As for the other three, Baron Harry Mellic was a rubber freak, Joel Symes liked being beaten, and Dunstan Ngwan seemed to like anything.

This little group Rocq termed his 'A' team. Below them, he had a hundred lesser clients, whom he ranked in diminishing order; at the bottom of the pile was Sidney Chilterley, whose account normally stood about $1 over the $7,000 minimum that was required to have an account at Globalex.

During the past two years, the other brokers in this office had earned an average commission of £12,000 on top of their annual salaries of £10,000; the volume of Rocq's 'A' team was such that he had netted an average income over the past two years of £105,000 a year. After tax and overheads, such as call-girls' fees, which Globalex was not interested in splitting with him, he had stashed away some £53,000. By lucky investments, he had managed to turn that sum into £90,000, which he had sunk into down payments on a flat in Redcliffe Square in London, and a cottage in the village of Clayton, in Sussex.

Whilst everyone else drove their company cars and worked a rigorous five-day week, he drove a £32,000 Porsche and spent two afternoons a week on the golf course. He might have been the blue-eyed boy of the board room, but in this office, where the legend *success is not everything – even your best friend must fail* hung like the blade of a guillotine in the air, his lack of popularity was not altogether surprising.

He looked at the battery of flashing lights, and then at the Reuter Monitor video screen, on which, by entering a code, at the tap of a button he could call up the price of any commodity on any market in the world, as well as foreign exchange rates, share prices, and a continuous update of all world news and general information.

The Reuter Monitor system, apart from being connected to all the world's commodity exchanges, receives data input from hundreds of banks, bullion dealers and brokerage houses who use the system as well. Rocq tapped a button for a read-out on the latest metal prices.

'Bloody hell. Gold up nine dollars,' he said. 'Over the five-hundred. What happened? Did Moscow nuke Washington?'

'Almost as good.' Slivitz talked over the mouthpiece of his two telephones. 'Remember in 1981 when the Israelis blew up Iraq's nuclear power reactor at Osirak?'

'Yes, I remember.'

'Well they've just gone and done it again.'

'Shit.' Gold moved up another dollar. 'When?'

''Bout three hours ago. Reckon you lost yourself about thirty-five clients since then. Moses has been going apeshit trying to find you.'

Moses Rondell was Rocq's direct boss; relationships between the two were not good at the best of times, ever since he had overheard Rocq's description of him as having metal balls.

'Reckon you'd better stop talking and start buying,' said Mozer, 'or else there isn't going to be anything left for you to buy.'

Rocq punched out the code for World News on the Reuter terminal. The green computer-typed words on the screen told him of the Israeli raid on Osirak, gave the Prime Minister of Israel's reasons for this second attack, and gave the Iraqi Foreign Minister's fury at this second outrage, and the destruction of their almost completely rebuilt reactor.

Rocq next pushed a button on his switchboard marked Tor 2. It was virtually the only button that wasn't flashing. It automatically dialled Baron Mellic's home number in Toronto. The Baron did not have an office; he worked from a massive penthouse overlooking four motorway junctions on the outskirts of Toronto. Mellic Construction Corporation had built the fifty-seven storey apartment block on the top of which the penthouse was perched. Mellic had furnished the penthouse by going to the furniture floor of Downtown Eatons, one of Toronto's largest department stores, and ordering the entire floor. To further amuse himself, he ordered all the fittings as well, including the signs and prices, and had the entire penthouse laid out as if it were the furniture floor of Eatons.

Toronto was five hours behind London. It was only half past nine there, and Mellic was a late riser; maybe he hadn't heard the news yet, hoped Rocq. He had.

'What kept you? Were you delivering the missiles for Israel personally?'

'I'm sorry, Harry.'

'You're sorry? I'm sorry too. How much have I lost while you've been humping some broad?'

'Not a lot – and I haven't been humping, I've been at the dentist.' He paused. 'Anyway – gold's only gone ten bucks.'

There was a noise from the other end of the telephone; to Rocq's untrained but accurate ear, it was not unlike the sound of a Hungarian Baron scraping himself off the ceiling of a penthouse.

'I tell you, my friend,' said the Baron, 'if I bought you a hooker for every hundred dollars you've lost me this morning, you could screw your ass off twenty-four hours a day for the rest of your life, and not get through half of them.'

'There's still time, Harry; better buy right now.'

35

'Right now? Too late, you shmuck – it's going to start going down.'

'No – it'll go fifteen – sixteen at least; if there's any retaliation, then it'll go through the roof. We could be on the brink of a major war – if that happens, it'll be over the thousand mark by the end of the week.'

'What's September trading at?'

'Spot's $509. September's trading at a $6.00 premium to Spot: $515.'

'Gold closed at $498 on Friday. You said it had gone ten bucks – Spot should be $508, not $509.'

'It just went up another buck while we were talking.'

There was a pause while the Baron vented a mouthful of air into the receiver. 'So you reckon Spot's going to go to what? Twelve? Fifteen?'

'I reckon at least fifteen, and probably a bit higher than that – if nothing more happens.'

'Okay – buy me one ton. September.'

Rocq whistled to himself. One ton. Thirty-two thousand ounces. Three hundred and twenty contracts. Globalex charged a commission of 25 cents an ounce on gold, and he got ten per cent of that. He tapped some figures out on his calculator. He had just made himself £444.

'And you'd better sell out at the right time, you shmuck – don't want you leaving me high and dry.'

'You can rely on me, Harry.'

'I'd rather rely on a fucking mongoose.' The line

36

went dead. Rocq paused to think for a moment. Thirty-two thousand ounces was a large amount of gold. The average total daily volume for London was only one hundred thousand ounces.

He hit the button on his Dealer Board for the Globalex New York office. It answered immediately:

'Steve Rausch, Globalex.'

'What's gold running September?'

'Hi, Alex, how are you?'

'Busy.'

'You hear the one about the Russian in New York, wants a broker?'

'Fuck or knit?'

'Yeah, you heard it.'

'You hear about the three old men discussing their wives?'

'One's losing his taste, the other his memory?'

'Yes.' Having exhausted their latest supply of jokes, they got down to business.

'September's $514/$516.'

'Buy me three hundred and twenty Seps at the market.'

'Wow – who's that for?'

'Mind your own business. Work it gently – it's for one of my big ones, and he's already not too happy. If you get a good execution, I'll look after you.'

'Okay, Alex. Take it as done.'

'Good lad.'

Rocq hung up, then called Baron Mellic back,

confirmed to him that he had bought the gold and advised him that he was transferring $1.6 million from his deposit account at Globalex to pay for the ten per cent margin. Mellic grunted, and hung up.

Rocq thought for a moment about the easy life of the super-rich; about how true it was, the expression that 'money makes money'. The Baron hadn't had to do a thing; just pick up a telephone and state an amount. One ton was the amount he had stated: thirty-two thousand ounces at $515 an ounce. Sixteen million dollars' worth of gold. If it rose another $15, that would be a cool $480,000 profit, and the Baron wouldn't have had to stump up one cent above the money he already had on deposit and earning him interest at Globalex. Long before the September delivery date, when the balance of the sixteen million would be due, the gold price would have peaked out and begun to slide back down; before the slide happened, Rocq would have closed out the Baron's entire position and credited his account with the profit.

He could understand the Baron being angry at his inefficiency in being out of the office at the time of such a crisis. He knew he should really have an assistant, but he preferred to carry the whole can himself. Like many account executives, he kept the identity of his clients a closely-guarded secret. He started to tap on his calculator keyboard. If he had bought within minutes of the news of

38

the attack, he could have got in right at the bottom – $8, $9, maybe even $10 earlier, and added a quarter of a million to the Baron's bundle.

Gold is one commodity that is almost certain to rise whenever there is trouble in the world. It always retains an attraction to the individual investor because behind every paper currency in the world are the gold reserves the paper represents, and there is an inherent mistrust in the value of the paper. Governments can make the paper money of their countries worthless overnight – it has happened many times in the past, Vietnam being one of the most recent examples of paper money becoming one hundred per cent worthless. If the banks of the country of which the currency was issued would not give credit for the paper, then the banks of no other country would. There is little use in being a millionaire if it is all in a currency which can no longer buy anything. No government would ever make gold worthless, because someone, somewhere, would always be willing to accept it in return for food, goods, shelter or services. It is an international marker and holds its value against all other currencies.

In theory, if the United States of America were wiped out, or taken over by the Soviet Union, the mighty dollar bill could become a meaningless document overnight. The only Americans, however rich they might be in theory, who could buy anything at all elsewhere in the world, would be the ones that had gold. Gold is the only currency that is universal – that everyone, everywhere, will always accept, just as they did long before paper money was ever invented to save gold being lugged about; when the going in the world starts to look bad, it is gold that everyone wants to buy.

There is, in fact, surprisingly little gold in the world; all the gold that has ever been mined would fit easily inside a cube fifty-seven foot by fifty-seven foot by fifty-seven foot – the size of a not particularly large house. The illusion that there is more comes from the amount of gold plated articles there are around, and the fact that gold is extremely malleable: from a single ounce, fifty miles of gold wire can be produced.

In spite of this small amount of gold, an enormous volume is traded in the world money markets each day; many times all the gold in the world changes hands, on paper, in the course of each year. In times of international tension, the public traditionally begin to horde, the speculators stop selling, and a shortage is created. With the addition of a vast amount of extra buyers, there is only one way the price at such times can go: up.

Rocq had a not dissimilar conversation to his terse one with the Baron, with the five other members of his 'A' team, interrupted by earfuls of abuse from a good thirty of his lesser clients. A number of the accounts he had were discretionary accounts – he had full power to buy and sell as he thought fit, within the individual budgets

40

– and normally these clients left him to get on with it. But not today.

The loudest earful of all that Rocq received was from his smallest punter, Sidney Chilterley. He telephoned Rocq, instructing him to buy one ounce of gold when it was at $517, and then telephoned him and ordered him to sell it when it reached $520, making himself a gross profit of $3 – a net profit, after brokerage, of $2.75, and a commission of $0.03 for Rocq. Rocq was so fed up with him that he didn't bother to remind him that the minimum handling charge for any single transaction was $10, thus rendering Chilterley's net profit of $2.75 into a net loss situation of $7.25. Before Chilterley had bought the gold, his account with Globalex had stood at $7,002 exactly. It now stood at $6,994.75 – exactly $5.25 below the minimum required to maintain an account at Globalex. Rocq looked forward, to turning down Chilterley's next order until he had received a cheque to rectify the inadequacy of his account. Chilterley was part of an unsuccessful experiment at Globalex to develop a business out of small punters.

For a few moments the lights on his switchboard stopped flashing. Rocq opened the Yellow Pages directory, thumbed through it, and then dialled the number of an Interflora florist. 'I want to send ten pounds worth of cut flowers to the following person: Amanda Lowell, Garbutt, Garbutt and Garbutt, 292A Hans Crescent, Knightsbridge.

Message: "Missing you madly, are you free for dinner?".'

He hung up. Slivitz looked at him. 'Another satisfied customer?'

'What do you do with yours at night, Slivitz? Stick it out the window and try and screw the world?'

Slivitz's phone rang before he could reply. He glared at Rocq as he answered it.

'You sure picked a good morning to play truant,' said Henry Mozer.

'Unfortunately, Henry,' said Rocq, 'the Israelis forgot to tell me their plans.'

CHAPTER 4

It was strange, the atmosphere in the office that afternoon of the day of the second Osirak attack, thought Rocq. A curious mixture of jubilations. The Jewish element among the staff was ecstatic over yet another positive blow being struck by the Israelis. The non-Jewish were overjoyed to have some action in the markets; all bad news was good, so far as they were concerned, for bad news meant movement of prices, and movement of prices meant buying and selling for their clients, and buying and selling meant commissions. When bad news was good news at the same time, so much the better. The only really bad news for a commodity broker was no news.

The only person in the office who didn't become the least bit flippant as the afternoon wore on was Clive Kettle. Kettle didn't know how to be flippant; no one had ever told him. From the age of eight onwards, he had turned up each day at school clutching a *Financial Times*, a black briefcase and a rolled-up umbrella. Whilst his contemporaries read Enid Blyton and Biggles, he ploughed through the *Wall Street Journal*. His classmates

43

ent their free time on games fields, in parks, in cinemas, playing and romping. He spent the free hours of his childhood having meetings with bank managers, discussing the investments and acquisitions on which his pocket money was spent. Throughout his entire life, to the twenty-seven-year-old he was today, he had one desire and one desire only, and that was to be a successful businessman. So far he had not succeeded. His main problem was that he took everything so seriously that he could never make a decision. When a metal began to rise in price, he did not want to buy, because he knew it might drop again. When it began to go down, he was reluctant to sell, in case it went up again. Many of the clients he had acquired over the past five years had left him. When they had first started with him, they backed him, thinking he was an infant prodigy, the original whizz kid; five years on, with a performance twenty per cent below the Dow Jones, they were coming, one by one, to the reluctant conclusion that he was an idiot. He replaced his phone on its hook, and proclaimed loudly, to no one in particular, 'I don't know what you are all looking so happy about – this could be the start of the Third World War.'

'Sooner the better,' said Slivitz, 'with the amount of gold I've just poured into my clients' troughs. A good international nuke war would send gold through the roof.' Then his face dropped. 'But I don't suppose it will happen,' he said, gloomily.

'Gold up two more dollars,' shouted a voice from the far side of the console.

Rocq was nervous. Gold was now $522; it had been climbing steadily. The pattern was such that he knew he had to stay in for a while longer, and shelve the plan he had made to start unloading when the price reached $523 – an increase of $25. He wanted a cigarette badly, but he had quit two months ago, and he wanted to stay quit. He wondered whether he might be more sensible to stick to that plan, but having caused his clients to miss out earlier in the day, he needed at least to regain some of their favour by taking them right to the end of the rise. His phone rang. 'Rocq,' he said, answering it.

There was a crackle, then the quiet voice of Prince Abr Qu'Ih Missh of Umm Al Amnah. 'How is it going, Alex?'

Rocq was relieved that he had called; the prince was in very deep, and now he could pass the buck to him. 'Still rising – just jumped two more dollars – my hunch is that we're near the top, unless there's going to be any retaliation by the Iraqis. What do you want to do?'

'Up to you, Alex.'

Rocq cursed; that wasn't the answer he wanted.

'I'd be inclined to sell pretty soon.'

'Five more dollars, then sell,' said the prince.

'Okay – but it might not go.'

'Chance it.'

'Okay.' Rocq hung up, and breathed a little; he

45

was off the hook on that one. The light on Tor 2 flashed.

'Hallo, Harry,' he said to Baron Mellic. 'Still got your hair on?'

'No – I scratched it all out thinking about that two hundred and fifty thousand bucks you cost me.'

'Well – I've made it up for you – gold's five hundred and twenty-two and we're still in the game.'

'So who's doing me favours? We're thirteen up and we should be twenty-four.'

'Harry – if I hadn't let you down this morning, I'd have taken you out at five hundred and ten, and saved myself the ulcers waiting here, watching every second to see if it starts to move back down.'

'You're full of shit.'

'Damned right – and I haven't dared leave my chair to go to the bathroom all afternoon. I think it's time to sell.'

'No. You can sweat it out a little more. I expect at least five thirty, Alex, and if it goes more, I want more. I don't want to read tomorrow's papers and discover gold went five fifty and you closed me out at five thirty-one – and all because of a complaint with your bowels.'

'I didn't know *Rubber Weekly* carried the gold prices.'

'Just keep bouncing, Alex, will yah?' The Baron hung up. Rocq's intercom light began flashing and he picked it up. The voice down the other end didn't need any introduction; it was Sir Monty Elleck, the chairman of Globalex:

'Come up and see me right away, Alex, please,' he said, curtly.

'Yes, sir.'

Rocq scribbled some buying and selling instructions down on his pad and handed them to Boadicea, the nickname they had given to the flame-haired girl order clerk. She looked disdainfully at the scrawl on the pad. ''Ere, Alex,' she said, in her thick East End accent. 'You oughter spend some of your million pound bleedin' commission on learning how to write.'

'I'll do a deal with you – you learn how to speak and I'll learn how to write. Maybe we could go to college together.'

A ball of paper hit him in the nape of his neck as he walked out of the door; he sincerely hoped it wasn't his list of instructions.

Sir Monty Elleck was not only the chairman of Globalex; he owned the company lock, stock and barrel. He was also the managing director, presiding over a board which met once a year for one hour. Of the eleven other directors on the board, only two had any practical knowledge of the commodity business. All eleven men had been selected by Elleck because of their high ranks, some by birth, some by merit, that made them in a position to be able to recommend and introduce new clients from the pick of the nation's wealthy and successful. The board comprised one duke, two earls, four knights, three self-made multi-millionaire heads of international public companies, and the shadow Secretary for Trade and Industry. All of them received handsome introductory fees from every new client they introduced, together with a percentage of Globalex's brokerage fees on all their subsequent transactions; although they never knew it, Elleck screwed them all blind on this part of the deal.

Sir Monty had come a long way since his grandfather, Baruch Elleckstein, a Lithuanian immigrant to England, had sold his first hundred-weight of pig-iron from a barrow in Leadenhall Street. The physical distance had not been far – 88 Mincing Lane was a mere couple of hundred yards from the spot in Leadenhall Street – but the financial distance was vast. It was Elleck's father who had realized there were easier ways to make money out of metal than humping around hand-carts loaded with the stuff, and it was he who founded Globalex, anglicized the family name, and put the Elleck family on the motorway to fortune. Seventeen years ago, whilst plugging-in a Kenwood food mixer for his wife, in the kitchen of their Mayfair flat, Joseph Elleck had inadvertently allowed his index finger and thumb to slide too far around the plug, and they had made contact with the negative and positive pins at the exact moment of insertion. When his wife came into the kitchen fifteen minutes later, she found no life in either her husband or the Kenwood mixer.

It would have been of little consolation to her to have known that the wiring to the socket into which Joseph Elleck had inserted the plug had been manufactured by a firm which bought all its copper wire through Globalex.

Monty Elleck was Joseph's only son, and he succeeded immediately to the throne, taking to his job with great zeal. During the next decade, he opened branch offices throughout the world, and made one Prime Minister of Great Britain a £500,000 profit in less than six months, for which he received his knighthood. He was married to an overweight wife, who spent her time waddling around whichever of the Elleck residences – either in St John's Wood, Gloucestershire, Gstaad, Sardinia, or Miami – took her fancy. He had an underweight son, who, as a result of a congenital mental defect, was attempting to start a kibbutz in the Shetland Isles, and two plump daughters whose main ambitions in life appeared to be to become fatter than their mother.

Elleck had coined the advertising slogan for Globalex: 'At Globalex, we make you richer whilst you're just dreaming about it.' And it was his proud boast to all potential new clients that 'We have offices in every time zone in the world. Wherever in the world you are sleeping, Globalex is awake somewhere else, making you money.'

Sir Monty Elleck was not only good at making money, reflected Rocq, as he walked up to the sixth floor of 88 Mincing Lane, he was equally talented at spending it. The change in atmosphere from the fourth floor was similar to that of walking from economy into first class in an aeroplane. There was nothing dramatically different, but there were subtle changes, creating a most definite aura; for instance, thought Rocq, anyone much below six foot tall would have greatly benefited from a pair of stilts, which would have enabled them to see over the top of the pile of the carpet. It was when you got nearer to Elleck's office itself that things began to change appreciably. Suddenly, the walls became oak panelled, and hung with paintings; anyone who did not know much about art but could read signatures would learn that gentlemen by the names of Gainsborough, Titian, Reynolds, Claude, Constable, Vermeer and Hals had been responsible for these paintings – originals, all.

Money dripped off the walls like running water; each time Rocq walked down here, he had the same feeling of awe, envy, and lust for money. Just in those twenty feet of corridor, he had walked past more money than almost any ordinary human being was ever going to have in a lifetime – even if he or she won the football pools every week for a year.

Elleck's office looked like the boudoir of a successful whore – probably because it was his wife who had been responsible for the decorating. It was a curious blend of Louis XIV, Louis XVI, Robert Adam, Thomas Chippendale, the Bauhaus, and Harrods. The walls were lemon yellow, and pastel pink, with gilded friezes. The carpet was cerise, and sprinkled with Persian rugs.

Elleck's secretary of seventeen years – and his father's secretary before that – Miss Jane Wells, ushered Rocq in and then left, closing the door behind her.

Elleck sat in the middle of the room, behind an ornate carved mahogany desk that looked like a dressing table, on a mountainous chair which looked as if it had been stolen from an African tribal chieftain; it was so thickly upholstered that even with several inches shaved off its legs, Elleck's short legs were still suspended above the ground.

The diminutive chairman of Globalex spoke in a high-pitched voice and as he spoke, his face always moved with a combination of nervous energy and nervous twitches that were so intense, it was always quite impossible for anyone opposite him to tell in which direction he was looking at any given time. His head was almost completely bald, but he had massive bushy eyebrows, and when he screwed up his forehead tightly, which he did every five seconds, the eyebrows shot almost to the dome of his head.

'Good afternoon, Alex, sit down.' He waved his pudgy fingers expansively about; Rocq cast his eyes around the room, noticing a pair of pink Victorian love-seats, a saffron chesterfield, and a small lime green armchair over by the window.

There was no chair close to the desk. Rocq decided on the lime green armchair, and sat down.

Elleck never bothered with formalities – he went straight in: 'This Israeli raid, Alex – it's pushed quite a few metals up.'

Rocq nodded. 'Particularly gold, Sir Monty.'

'And silver, zinc, lead and copper.' The Chairman proceeded to reel off from memory the current market buying and selling price of all the major metals. Rocq nodded his agreement to the prices.

'You must be pleased to see life in the market,' said Elleck.

'It has been quiet recently.'

'You still got that car of yours?' There was disapproval in the Chairman's voice. Although Alex qualified for a company car, the Chairman strictly forbade buying foreign; if employees wanted foreign cars, they had to buy them with their own money.

'Yes, Sir Monty.'

'Why don't you buy something British? You know we would buy it for you.'

'That's very kind of you, Sir Monty, but there is no British car that I want.'

The Chairman shrugged, and looked at his watch. 'It is now four-twenty. At exactly four-thirty, I want you to start selling your gold. I want you to have unloaded your entire gold position by five o'clock. You have some big customers – I don't want to see them upset.'

'Personally, I think the price will climb several

52

dollars higher.' Rocq spoke with a trace of petulance and a trace of arrogance in his voice.

Elleck's eyebrows shot to the top of his head and hung there like two large moths; he pursed his lips and made a sound not unlike a Wellington boot being extracted from a ditch of thick mud. 'Would you like to assume personal responsibility for any losses incurred if the price does not rise?'

'Of course not, no.'

'You've made a good profit for your clients so far today?'

Rocq nodded.

'You bought for all your clients at four hundred and ninety-eight, I trust?'

Rocq stared at him for a moment. He wasn't sure what was coming next. 'No, Sir Monty, I didn't. I waited until five hundred and nine.'

'Why?' asked Elleck, politely; too politely.

'I wanted to wait until there was a definite rising pattern.'

'I see.' Elleck still spoke very politely. 'When the Israelis bombed Osirak in 1981, the world press called it the greatest single act of aggression since the Japanese bombed Pearl Harbour. Now the Israelis do the same again, which presumably makes this morning's raid on Osirak the second greatest single act of aggression since Pearl Harbour; the entire world starts beating a path to its nearest bullion dealer, and you alone decide to sit tight?'

'I felt it was the right thing to do.'

The eyebrows sank down and rested on the bridge of his nose. Elleck was becoming less polite by the word. 'You lost six of the biggest clients this firm ever had a ten dollar rise in gold, because you felt it was the right thing to do? And now you expect me to listen to your advice? You just get back down there, Alex Rocq, and at half past four, you start selling; any gold you have left in any client account by five o'clock, I am treating as your personal property and I am going to invoice you for it. Is that clear?'

'Perfectly clear,' said Rocq.

The chairman looked down at his desk, turned over some papers, nodded his head twice, and dismissed Rocq with a wave of his hand.

As Rocq walked down the corridor, he smarted with anger, although he knew that in view of what had happened, he had actually got off extremely lightly. He had been convinced that gold would continue to rise and would go several more dollars; he wondered why Elleck was so sure it would not, and why he was so insistent on the times. He was no prophet, thought Rocq, so what did he know? He was very interested to see what would happen to the price. Very interested indeed.

At exactly four-thirty, Daniel Baenhaker's heart stopped beating. The surgeon at the operating table in Theatre 1 at the West Middlesex Hospital injected the heart with adrenalin; it beat again, for thirty seconds, and once more stopped. The

54

surgeon, Harvey Johnstone-Keynes, shook his head, and looked at the clock on the wall; he was going to the theatre with his wife tonight, to see an Alan Ayckbourn play; she was mad as hell with him at the moment because, on the last two occasions when they had arranged to go, he had had to cancel out because of urgent operations. There was a danger of the same thing happening again now. If the man did die, it would solve an awful lot of problems, and with the condition he was in, the chances were, that even if he spent the next five hours operating, it would still be a waste of time; the guy had lost so much blood, he had absolutely no resistance left in him. Johnstone Keynes wanted to pull off his gloves, and say 'That's it.' But he couldn't bring himself to do it. 'Calcium' he said, instead, and began injecting the heart again.

Within thirty seconds, Baenhaker's heart was beating rhythmically once more.

By five o'clock that afternoon, the only gold that Alex Rocq's clients possessed was what they had stashed away under their beds and in their teeth. They no longer had any on paper at Globalex. Some, particularly Joel Simes of Country and Provincial, disagreed strongly with Rocq's advice to sell, and the Baron was among the most vociferous. 'You just want to unload, and go off home early to start humping again,' he yelled down the phone.

'Relax, Harry; I've had a word with our soft commodities department: we're putting you deep into latex.'

By 5.15 the price of gold had not moved for an hour and ten minutes. At 5.25, it dropped one dollar. It fell another two dollars at 5.35. Rocq stayed glued to his Reuter-System screen. The London market had closed, but, if he wanted to, he could have watched prices move all night. New York, five hours behind London, was in full swing. When New York closed, Chicago, which was an hour behind New York, would still be open; when that closed, it would be morning in Hong Kong, and that would be opening. When that closed, it would be morning in England, and London would be opening.

Rocq did not stay through the night, but left the office at 7.30 that evening; by the time he got up from his desk, the price of gold had dropped twelve dollars.

It was raining as he eased the Porsche out of the meter bay, and down Mincing Lane, and he drove slowly, thinking hard. Elleck had not given him advice, he had given him instructions, and he had been pretty damned sure of himself. Elleck was Jewish; he gave a lot of money to Israel. Maybe someone was paying him back a small favour; it was possible. But he was puzzled. If Elleck had inside information, he would have known the raid was going to happen, so he would have known when to buy – but how could he have known when to sell? What kind of information could Elleck have obtained that made him know when to sell? Something was making the price of gold drop, and drop hard. There was one thing that was always certain to make it drop, and that was massive selling: but it would have taken far more selling than he had been doing for his clients – even though he had sold a substantial amount, it could not on its own have had any significant effect on the market. There were a lot more sellers besides himself – there had to be – but how did Elleck know? Was it merely a hunch, the result of years of experience, of reading the signals, or was there a lot more to it than he knew? He had the certain feeling that whatever it was, it was not merely Sir Monty Elleck's hunch.

Rocq switched on the stereo, and punched in the old Elton John tape. The music took him back to the seventies, and he began to feel nostalgic, and a little sad. He thought about his twenty-first birthday: a lot had happened in the decade since then. He'd married Pauline, buried his parents, almost gone bankrupt, divorced Pauline. Memories of his parents came flooding back to him, and he felt sad, as he always did when he thought about them. His father, Anton Rocquinitiskichieov who had struggled through his life with two massive handicaps – one being his name, the other his lack of money. His father was Polish and had come to England in 1938 to flee Hitler, and had met and married Rocq's mother, an English nurse, in 1940.

She was not a strong woman and it was over a decade, and many miscarriages, later that Alex Rocquinitiskichieov was born. When he was fifteen, his mother contracted a rare kidney disease. To remain alive, she needed to be kept on a kidney machine. The hospital in South London, where they lived, did not have enough money for a kidney machine; nor did her husband. Alex, although in the midst of preparing for exams, did a newspaper round before school in the morning, and then worked a night shift, six days a week, in a glucose factory after school finished in the evening. His father, a tailor, also worked around the clock. Three weeks before they had saved up the fifteen per cent deposit the hire purchase company wanted for the machine, his mother died.

Four years later, his father, then aged sixty-two, suffered a series of heart attacks. The doctors told Alex that his father's heart arteries were damaged beyond repair; he needed a major operation in which healthy arteries would be grafted from his legs onto his heart arteries. If the operation succeeded, he would be able to return to a normal existence; without the operation he had only months, at the most, to live. Because of long waiting lists, the operation could not be performed on anyone over the age of sixty, on the National Health. If his father was to have the operation, he would have to have it privately. The estimated cost was £7,000.

Rocq and his father simply did not have that amount of money. His father had always rented his premises and the flat above, where they lived, and had never been able to amass any money. Although now working as a runner on the London Stock Exchange, Rocq again took an evening job, this time, in a bottling factory. He worked a night shift during the week, and a double shift during the weekends. Before he had even the first five hundred pounds saved up, his father had another heart attack, and within three days had died.

Rocq remembered as he had watched his father's coffin slowly lowered into the ground; he remembered the sadness and the bitterness that he had felt. The only two people he had ever loved in the world, the only family he had ever had were dead because there had been no money to save them. He stood and he made a vow: never again, as long as he lived, would he allow himself to be in a position whereby he could not afford the money to save the life of someone he loved.

He knew he had made the right decision going into stockbroking, but he equally knew that if he was to get anywhere in that field, he was going to have to plan carefully the way he could get to climb each rung. The first thing that he did was drop fifteen letters from his name. Although he felt sad in some ways to be severing what he now felt was his only link with his past, at the same time, he felt as though he had suddenly been cut free from a pair of handcuffs. When, to his surprise, and pleasure, his workmates stopped referring to him as 'the Polack' and began referring to him as

'Alex Rocq' he knew that although he had by no means arrived, he was, at last, on his way.

Memories of the afternoon's hectic activity came flooding back to him, interrupting his thoughts. He tried to ignore them, but they were persistent; his work was never far from his mind, as it never is with any metal broker. With violent fluctuations liable to happen at any moment of the twenty-four hour day, they can never completely switch off. Most of them quit broking and move into management before they reach forty; either that or into the intensive care unit of the nearest cardiac department. There was no such thing as an unscheduled morning off – everything needed to be planned and catered for. He'd gambled this morning, and lost; but, he decided, Amanda was an exceptional bird, and worth all the stick he'd received in the office. It had been a good weekend, a damned good weekend staying with his friends in Berkshire, and it was the first time since he had started going out with her that Amanda had actually gone a whole two days without mentioning that damned name, Baenhaker.

What the hell she had seen in him, he did not know. It certainly wasn't in his pock-marked face – not that he had ever met Baenhaker, nor seen his photograph – he just imagined him as having a pock-marked face. 'A nasty little piece of work,' was how Rocq had summed him up.

'You're just saying that because you're jealous of him,' she said.

'Nasty little Commie,' he said.

'He's a bit left, but hardly a Communist.'

'Well, I think insurance assessors are a very strange breed of people.'

'I doubt that he thinks too highly of metal brokers. Come on, Alex, let's not talk about him; you've won, haven't you? Why be bitter about him? He didn't try and take me away from you – I'd been going out with him seven months before I met you. What have you got to gripe about? He's the one that's doing the griping – and I can assure you, he is griping.'

'Does he know who I am?'

'No, he most certainly doesn't, and I'm going to make sure he doesn't find out.'

'Why?'

'He's very strange. He has an almost vicious streak in him – I don't know how to describe it, quite – it's weird.'

'Terrific.'

'I wouldn't worry,' she smiled.

'I'm not worried,' he said.

Rocq remembered that conversation now. He stopped the Porsche at the red traffic lights at Westminster Bridge. On his left was a young man, about his age, in a shiny Mazda sports car. He was dressed flashily, and obviously thought highly of himself and his motor car, judging by the amount of bolt-on goodies attached to himself and to his vehicle. Rocq could see him out of the corner of his eye, attempting to study the Porsche and its

61

occupant without giving any impression of envy. On Rocq's right was a massive white Rolls Royce, with smoked-glass windows and a vast television aerial on the roof. It made him think of Elleck, and the vast empire he owned. Rocq was thirty-one now; he had, at the very most, another ten years of broking before he moved into management, and there was no opportunity to earn commission in management. For most brokers, management was a welcome release from the tension of broking – as well as paying better – but for Rocq it was different. His broking commission was far higher than he could ever earn in management.

He thought hard; it was something that was troubling him more and more just recently. For the past three years he had been lucky and done extremely well. He had paid good deposits on the flat in Redcliffe Square, the cottage in Clayton and the Porsche, but they all cost a lot of money; he had two mortgages plus the H.P. on the car and, in addition to that, the alimony to Pauline. He needed every penny of his income just to stay afloat, and he didn't just want to stay afloat. He wanted to be rich, like Elleck, and he knew there was a gap that would take a bridge bigger than the Golden Gate of San Francisco to span between the likes of Sir Monty Elleck and himself, and if he was going to do something about spanning that gap, then he was going to have to get on with it and start now.

★   ★   ★

He took Amanda out to dinner to the Grenouille, and spent forty-five pounds on a bottle of 1957 Pouget. The wine smelt of stale tea, tasted of old dusters, and they both decided it was delicious and got very drunk on it.

He drove her to Tramp, and ordered a bottle of Krug and fresh orange juice. They sat back in the leather bench, in the far corner of the room, under the chandeliers and the soft lighting and the opulence, watching lazily as a particularly frenetic dance took place, and he put his arm around her shoulder and kissed her. 'Happy?'

'Yes,' she replied. 'And you?'

'Very.'

'Are you really?' she quizzed.

'Can't hear you!' The noise of the music made conversation, even at close quarters, a shouting match.

'I said, are you really?'

'Yes, I am.'

She looked at him. 'What do you want most in life, Alex?'

'Next to you, do you mean?'

She grinned, and nodded happily. 'Do you want to be a millionaire?'

He was silent, for a long while, thinking. 'No,' he said, finally. 'I don't want to be a millionaire: I want to be a billionaire.'

She paused, reflecting; 'You know, it's funny,' she said. 'I really am not interested in money.'

'You would be if you didn't have any.'

She stubbed out her John Player Special. 'Shall we make tracks?'

At four o'clock in the morning, a cheese-knife sliced through Rocq's head; a few seconds later, it plunged through again. He opened his eyes and closed them; the alarm clock was ringing, and so was his front door bell. The cheese-knife sliced through his head once more. He put his hand out to switch off his alarm clock; a glass of water on his bedside table fell over, rolled off the edge, and fell onto the carpet.

'Blast!'

There was a dull clank and a tin of Mazola cooking oil began disgorging its contents onto the already sodden objects on the table top.

'Shit!'

The candle, which had still been burning, fell over, pouring hot wax over his hand. He fumbled further for the alarm clock, and then he remembered that he did not have an alarm clock. The bell persisted. His hand came to rest on a large plastic object; it clattered and fell into the rest of the mess with a thump; the bell stopped.

'Telephone!'

He fumbled for the object he had just dropped, grasped it with some difficulty in his slippery fingers, and brought it to the side of his head.

'Hallo?' he mumbled, feebly.

'Rocky! How are yah?' The voice boomed down the telephone, like thunder.

'Who's that?' Rocq knew full well who it was; it was easier to ask the question than to return the enthusiasm.

'Theo! I'm in New York, and I'm with a gorgeous girl who wants to meet you. She's gonna say hallo!'

The voice of a very drunk girl with a strong Californian accent, came down the phone: 'Hi, Rocky, how are you?'

'Fine, just fine,' groaned Rocq.

'Theo told me all about you; I feel like I'm talking to an old friend.'

'Then do an old friend a favour, sweetheart, and let him get some sleep.'

'Okay, Rocky, it's been beautiful talking to you; you sound like a beautiful guy. Next time Theo comes over here, I'll make sure he brings you with him. Nighty night!'

'Grnight.'

'It's me, Theo, back now,' boomed the thick Italian acccnt.

'Did you say you're in New York?' Rocq mumbled to the Italian commodity broker and Globalex's largest Italian client, not only in money, but also in girth; Theo Barbiero-Ruche was a good pair of cement shoes the wrong side of twenty stone. Barbiero-Ruche used Globalex for some of the many transactions he did not want the Italian Revenue to know about.

'Got a horse running at Sandown, Thursday, thought I might come over.'

'Nice of you to call me, you fucking fat wop. Do you know what time it is here?'

'Do I know what is what? I can't hear you too good.'

Amanda stirred and grunted.

'Forget it,' said Rocq. 'Why don't you stay the weekend – bring your friend.'

'Okay! I bring her husband too!' the Italian roared with laughter down the phone.

'Thanks for calling, fat man. Call me when you get to England.'

'Okay, Rocky. Hey? What you doing this evening? Going out with some broads?'

'I've already had this evening – several hours ago.'

'Ciao, Rocky.'

'Bye, fat man.'

Rocq tried to hang up the phone, and missed. The receiver clattered to the floor; as he lunged after it, the entire telephone fell off the table.

'Who was that?'

'Bloody Italian client; been travelling the world for the last fifteen years and still hasn't figured out the time zones yet.'

Amanda went straight back to sleep. The cheese-knife sliced through Rocq's head once more; he lay there, wondering how long he could prolong getting up and going to the bathroom in search of some Paracetamol. He felt very wide awake, now. Elleck and the events of the afternoon came back into his mind. He thought about Elleck, in

66

his palatial office, and thought about the wealth of the Elleck family, and he tried to compare it with his own wealth. The Ellecks had a house on the St John's Wood side of Little Venice, overlooking the canal; they had a mansion and a couple of thousand acres of land near Stroud, in Gloucestershire. Their villa on the Costa Smeralda was permanently staffed, as were their Miami duplex and their Gstaad chalet, and these were just their private residences. There were, in addition, sumptuous and permanently staffed company apartments in Park Avenue in New York, in Chicago, in Hong Kong and in Zurich, as well as one hundred and thirty feet of company yacht. These small company perks were used by one employee only: Sir Monty Elleck. For transport, Elleck had a Mitsubishi Solitaire twin-engined plane, an Elvstrom helicopter, a bronze Rolls Royce Silver Spirit, a burgundy Mercedes 500 SEL, plus a fleet of lesser vehicles for purposes ranging from driving up the unmade tracks around his estate to negotiating parking meters outside Harrods.

He was worth, personally, Rocq guessed, at least £200 million. Rocq thought about how much money he could accumulate himself. He had made just over £50,000 during the past year, which he knew was because of the client list he had: if he lost any of these clients, his income would drop dramatically. But, assuming he could continue at this rate and even better, he figured that by the time he was forty, the most he could possibly have accumulated, assuming he saved assiduously and invested cautiously, would be, net after tax, in the region of £200,000 – approximately point nought one per cent of Elleck's wealth. His last thoughts before he slid into an uneasy sleep were that if he was to become rich, really rich, anywhere near as rich as Sir Monty Elleck, then he was going to have to do what Elleck clearly seemed to do. He needed to get hold of inside information about what was going on: some inside information that would tell him when a commodity – any commodity, it didn't matter which – was about to go through the roof, so that he could buy it, quietly, himself, and make a killing.

CHAPTER 5

The dimples glinted in the sun as the Dunlop DDH golf ball nestled in the cup of the gold plated tee. In small black lettering down the side of the tee, and across a small area of the golf ball, were the initials T.B-R. The immaculately polished head of the graphite Ping driver wavered uncertainly about three inches off the ground, just behind the ball; it moved slowly up to the ball and sank down onto the ground, the top of the face nestling halfway up the ball. Almost immediately, in a slow, steady sweep, it moved backwards, and then began to arc upwards. Smoothly his shoulders turned until the club was held in the perfect position, pointing directly at the yellow flag four hundred and fifty yards away.

'Coffee,' said Theo.

As quickly as it stopped, the club head began to reverse down the same arc in which it had just travelled, accelerating powerfully and twisting, slightly, to approach the ball square-on. It was a text-book golf swing for a full two inches as, by coincidence, in its sweeping descent from the sky, the club found, for this short distance, the correct oove, and then departed from it again. As the head raced the final two feet to the ball it veered, almost imperceptibly, to the left. The far right hand edge of the face connected with the bottom left hand dimple of the ball, sending it tumbling three feet, six inches at a ninety degree angle to where Theo stood, in front of his shattered tee. The club continued its journey and the face ripped into the virgin grass of the first tee, and hurled a foot-long divot out.

The grossly overweight Italian multi-millionaire emitted a sound not unlike a bull elephant that has been stung in the balls by a wasp and, in a fit of rage, proceeded to hack a further large divot out of the unfortunate grass. He looked around him; a dozen stony-faced golfers returned his gaze. He knew what they were thinking, and they were probably right: they were in for a slow afternoon stuck behind him.

'Bad luck,' said Rocq, trying to conceal his grin. With one hundred pounds on the game, any sympathy was liable to be lacking in any great degree of heart-felt sincerity.

Rocq's own ball lay in the centre of the fairway, two hundred and ten yards ahead; he looked down from the first tee of the Dyke Golf Club, across the panorama of Brighton and Hove, towards the tall chimneys of the power station at Shoreham Harbour and the hazy sea beyond.

'Coffee, you reckon?'

'For sure,' said Theo, tugging his three-iron out of his Gucci golf bag and strutting to the edge of the tee, where the ball lay. He lowered his head forward so that he could see the ball over the vast hulk of his stomach, pulled the club back, and swung it ferociously forward. A divot travelled twenty yards; the ball remained stationary. He swung again. In a flurry of grass and mud, the ball travelled in a straight line, towards the pin, for a good nine feet. The Italian grunted and, brandishing his three-iron like a tomahawk and tugging his trolley behind, as if he were a mother tugging a reluctant child, he stomped off forwards.

Rocq and Barbiero-Ruche walked up to the ball; the Italian scooped it up in his fist. 'I concede ze 'ole.' He put the ball into his pocket, and the two of them marched off down the fairway.

'Why are you so sure about coffee?' asked Rocq.

The Italian stopped and stuck his three-iron back into his bag before answering. Rocq eyed his grotesque shape for some moments, a shape that had been bought and paid for by the Italian's now legendary capabilities in the world's commodity markets. Out of the ten most spectacular rises on the world's commodity markets in the previous ten years, Barbiero-Ruche had published articles, well in advance, predicting not only the rises but, in nine of the ten, the exact days on which the commodities began to rise and the exact dates on which they began to fall. His book, *Me and My*

Frozen Pork Belly might not have knocked any of the international best-sellers off their perches, but there weren't many commodity brokers in the world who couldn't quote at least half a dozen lines from it.

'Brazil supplies approximately one third of the world's coffee – last year her output was two and a half million pounds of coffee.'

They reached Rocq's ball, and he picked it up; they carried on walking.

'Ze 'arvest is in July. Two things can kill coffee – coffee rust disease, and early frost. Even viz a full 'arvest from Brazil, there will still be a shortage of coffee for ze nex' year. Ze reasons are increased demand, together with ze coffee rust in several other major producing countries – particularly in Columbia, Mexico, El Salvador and Ecuador. So anyway, ze price must go up.' The Italian stopped for a moment, pulled up his trouser leg, and scratched his ankle. Then they continued, and approached the second tee. 'I have ze very elaborate computer system in Milano, and I 'ave just had analysed all the weather reports for Brazil for this time of year for the past fifty-five years – as far back as there are records. Ze pattern is exactly as in 1976, when there was a disaster because of early frost in June. You go.' Barbiero-Ruche waved his hand.

Rocq took his driver and bent down, teeing his ball high; he then stood well back from the ball, swung the club gently a few times, then took a full, hard, practice swing; the bottom of the head cracked across the surface of the grass on the exact spot at which Rocq had aimed. Satisfied, he stepped forward, took careful aim at the marker pin, beyond which the fairway dipped down, out of sight, and steadied the club head behind the ball; he took a slow backswing, winding himself up extremely taut, then brought the club hurtling around and down in a near perfect stroke. The sweet-spot of the club face hit the exact rear centre of the ball, momentarily flattening it into a thin saucer-shaped object as it lifted it clear of the tee. As it sprung back into its round shape, it accelerated for one hundred yards low across the ground and then began an arcing climb for a further hundred yards, and then descended gently for thirty yards, bounced on the dry grass, and then rolled along the fairway, curving almost imperceptibly to the left, and then halted. Rocq stood, club held out in the air in front of him, and watched the ball drop out of sight behind the marker with not a little pleasure.

'Shot!' said Barbiero-Ruche, with only the tiniest trace of malice in his voice. He pulled his Ping driver out of his bag and then surveyed the fairway; to the right was a clump of trees, and he eyed them nervously. 'How far do the trees go?'

'Quite a long way. Keep to the left of the marker – you'll be in trouble if you go anywhere near them, because there's thick rough to the side of them.'

'Okay,' said the Italian, uncertainly. He shot the trees another furtive glance, stabbed his tee in the ground and placed his ball on top. He then stood back, and began to line himself up. To be absolutely safe, he turned a forty-five degree angle away from the trees; if he hit the ball straight, it would go off the left hand side of the fairway.

He made three practice strokes, each ripping a six-inch divot out of a different section of the grass, and then he lined his club head up behind the ball. Almost in slow motion, he swung the club back and as it swung, he swayed along with it, so that by the time the club head was at the top of the backswing, he himself was leaning at almost forty-five degrees to the ground. Then, with a loud grunt, he let rip at the ball with all his force, unwinding his body, swirling his wrists, wrenching his shoulders down, blistering the club head through the air and swaying his body back with one sharp jerk. The club head, travelling well over one hundred miles an hour, passed six inches over the top of the ball, and ripped into the virgin grass two feet in front of it.

Barbiero-Ruche spat out a mouthful of air and angrily smacked his club head down again, ripping out yet more grass. Rocq winced, and was glad they weren't on the first tee, in full view of everyone. If word got back to Paul Longmore, the club pro, of the calibre of guest he was bringing along, he had a feeling his days at this club would be numbered.

The Italian calmed down, and lined himself up again for another attempt; this time, the club face connected with full force with the ball, which, along with the remains of his shattered tee, hurtled into the air.

'Shot!' said Rocq.

They both watched as the ball climbed, Rocq with mounting glee and the Italian with mounting gloom, as it began to veer sharply to the right, traversing the fairway and then, as sharply as it had climbed, it began to drop, straight into the very midst of the trees on the right. They both stood in silence as the ball dropped out of sight and then, after a moment, there was the resounding crack of a ball bouncing off a tree trunk, followed by the lesser crackling sound of a ball tumbling into thick undergrowth.

'Mamma mia!' The Italian took a deep breath, put down another ball and again took aim. He despatched this ball to a spot in the same trees, which, Rocq and he guessed, was within six inches of his first ball. 'I concede ze 'ole', said the Italian, angrily ramming his club back into his bag. Rocq turned his face away so that the Italian could not see his grin, and they again set off down the fairway.

'How sure are you about the frost?' asked Rocq.

'For sure, frost. It is impossible, with these conditions, that there cannot be frost. Impossible. You should buy a little coffee yourself. It's going to go – how you say – bottoms up?'

'"Through the roof," Theo, is the right expression.'

'Okay, for sure, through the roof.'

Three hours later and one hundred pounds richer, Rocq climbed into the driving seat of his Porsche. Barbiero-Ruche lowered his dejected hulk into the passenger seat. 'Stupid game, golf,' he repeated for the tenth time. His tally for the round had been two pars, one eagle, three nines, twelve unfinished holes and sixteen lost balls.

'You'll have the chance to get it back tomorrow, Theo.'

'For sure,' he said, not at all sure.

The Porsche took off, and the Italian winced as the weight of his stomach pressed against his backbone; he clawed nervously for the seat-belt. 'You have a pilot's licence for this thing?'

Rocq grinned. They tore down the steep hill, then he slammed the gear lever down into second, and stood on the brakes. As they started to enter the sharp left-hander, he pressed the accelerator down hard; there was a pause for a second, and then the turbo began to deliver its pound of flesh. The limpet grip of the tyres held them rock steady as they accelerated out of the bend at eighty miles an hour. The Italian's eyeballs bulged. They came up behind a slow-moving car, and Rocq was forced to brake hard and sit behind it as they went into a blind corner.

'Who's this girl you fixed, Rocky?' said the

Italian, brightening up considerably at the thought that he wasn't necessarily going to be wiped out in a smash in the next few moments.

An old friend, Theo. Bangs like a shit-house door.'

'She look good?'

'Stunner. Just how you like them – 'bout five-eight, long blonde hair, blue eyes, gobblers lips.'

'What's her name?'

'Mary. She's got a great sense of humour.'

'Could be better than the golf, eh?'

'Maybe you'd better start practising, fat man.'

She was five-foot two, with short dark hair, brown eyes, and her name was Deirdre. If she had a sense of humour, she did a good job of keeping all trace of it from her face when she was introduced to her bedmate for the weekend. The expression on her face told one thing and one thing only: the two hundred and fifty pounds she was getting paid for giving Theo a good time for the next couple of nights was not enough.

'What happened to the blonde hair?' Theo asked Rocq as he followed him through into the drawing room of Rocq's cottage.

'Must have dyed it,' hissed Rocq.

'And her eyeballs too?'

'Any more complaints, and you're in the garage with a pot of vaseline and the local cat.'

'Which way is it?' asked the Italian.

'Come on, Theo, I think she's stunning,' said Rocq, lying through his teeth, and making a mental note to sue a certain madame when he got back to London on Monday.

'You always fix me with dogs, Rocky.'

'Shut up, she'll hear you.'

'I think you should hang her out of the window – scare the birds off your garden!'

'Shut up. What do you want to drink?'

'Scotch.'

'Deirdre?' said Rocq, turning to her.

'I'll have a beer,' she said.

Rocq went into the kitchen; Amanda was rummaging in a cupboard. 'Have you ever cooked in here, Alex?'

'Think I boiled an egg once.'

'What in – an ashtray or an empty bottle?'

'Theo's tummy button.'

She grinned. 'That's a beauty you fixed him up with.'

'Don't think she's too crazy about him either.'

'Where the hell did you drag her up from?'

'Twenty-two stone Italians aren't in big demand.'

'I think she's on the game.'

Rocq didn't want to tell her she was right. 'Rubbish. She's a friend of an old friend of mine – I had a very nice bird lined up for him, and she blew out at the last minute.'

'Lucky Theo.'

Rocq's cottage, in the hamlet of Clayton a few miles outside Brighton, was listed in the Doomsday Book; it had withstood everything that had been chucked at it for the past seven centuries, but now the tiny building was in grave danger of having met its match.

Through the eighteen-inch-thick flint wall, Theo sounded as if he was trying to blow up some gigantic balloon whilst having a red-hot poker thrust up his back-side. This sound was punctuated every seven seconds by what sounded to Rocq and Amanda remarkably like a knight in armour doing somersaults on the bare springs of a trampoline. Throughout the shaking cottage, books were falling off shelves, crockery was crashing to the floor. Suddenly, the Italian emitted a series of ear-piercing wails out into the sleeping Sussex countryside and then for a few minutes all went quiet. A similar thing had happened half an hour ago, and again, an hour before that.

'Seems the fat man's got over his hang-up about brunettes,' said Rocq.

'I'd noticed,' said Amanda.

Rocq slid his arms around her and moved over towards her.

'You're not feeling horny, are you?'

'Yes – aren't you?'

'Not with that racket – and I'm very tired, Alex.'

'What's the matter? You haven't been looking happy all evening.'

'Nothing.'

'Must be something. Did that girl upset you?'

'No.'

'Theo?'

'No. I like Theo.'

'Something's upset you.'

There was a long silence before she spoke: 'It's Danny,' she said at last.

'Baenhaker?'

'Yes.'

'Has he been calling you?'

'No. I got a call from a hospital – the West Middlesex – this morning. He's been in a car smash. I went to see him this afternoon. It happened on Monday – he's been in a coma for three days – only came out of it yesterday. He's in intensive care still.'

'What happened?'

'I'm not really sure – went through the central reservation of the M4.'

'We drove down the M4 on Monday.'

'Oh Alex – he looked so terrible.' She started to cry, and he hugged her tight. 'I'm sorry – I don't want to ruin our weekend.'

'That's okay. I'm sorry about Baenhaker too.' He leaned over and kissed her on the forehead. An ominous clanking started up again in the next bedroom.

'You know,' she said, brightening a little, 'I think I prefer that rubber-freak friend of yours from Toronto – he's quieter!'

CHAPTER 6

Somewhere in the murky half-light in the whirling sandstorm that had been the past forty years of his life, something deep inside his brain had snapped. Sometimes, on the shrink's couch, he looked back into the vortex, but terror always made him turn away.

General Isser Aaron Ephraim, head of the Mossad, Israel's secret intelligence service responsible for overseas intelligence, had thought that maybe, as the years advanced, it would go away. But now he was sixty-four years old, and it had shown no signs of going away. The hatred that burned inside him, as he lay there, burned as fierce as the day it had begun, on a hot, dry day in 1938, when he'd returned with his father to the farmhouse, after a day at the market in Shedema, to discover the butchered bodies of his mother, two brothers, three sisters, grandfather and grandmother, victims of a Syrian vengeance raid.

That hatred was compounded more times than he could ever comprehend two months later, when he saw his father standing with a rope around his neck on a scaffold in Tel Aviv. His offence had

...eal a machine-gun from a British post
...n fire on a Syrian army truck. It was a
...ng offence under the British rule, and they
...nged him.

Ephraim had spent most of the Second World
War killing Englishmen, first for the Stern Gang
and later for the Irgun, under the leadership of
Israel's future Prime Minister, Menachem Begin.
In 1944, whilst on a mission to Germany in an
attempt to free Jewish prisoners of war, he was
captured by the Germans and imprisoned in
Auschwitz. After the surrender of Germany,
Ephraim was sent by Begin to Rome, as part of
a team to infiltrate the Vatican and expose the
lucrative racket the Vatican was running, under
the full sanction of the Pope, of organizing the
escape routes and safe destinations for fleeing Nazi
officers.

After the formation of the State of Israel in 1948,
Ephraim was recruited into the Mossad and placed
in Syria as a mole, in the guise of a highly successful
businessman with a lavish lifestyle. He married
the daughter of the Syrian Minister of Technology,
and rose to become an influential economics
adviser to the Syrian Parliament.

In his seventh year in Syria, whilst his wife was
out shopping, the Syrian intelligence service kicked
down the attic door of his house, and found him
crouched over his radio, tapping out his weekly
transmission to Tel Aviv.

He wanted to die, but that was a release they

had no intention of granting. Beginning with the rape of his pregnant wife outside the locked door of his cell, by a dozen prison officers who did not stop until long after she and the child were dead, he spent four years in which his mind was progressively disembowelled. From the young prison warder who used to grin and urinate on his food before passing it through the bars, to the other Israeli agents, the names of whom his torturers extracted from him one by one, who were brought up and tortured to death in front of him, a hatred welled up inside him, a hatred of the Arab race that was so strong, it became the only thing that kept him alive.

In 1958 he was suddenly returned to Israel in exchange for eighty captured Syrians and, after a long recuperation period, he was given a desk job in the Tel Aviv headquarters of the Mossad.

The fervour that he threw into his work brought him rapid promotion and he rose up through the ranks until finally, one year ago, he had been appointed its Director.

Ephraim had married an Israeli girl, Moya, who had produced four children, two sons and two girls. The eldest son was already a captain in the army, the second son had begun a promising political career, and his eldest daughter was engaged to be married to one of the most prominent young rabbis in the country. The solidity of his family, his respectability, the warmth and the achievements put a barrier between him and his past, but however much he immersed himself in a family life, and he had time for very little, the barrier, he always found, was ever only paper-thin.

The Head of the Mossad raised himself gently off the Arab's back and ran a caressing finger down the young man's spine. 'You know,' he said, in a strange, flat voice, 'it's too bad we never had longer together, time to get to know each other, perhaps, a little; we might have become really good friends.'

General Ephraim put his trousers back on, and pulled the sheet up over the bare back. It was very quiet in the room, except for the steady hissing of the air conditioning. Ephraim could hear no other sound, not even the faintest hint of a whirr from the tape that slowly revolved in the Sony video-camera, whose 28mm wide-angle lens peered down through the tiniest crack in the ceiling.

Ephraim walked through the eerie stillness with a strange smile on his face; all the weird nightmare feelings that welled within him, threatened at times to overpower him and smash his brain to pieces, were calm now, completely calm. He walked towards the door, stopped just before it, and sat down on the step. All of a sudden he felt weak – weak and very sick. He bent his head forward and cradled it in his arms. He began to sob, slowly at first, then faster and louder, until he was near hysteria. He wept for ten minutes and then, still in the same position, he slept.

When he awoke, he did not know how long he had slept; it was always the same when he came here, drawn by a magnet he did not understand and could not resist. He awoke full of a deep sense of dread, full of fear in the pit of his stomach and fear in his eyes. He looked around the room. Nothing had changed since he had slept. The slow whispering hush continued. He rose to his feet and went through the door, into the corridor.

At the end of the corridor, he ignored the lift with its massive wide doors and climbed the long flight of stone steps. At the top was another corridor which he walked down, and then came into a slightly brighter ante-room. There was a small office beyond the ante-room, and a man came out of it; he had a hideous expression in his face, deeply engrained. It was the same expression he always had: a mixture of disgust and apathy. The General pulled out a roll of bank notes from his jacket pocket. It was a thick roll, and he gave the whole roll, complete with elastic band, to the man, avoiding his gaze; he could not bear the man's gaze. The man nodded once, almost imperceptibly, and pushed the button which opened the electric lock of the front door.

The General walked outside, shut the door behind him and stood on the steps, gulping in the midday Tel Aviv heat with the gratitude of a diver who has just returned to the surface of the ocean. He looked up at the sky, at the hot sun, at the traffic that thrashed down the road, at the pedestrians, at the buildings opposite – and stood like a man starved, greedily gulping it all in.

Behind venetian blinds on the second floor of the building directly opposite, a 200mm lens on the front of a Sony video camera was trained and focused on him. The electric motor relentlessly drove the cartridge of tape over the head of the recorder built into the back of the camera. Through the viewfinder, the cameraman concentrated on keeping two subjects in the centre of the tiny television screen in front of his eye: the Head of the Mossad and the small plaque attached to the wall, a few inches to his left. On the plaque were the words: 'Hadar Dafma House'. Hadar Dafma House is the Tel Aviv morgue.

Ephraim took a taxi back to his apartment, which was empty. His wife and family traditionally spent the month of June at their house outside Haifa, and he joined them at weekends. He bathed and then lay down on his bed and slept until three o'clock. When he woke, he was calm; the hatred that had been building up inside him to a point where it threatened to tear him into pieces was gone. It would be back again, he knew; in a few weeks it would start up again, slowly begin to grow again; but now, at least, it was quiet.

He arrived back at his office, and there was a Priority sealed envelope waiting on his desk; he cut it open, and pulled out a decoded report. He read it quickly and then put it down; he rested his left hand on the top of his mahogany desk and started, slowly and rhythmically, to pound it with his right hand. Sometimes, it seemed to him, everything in life was against Israel – not just the hatred of her enemies farther afield. It was the very soul of life itself that seemed at times to be against her.

Before the six-day war of 1967, Israel had been a minute country, smaller than Wales. Since that war it had doubled in size, but Ephraim knew that the land could just as easily, one day, be snatched away again, and Israel could be back to where she was before, a mere seven thousand, nine hundred square miles, the only true home for the fifteen million Jews in the world – a home which one day, it was not inconceivable, they might need.

Ephraim's job was to listen in on the rest of the world, find out just what anyone might be intending to do that could harm Israel, either by propaganda or by force, and either arrange for them to be stopped himself, or advise the Prime Minister on what action to sanction.

His moles were his ears, and just as he himself had been planted in Syria over thirty years earlier, he in turn had planted men – young, dedicated men he could trust, intelligent men with the ability to rise far – in all the countries where he felt danger could lurk or good information could be obtained. With a population in Israel of only three and a half million to draw from, and a tiny budget, he had a tough task, and could not afford to carry passengers on his team. In some countries he kept better moles than others: Britain was a key country to him, both because of its own status in the world and because of its large Arab population and connections. One of the men he had placed in England was a man in whom he had originally had particularly high hopes, someone whom he had singled out as a true chameleon, able to adapt and blend into any situation – a dedicated man, and a ruthless man.

During the past few years this man had disappointed him; somehow, the zeal for Israel had deserted him, and been replaced by a bitterness with his lot in life. He had become careless in his security, lazy in his work. He was a bad agent, and it was Ephraim's strong view that a bad agent was a dangerous person to have.

The decoded message on his desk told him that this agent was at the present moment in the intensive care unit of a hospital outside London, following a car accident.

The report of the accident made no sense: the man had apparently driven into the back of a road-laying lorry in broad daylight on a clear day. He could have fallen asleep at the wheel – or equally as easily, he could have been drugged. Ephraim had a good young man he wanted to put into England, but his budget was already overextended; he decided that soon he would swap this man for Baenhaker. He smiled. Some occasion would arise soon in London which would involve an agent in the risk of having his cover blown these situations cropped up all the time. As soon as Baenhaker was out of hospital, he would be put at the top of the 'candidates for blown cover' list. The first assignment that came up, he would give Baenhaker, and then afterwards transfer him out of England to an unimportant country, on the grounds that his cover had been blown. He smiled, and wished all his decisions could be made so easily.

CHAPTER 7

One naked blonde English girl held his ankles and ran her tongue slowly up and down the soles of his feet. He wriggled and giggled hysterically, thrashing around, trying to free his wrists from the pincer-grip of the second naked blonde English girl at the head of the massive bed. The third naked blonde pulled away his djellaba, climbed on top of him, and lowered herself down over him.

Ten minutes later he lay there, gasping in exhaustion. She leaned forward and untied his blindfold.

'Judy!' he smiled, weakly.

The other two began to sponge him down with hot towels. 'Come on, Abby, take us out today,' said one.

'Yes, let's go down to that beach at Quommah,' said the other.

'I planned to stay in and do some work,' said Prince Abr Qu'Ih Missh, the thirty-one-year-old son and heir of Sheik Quozzohok, divine Emir of Umm Al Amnah.

Prince Abr Qu'ih Missh was a tall man with a

handsome, if rather weak, face. The pursuit of English blondes in their homeland, and the persuading of them to come, for not inconsiderable sums of money, for extended stays to the Palace of Tunquit, the capital of Umm Al Amnah, was his consuming interest in life. It was also a sport to which his passion for playing, on the world's stock and commodity markets, some of the $9 million Umm Al Amnah earned every day from its oil sales, took a firm second place.

The Quommah Beach Club is one of the few spots in Umm Al Amnah that has anything approaching western style. It was built by Missh to impress visitors, and relieve them of some, if not all, of their dollars, by virtue of its containing the only casino in the country. It is a handsome oasis of green trees and smoked glass, built around a sheltered white sand bay that faces the shimmering Persian Gulf. Impressed by his visits to the Playboy Clubs, Missh staffed the place with blonde girls dressed in two piece bathing costumes made from camels' skin, with camels' ears attached to their heads and tails to their behinds.

The Beach Club is midway between Tunquit, the capital, and Al Suttoh, the chief port of Umm Al Amnah. An immaculate four-lane highway connects the two towns; it is the only four-lane highway in the country and it runs no further in either direction than the airport, the seaport and the capital, passing the Beach Club on the way. Like the road, the airport, the seaport and the capital are ultra-modern and immaculate; Sheik Quozzohok wanted to impress visitors to his country and, provided they didn't stray beyond this part, which, if they didn't have camels they were unlikely to, he usually succeeded.

The total population of Umm Al Amnah is 17,000 of whom less than 1,500 can read or write. For ten years Sheik Quozzohok had been busy ploughing the oil revenues back into modernizing his country. He wanted to take his people out of the rock, tent and shanty dwelling that had traditionally been their homes and bring them into his city, Tunquit; again, it was not so much for their welfare, but more to impress visitors. He wanted visitors to see how modern and progressive his country was because he wanted foreign investment, foreign industry. One day, he knew, the oil would run out; long before that, he wanted Umm Al Amnah to be an industrial nation. Twenty years ago, his country's export revenue had amounted to the grand total of $180,000 achieved through the export of dried fish, dates and pearls. For the previous five years, the annual average was $3.5 billion, all except $800,000 of which was from one product only: oil. The fish and dates had quadrupled in size, and he had scrapped the pearl farming as being uneconomical. In the next twelve months, revenues from sources other than oil would, he confidently expected, be upwards of $5 million – an increase of over six hundred per cent. This would come from the export of goods made by companies that he had persuaded to build factories in Umm Al Amnah – from the manufacture of car batteries for Australia, pocket cameras, ceramic flower pots, woven rugs, light bulbs, vacuum cleaners, deep freezers, camping gas stoves, oral contraceptive pills and a host of other items.

He had induced these companies to build plants in Umm Al Amnah by bartering oil licences, favourable terms for oil sales, and supply guarantees.

To impress upon the captains of foreign industry that his country was not a tin-pot nation of bedouins and camel shit, he had spent vast sums of money in constructing, in Tunquit, as modern a city as money could buy. Anyone who ever dreamed of finding a city with its streets paved with gold would be unlikely to come closer to his dream than to visit Tunquit. Although not gold, the pavements are entirely marble and mosaics, and above them, rising high into the sky, is a forest of smoked glass and steel skyscrapers, with every building unique, and many displaying stunningly handsome architecture. The shorter ones are fifty to sixty storeys; the taller ones, eighty to ninety storeys. All, with few exceptions – which are the office buildings and the Royal Palace – have no occupants above the ground floor.

It had not occurred to Sheik Quozzohok that the bedouin nomads, for whom these dazzling palaces in the sky had been intended, could not get their camels into the elevators, or that their goats and sheep would not enjoy high-rise living. Many tried the apartment style of life; few stayed for more than a few days before returning to their hills and communities.

Quozzohok's reaction to this was the same as his reaction to any act of infidelity to him, whether by an individual or by an entire community: a fit of rage followed by swift retaliation. The method of retaliation was always the same: he would cut off the water supply. For the communities that lived in the desert or in the mountains, the way he did this was to instruct his army to concrete in all the waterholes in the surrounding area; the effect for them, normally, was devastating. Not only would the occupants of the immediate vicinity face dying of thirst, but many communities all around, who would frequently depend on one waterhole in hundreds of miles of inhospitable and barren desert, would have either to uproot and move – completely – elsewhere, or die. Cutting off the water supply for the town dwellers was easier for Quozzohok – it required only the turning of a mains tap. Frequently, he caused the whole of the nation's capital to be without water for days on end.

It was not surprising that Quozzohok's popularity was on a steady wane. His intolerance towards his people and his open capitalism angered and upset many of his people, going against their Muslim grain. There was a rising tide of rebellion growing in the country, carrying inside it a bubble that was dangerously near to breaking point. Quozzohok spent most of his days closeted in the palace, working out new ways to woo major industry to Umm Al Amnah and playing with his massive assortment of gadgets that were his passion. He was an old man, a seventeenth generation ruler, who, unlike most of his predecessors, did not like the desert or the heat. The Royal Palace is a ninety-seven storey building, constructed from smoked glass and bronze-coated steel, rising from the centre of Tunquit like a massive altar. From his penthouse study, he could, on any one of the three hundred and thirty eight clear days of the year, survey all the corners of his land; but he rarely bothered to have any of the closed shutters over the windows raised.

If he had looked out or, better still, actually gone out, he might have picked up a few of the warning signs that his son, Prince Abr Qu'Ih Missh, spoke about at dinner almost every night. But he stayed inside, eyes firmly entrenched in the tomes of John Kenneth Galbraith and other financial architects of the major industrial nations of the world, dreaming of a gross national product which would leave the Japanese wringing their calculators in envy, and ordering the filling-in of still more waterholes for his ever-diminishing population.

Prince Missh and his three blonde ladies left the Quommah Beach Club at five o'clock, and walked to the palm-shaded car park where he had left his gleaming white replica pre-war Mercedes.

As they reached the car, two of the girls screamed in horror, and Missh froze: the tyres of the car had been slashed to ribbons, and every inch of the paintwork, and the leather interior, was smeared in excrement.

For some minutes, Missh did not move; then his eyes began to moisten. He walked silently around the car while the girls stood watching him, fearful. Then he swivelled on his Moreschi heels and walked swiftly back to the Club. He dialled a number at the reception desk and ordered a car from the secret police. As he waited for it to arrive, he stood still in silence, deep in thought. The day was not long now, he knew; something had to be done, and done fast.

Throughout the ride in the armour-plated Lincoln, back to the palace, and throughout the nightly ritual of dinner with his father, he remained in almost complete silence. After dinner he went to his quarters, occupying the sixtieth to seventy-fifth floors of the Palace, and sat awake, on his own, throughout the long night. There was revolution in the air, he knew; an idiot could have sensed it. He thought back to 1979, to Iran – the evening of that year when he had sat with his father and with the Shah of Iran, one of his father's greatest friends, and the man in the world that his father had always said he admired the most. He remembered the Shah talking about unrest, and his father poo-pooing it as nonsense and telling the Shah not to be concerned. And yet his father had learned nothing from all this. He was right, thought Missh, the man who said, 'The lesson of history is that man does not learn the lesson of history.'

Iran was many hundreds of times the size of his own country but the policies were much the same, the people much the same, and now the signs were much the same. He needed help, a lot of help, and quickly – and he did not know where to turn. The Umm Al Amnah army was strong, but small; and although, because of the size of their pay packets, most of the soldiers were undoubtedly loyal to his family, he was equally certain that when the crunch came, there were many who would not turn their guns onto their own people, just as he knew there were many who disobeyed their instructions to fill in waterholes. They needed help from the West, but he knew the West wouldn't help. When his father had declared Independence and broken away from the Emirates, he had upset just about the entire Western World.

At that time, he had drawn help from the Libyans and the Russians, a fact which more than anything had prompted the pro-West United Arab Emirates to disown Amnah. Ever since then, relationships with the UAE Government had been strained at the best of times, with frequent border skirmishes, on Quozzohoks's instructions, at the slightest hint of territorial infringement. The West would now not dare lift one finger to help them for fear of upsetting the UAE, with whom the West now had major economic ties.

It had taken Amnah eight years to throw off the claws of Libya and Russia. Neither country was pleased with the way it had been treated by Quozzohok after helping Amnah to gain Independence, and it was unlikely either would be willing to help again, on anything other than complete take-over terms.

He wished he could discuss the situation rationally with his father, but he knew his father would not listen. His father would not believe that his people, whom his family had led for eleven hundred years, could even contemplate rising up against him. If he told his father about the incident with his Mercedes, it would only lead to even more waterholes being filled in, and create more misery and greater resentment still.

At dawn, Missh came to a decision: he would have to bring in a private army, one whose loyalties were to money and money only, one which would not be influenced by political or religious views. He needed someone thoroughly experienced in the field of mercenaries to advise him on the numbers and types of mercenaries he needed, and to set the whole thing up for him. There was one man, he knew, who might be able to help. He was the man through whom they had bought most of their military equipment during the last eight years – a man who was able to produce gun-boats, tanks, aeroplanes, with the ease of a village shop delivering a weekend grocery order. He lifted the telephone receiver an started dialling an Athens telephone number. The phone rang three times, and then a voice answered.

'Jimmy Culundis?' said Missh.

'Speaking', said the Greek arms dealer.

'This is Abby Missh. I have some business to talk.'

CHAPTER 8

The white golf ball climbed gracefully through the air, high above the manicured fairway, and seemingly high above the peaks of the mountains that surrounded the course at Crans Montana, in the Swiss Alps. The man who stood on the eleventh tee, peering over the top of the lacquered head of his three wood at his ball's flight, was short and plump. He wore a bright red Lacoste T-shirt, green tartan trousers, white shoes, a yellow peaked cap, and was festooned with heavy, vulgar jewellery. As his ball dipped down towards the fairway, it was momentarily obscured from his vision by a cloud of Bolivar smoke that belched out of his mouth and out of the damp stump he held clenched between his tobacco-stained teeth.

The ball bounced onto the green, ran forwards towards the pin and stopped what appeared, from where they were standing, to be only inches from a hole in one. Jimmy Culundis, the multi-millionaire Greek arms dealer, chuckled, removed the stump from his mouth and spat onto the ground. His companion, a tall man with a handsome, if slightly weak face, dressed in a cream silk shirt, paisley cravat, yellow cashmere V-neck cardigan and well-cut beige trousers, frowned at the perfect shot, and then glared down at the puddle of spittle on the ground. Slightly embarrassed, he looked behind him; the Moroccan Ambassador to Switzerland, the French Foreign Secretary, the French Commercial Attaché to Switzerland and the Couve de Meurville stood behind them with their battery of caddies, patiently waiting for them to move on, and with expressions of undisguised disgust on their faces.

Claude Louis Santenay Jarré du Charnevrau Ducarme de Louçelle, fifteenth Viscomte Lasserre, beamed a crushing aristocratic expression at the Greek, which, without words, told Culundis that the Viscomte approved neither of the shot nor the spitting.

'Shot!' said the Viscomte in a curt, grudging tone.

'Good, hey!' said the Greek, twiddling his finger in his ear.

The Viscomte placed his ball, and took his four wood. He cracked the ball high and hard over to the right, and it dropped neatly between the roots of a fir tree about eighty yards to the right of the green. He pushed his club back into his bag and, pulling their trolleys, the two men set off. They had no caddies because they wanted to talk, and did not want an audience; for it was here at Crans Montana, home of the Swiss Open Championship, that the two men met once a month during the summer months, to discuss their business.

Neither of them stood out particularly from any of the other rich people who hacked and bashed their way around some of the most exclusive kilometres of cultivated grass in the world, neither in appearance nor in standard of play. The Greek's handicap was nine, the Viscomte's twelve. The backgrounds of the two men could not have been more dissimilar. The Greek was the son of a twelfth generation lobster fisherman; when he was born, his family owned a single-storey cottage with no running water and no electricity. When the Viscomte Lasserre was born, his family owned Chateau Lasserre, a massive grey and white stone chateau, set in front of a two hundred acre lake, in a seventeen thousand acre estate which included fifty-five acres of *cinquième cru* vines. To most people, Chateau Lasserre was possibly the most beautiful of all the chateaux in the Médoc region of France. To all Frenchmen, its claret was, without doubt, one of the worst. The current Viscomte's grandfather had, some sixty years previously, upon discovering that fewer and fewer people in France would buy his wine, succeeded in selling the entire output for one hundred years to an English shipper who knew that with a smart name, an old year and a cheap price, there would be no shortage of punters in the English restaurant trade.

The Greek, like many sons of fishermen, had gone into shipping. But whereas that other man from his country, Stavros Niarchos, had gone in for tankers, Jimmy Culundis had gone in for vessels for gun running. At first it had been on a local scale, providing boats to carry guns into Turkey, but soon he built it up into an international business, illegally shipping at first guns and ammunition, then graduating to all types of warmongering hardware, from armoured vehicles to jet fighters. His clientele comprised mainly terrorist organizations and guerilla outfits which legally no one was allowed to supply, or which were politically sensitive. He shipped guns to the IRA, gunboats to Israel, uranium to Libya.

It took him a mere five years to graduate from being the carrier to arranging the entire deals from start to finish. By the time he was thirty-three years old, he had completely equipped the armed forces of nine African countries, three Arab countries, and six South American countries. There was scarcely a terrorist in the world that had not at some time carried a weapon purloined from Jimmy Culundis.

Right from the very start, Culundis had always taken great pains to conceal his clandestine activities behind a carefully-maintained respectable front, although now it was a front that was in the process of crumbling fast. For over twenty years he had been one of the world's leading bona fide arms dealers, and had been trusted widely by many governments. But stories of the murkier side of his business had been coming to the surface in many parts of the globe. The British *Sunday Times* Insight columns had plucked truckloads of skeletons from his closets, as had the *Washington Post*. So that at the age of fifty-three, he had been black-listed by most of his major clients; and whilst there was still plenty of business for him in supplying the more dubious of customers, the massive empire he had constructed had lost the support of his biggest punters, and was in grave danger of collapsing.

Culundis walked onto the eleventh green, and smiled with satisfaction when he saw his ball was a mere six inches from the hole. He stood and watched the Viscomte take three shots to extricate his ball from between the roots of the fir tree and then, with his next shot, drop it neatly onto the green, about eight feet from the pin. He walked up to Culundis.

'I give you the hole.'

The Greek grinned and pulled the cigar out of his mouth. 'Two up!' he said.

'You're playing well, Jimmy,' said the Viscomte. 'You don't give me a chance.'

'I can't make any profit out of doing business with you, Claude – this is the only way I get to eat!'

'If you can't make a profit out of the prices I let you have goods at,' grinned the Viscomte, 'then you are in the wrong business.'

The Greek shrugged his shoulders, and stopped by the twelfth tee. He looked with more than a little envy at the Viscomte, the chief executive of Lasserre Mondiale, one of the largest private companies in the world. Claude Lasserre had it cushy, he thought. Straight in at the top. Not for him those early days of battling to build up a business from scratch. Sailing blacked-out boats into pitch dark bays in the middle of the night, never knowing when a battery of searchlights might blaze into life, floodlighting them in the empty sea as the guns pounded at them until they had sunk. Lasserre had never had to do a bloody thing, he thought. Ever since the Fourth Viscomte had bought his family's safety through the French Revolution by supplying arms to the revolutionaries, the Lasserre empire had flourished without a hiccup. Today it had many tentacles, all to do with the business of killing: Lasserre Aerospatiale, which manufactured military specification jet helicopters and short-range strike jets; Lasserre Nautique, which manufactured gunboats and navy-specification submersibles; and Lasserre Industriel, which manufactured a vast range of pistols, machine guns, mortars and artillery guns, bullets, shells, grenades, land and sea mines, and also was one of the French Government's principal nuclear weapons contractors.

In spite of the vast amounts of money the Lasserre empire earned him, the Viscomte was not a man for stashing his bundle idly away in the coffers. He liked to see his money work; he liked to see it multiply. Lasserre was a great believer in commodities as a way to make money grow, and there was one commodity-broking firm in whose abilities he had particular confidence, both in the boss and the calibre of those beneath him. The man was Sir Monty Elleck, and the firm was Globalex. Although based in London, he had always found that the performance of the firm more than made up for the nuisance of having always to deal at a distance.

'I received a telephone call last night,' said Culundis, bending down to push his tee into the grass and lay his Titleist ball on top; he grunted as he stood up again. 'From no less than Prince Abr Qu'Ih Missh of Uram Al Amnah.'

The Viscomte froze for a moment, and his face went white. He stared at Culundis. 'From Umm Al Amnah?'

Culundis nodded. He stepped back, removed his driver, took one short practice swing, then hit the ball badly; it travelled only a short distance, hooking sharply to the left, and fell into the rough.

'What was he calling about? The mines? Jimmy – was he calling about the mines?'

'No, no. Relax, Claude, it wasn't the mines.'

The Viscomte played a two-hundred-and-forty-yard drive straight down the centre of the fairway; it went over the centre marker pin and fell down, out of sight in the dip, into the perfect text-book position. He put his club head on the ground, and leaned on it. 'What did he want?'

'He thinks there is trouble brewing; he wants to make sure his family stays in power.'

'What sort of trouble? A coup?' Lasserre even paler.

'He seems to think so.'

'That would destroy everything.'

'So we have to make sure there is no coup.'

'And how do we do that?'

'I'm flying there tomorrow for the weekend.'

'I can think of places I'd prefer to spend my weekends.'

Culundis shook his head. 'You'd be hard pushed. That man has got the best crumpet in the world, and I mean that. In the world!'

'Maybe he should spend more time thinking about his neck and less about his genitals.'

'That's what I am going to discuss with him.'

'Well, I hope you remember to.'

CHAPTER 9

Rocq arrived at work on the Monday morning late and exhausted, having dropped Theo Barbiero-Ruche at Heathrow airport at eight and subsequently been stuck two hours in a jam on the Hammersmith Flyover behind a jack-knifed lorry. His weekend had been spent playing golf with Theo, drinking and discussing coffee into the small hours of each night and lying awake, trying to avoid listening to the fat Italian copulating with the sparrow-like Deirdre until dawn.

He put his briefcase down under his desk, nodded at Henry Mozer and Gary Slivitz who were busy trying to extricate a large number of their clients out of a £20 drop in zinc over the weekend and into a rapidly improving silver market, ignored the frantically flashing lights on his own switchboard and went out, and down to the next floor, the Soft Commodities department.

From the way the brokers and other staff were sitting, idly chatting, it had been a quiet weekend for their business. He sat down in an empty chair next to his one chum in this department, the Honourable James Rice. 'Morning Jimbo,' he said.

'Well, well, Rocky,' said Rice. 'What's up? Metals finally gone through the floor?' He guffawed at his own joke.

'Might have you a client, Jimbo.'

'Sensible, Rocky. This is the best place for any client – I mean, who the hell wants metal? Can't eat the bloody stuff.'

In spite of his frivolous conversation, Rice was the most successful soft commodities broker in Globalex. He was the only other broker in the entire firm whose commissions nearly rivalled Rocq's and, accordingly, just about the only other broker who was ever genuinely friendly towards Rocq.

'What do you reckon on coffee at the moment, Jimbo?'

Rice looked at him. 'Want a cup?'

Rocq grinned. 'Bit more than that.'

Rice shrugged. 'I'd go sugar at the moment. You can buy it at £160 – it'll be £180 by the end of the week.'

Rocq shook his head. 'I've heard that there might be a coffee shortage – coffee rust?'

Rice seemed cagey to Rocq. 'Who's your source?'

'The man who punches the holes in tea bags.'

'Maybe I should meet him; he's got his snout in the right trough. There is talk of serious coffee rust in South America – could hit the crops badly in the next few weeks – but it's very closely guarded talk. Problem is, coffee's already very high – been high for two years now, and the high prices have hit the consumers. Result – demand's gone down – and is still falling. I think the prices are due for a major tumble, and the rust'll hold them upright – but no more.'

'I think you're bullshitting, Rice.'

Rice grinned.

'I think you've got a fat one you're keeping for your favourites, and you don't want Uncle Rocky to get a look-in and set the market stampeding.'

'Tell me your source, and I'll flog you some beans.'

'Up yours.' Rocq stood up. 'I'll talk to you later.' He began to walk out of the room.

'Hey Rocky,' shouted Rice, 'cash only – no cheques.'

'Relax – I've got American Express.'

'I'm sure that will do nicely.'

Rocq had a 12.30 appointment with his own personal bank manager. The appointment was not in the bank, but in the Halls' Well Dining Club. Somewhere between his fourth glass of Chateau Palmer '62, and his third snifter of Hine '47, the bank manager agreed to loan Alexander Rocq £110,000 for three months, at fifteen and one quarter per cent. This was to be secured by a charge on Rocq's cottage at Clayton and on that part of his apartment in Redcliffe Square that the Bradford and Bingley Building Society did not own; and by a lien on his £32,000 worth of Porsche, and custody of the certificates for £10,000 worth of ordinary shares spread between Great Universal Stores, Valor, British National Oil Company, Foreign and Colonial Investment Trust, Moss Bros and Conrans, together with stock transfer forms. With the exception of two white gold crowns in his teeth, £300 of Piaget watch, five pairs of Gucci shoes, an assortment of Louis Feraud and Yves Saint Laurent suits, jackets and trousers, several dozen Turnbull and Asser shirts, twenty-six pairs of Henry Burton of Glasgow socks and a motley assortment of furniture, artefacts and inessential trappings, Alex Rocq had hocked his entire worldly goods.

At half past three he walked, slightly unsteadily, into the Honourable James Rice's office, and sat down beside him; he belched out a mouthful of expensive alcohol vapour.

'Changed your mind about coffee and went into booze, did you, Rocky?'

Rocq stared at him, and found he wasn't focussing too well. He sat back and squinted hard. 'What's the big news in coffee today?'

Rice tapped his keyboard and looked at the visual display screen. 'One thousand and twenty-two. September. Dropped £15 today.'

'So now would be a good time to buy?'

'Fifteen pounds cheaper than this morning.'

'That it for the day?'

'Thought you were the expert, Rocky.'

'I'm serious, Rice, don't mess me about. I've got a nice client for you – a real gentleman – that is, if you want him – would you rather I took him elsewhere?'

'How nice is he?'

'He drinks a lot of coffee.'

'How much?'

'Reckons he'll be needing two hundred lots in three months' time.'

Rice pursed his lips. Two hundred lots was one thousand tons. At the current price, that was £1,022,000. A damned nice deal to have at the start of what looked to be a quiet week, otherwise. At £10 per lot brokerage, that was £2,000 for Globalex and £200 in commission for himself. 'I'll place that on the market for you,' he said, 'with the greatest of pleasure. The margin requirements are £102,200, due tomorrow, and the balance of – er – £919,800 due September,' he said.

'Booked,' said Rocq.

Rice wrote out his order slip. 'Who's the client?' he asked.

'Me.'

Rocq celebrated the sale of his soul to the Midland Bank by taking Amanda to dinner at Le Capo, off West Halkin Street. It was, she pointed out, exactly ten weeks to the day since they had met, on Easter Saturday, at a point-to-point at Cowdray Park in Sussex. She had been arguing furiously with the Tote over why she'd only collected 97p on a 50p win-only bet on a horse which, according to the bookies, had come in at ten to one. Rocq had been at the queue for the Five Pound Win box next to her; he had attempted to explain the way the Tote calculated its payouts. At the end of his precise and accurate lecture she glared at him: 'When you lose, it hurts, and when you win, you don't get enough.'

'You got it in one,' he had said.

'So if you know so much, what are you doing it for?'

'It hurts less than not gambling at all.'

She frowned at him, and it was then he noticed for the first time her exquisite short straight nose, her beautiful mouth that was pouting cheekily, her blue eyes that were full of life and her fair brown hair streaked with highlights. She was about five foot seven in her high-heeled boots, Phillipe Salvet cord trousers, Jousse shirt and Cornelia James silk scarf. She had put her hands in her pockets and was looking at him. He had forgotten that there were girls on this planet who could look as good as she did. He had stared at her, taking her in, the soft skin on her face that radiated life, the couple of freckles and, apart from two light dabs of mascara, no make-up at all and, for a moment, he had thought back to his busted marriage – his stunning blonde wife who was only stunning after an hour of patience in front of the mirror, who scraped the gunk off each night before bed. He would go out to dinner with a raving beauty, a girl with the aura of an enchantress, a girl who would turn heads at any beauty contest; she was a girl who looked simply, incredibly sexy, until the one time that mattered to Rocq the most: the time when she came to bed. She would never come to bed until after her twenty-five-minute ritual in the bathroom, scraping every last molecule of make-up off her face so that it would not ruin her complexion. Thus it was that the woman, his wife, who filled him with lust at the dinner table arrived in his bed with a face like an uncooked turkey.

But Amanda was something else. Standing beside the Tote and looking at her under the grey April sky, he could see someone who would look as good waking up in the morning as she ever could in all her evening finery.

'Are you one of those compulsive gamblers?' she had said, when she had finished frowning; she was already turning, about to walk off. Rocq wanted to stop her, wanted to find the hook, did not want to give her a reply she could merely walk away from.

'Would you like to have a bet with me?'

'Do you always win?'

He liked her voice; she was well spoken, well-bred without having to flaunt it through her vocal chords.

'I always try to win.'

'But do you succeed?' She smiled, for the first time.

'You'll have to tell me; I'll bet you five pounds you wouldn't come and have dinner with me tonight.'

She turned back towards him, grinning almost shyly, then blushed just a fraction. 'That's not a fair bet. How can I win that? I'm not free tonight.'

'Are you going to accept the bet?'

'How could I win it?'

'By making yourself free.'

She shook her head. 'I can't,' she said. 'I really can't.'

'Would you like to come out some other time?'

She looked at him carefully, looked down at his shoes, then up at his face, then nodded her head. 'Sure.'

'How about breakfast tomorrow?'

She grinned. 'Lunch?'

'Why don't we compromise and have brunch?'

'Just as long as I don't have to gamble.'

'I wasn't planning to take you to a casino.'

'I wanted to be sure.'

Rocq toyed with his rich seafood crepe, wishing he'd had something less rich, like a salad, and regretting he'd ordered a tournedos in champagne, cream and mushroom sauce to follow, when he would have happily settled for a plain grilled sole. He was finding it difficult to concentrate on his evening out. Amanda looked more stunning than ever, and he wished he felt more relaxed. He was enjoying the buzz of the two large ice-cold vodka martinis and the taste of the crisp Sancerre, and he looked forward to a night of rummaging through the erotic treasure chest of Amanda's mind, body and bedroom cupboard, all of which contained a myriad of ideas, artefacts and liquids designed or adapted by her for the purpose of making the long dark hours of the night slip past in the nicest possible way.

One half of him was bursting to lean forward and tell her what he had done. The other half was very much aware of her loathing of gambling, and advised him, in the firmest possible manner, to keep his trap shut. So he did. Instead, he thought. He did his sums over and over again: for £102,000 he had bought one thousand tons of coffee, at a price of £1,022 a ton. The total value of his purchase was £1,022,000.

The commodity market is unique in that investors do not usually buy a particular commodity for immediate delivery, but buy it for delivery at a future date. For coffee, three to six delivery months forward is the norm. When buying a 'future,' the investor does not have to pay the full price until the delivery date. All he has to put down at the time of purchase is a deposit – normally ten per cent. This is known as 'buying on margin.' The investor is free to sell his 'future coffee' at any time. If, before the delivery date, the price has risen, and he does sell, he takes his profit not merely on the ten per cent deposit, but on the total value of the purchase. If Rocq's coffee, which he had bought at £1,022 a ton rose in price to £2,000 a ton and he then sold, on his £102,000 investment he would make a profit of nearly £2 million.

116

Conversely, if the price dropped to £500 a ton, he would still be obliged to buy the coffee for £1,022,000, even though he would only be able to sell it for £500,000 – giving him a loss of over half a million pounds. He had put down £102,000; if coffee dropped to £500,000, he would have to pay out a further £400,000; and that was £400,000 more than he had.

The waiter asked Rocq if he was finished, and removed the almost untouched crepe. Would Senor like something else? A salad, perhaps? Rocq shook his head. He wanted nothing; just some silence, for a few more moments, to do those sums again, for the one hundredth time since this afternoon.

Theo had reckoned coffee would go to £2,500 a ton, which would put the value of his investment at £2.5 million. He would pay back the £102,000 plus interest to the bank, and have near enough £2,400,000 profit. After tax, that would still leave him comfortably a millionaire. He smiled; he was on his way. He was going to whip Monty Elleck's ass.

The 1961 Chateau Lasserre arrived in its wicker basket; Rocq read the label, sniffed the cork, swirled a few drops of wine four times around his glass, held it up to the light, looked at it, sniffed the top of the glass, screwed up his nose, took a mouthful, swilled it around his mouth, opened his mouth a little to let in some air, closed it again, and swallowed. The waiter hovered the bottle over Amanda's glass, expectantly.

'Corked,' said Rocq.

'Pardon, Senor?'

'It's corked. No good.'

The waiter's eyes opened a fraction: he hesitated for a moment. 'Si, Senor.' He swept away with the bottle.

'I have never seen anyone send back a bottle before,' said Amanda.

'It was muck.'

'What's up?' she said. 'Why are you in such a ratty mood tonight?'

'I'm not ratty; that's a very expensive wine, and it's off. I know the wine well – I actually had some at lunch today – not such a good year and it tasted a hundred times better. I want a nice wine for us – not one that's off.'

'Well I'm glad something's caught your attention tonight, because I certainly haven't.'

'You look terrific,' he said.

'That's the third time you've told me that tonight; it's very nice to be told that, very flattering, thank you. You're looking very dishy yourself; maybe we should start the Alex and Amanda mutual appreciation society. You're pretty good at flattery, and I'm sure I could learn fast.'

He grinned. 'I'm sorry, I've had a heavy day. I'm unwinding a bit slowly.' He paused. 'How is work at Messrs Garbutt, Garbutt and Garbutt?'

'Frantically busy. They've landed a massive contract for an Arab country – Umm Al Amnah. There's some mad sheik who's decided that there

118

should be a squash court for every man, woman and child in the land – and the firm's been commissioned to design a seventy-five storey high rise squash complex, and the whole thing completely in smoked glass.'

The waiter reappeared with a belligerent look on his face and a new bottle, without wicker basket, brandished in his fist like a dagger. He cut the seal off the lip with all the grace of a rabbi performing his tenth circumcision of the morning, stabbed the corkscrew into the top as if it were a harpoon, and twisted it several times, like a monkey wrench. Then, with a triumphant gleam in his eye and all the delicacy of a plumber removing a plunger from a blocked lavatory, he wrenched the corkscrew out. The gleam soon faded. Attached to the corkscrew was a mere one-third of the cork. The remaining two-thirds stayed exactly where it had been wedged, on a day back in the early 1960s, when the Beatles were jeered for having long hair and the mini-skirt had not yet been invented.

There were storm clouds in Amanda's blue eyes; Rocq had not seen storm clouds in her eyes before. He wanted to defuse the situation, and defuse it quickly. 'How's Baenhaker?' he asked, not because he was interested, but because on the spur of the moment, he couldn't think of anything else to talk about.

'Why do you always call him "Baenhaker," Alex? I call him Danny, why can't you?'

The waiter now had the bottle gripped between

his thighs; he was bent over it at an angle which was provoking curious glances from a number of the other tables around, and was engaged in a long and subdued conversation with the bottle in a language that was not immediately recognizable to either Rocq or Amanda. At the same time, he was gently winding the corkscrew back in.

'Look, Amanda, I don't wish to be disrespectful about your ex-lover, and as I have never met him, it would be extremely discourteous not to call him by his surname.'

'In that case you should call him "Mr" Baenhaker.'

'Amanda, you're being ridiculous. If that's how you feel about him, then I suggest you go back to him.'

Her eyes began to well with tears, and she shook her head slowly. 'I love you,' she said, straining hard not to cry. 'I love you and I don't love him. But he was my boyfriend for a long time – over a year and a half, and it's one hell of a shock to see him in hospital in that condition. Can't you understand that?'

Rocq nodded. 'I'm sorry. I'll try to be nicer about him.'

There was the sudden loud yell of an Italian waiter crushing his index finger between the neck of a claret bottle and the blade of a corkscrew. It was followed in rapid succession by the sound of a cork being forced through the base of the neck of a bottle, followed by the sound of vintage claret,

under considerable pressure, shooting out
neck of a bottle and liberally dousing a party
ill-tempered German film producers.

'You know,' said Amanda, 'I think I'd be quite
happy to stick to white.'

CHAPTER 10

General Isser Ephraim, head of the Mossad, whilst heavily guarded at his office and home, relied on nothing but his wits when he was not in these places. He travelled frequently, and used a combination of disguises, spontaneous changes of plan, and illogical routes.

On this particular mid-June Tuesday morning, having flown the night before from Tel Aviv to Athens, he had hopped onto a Singapore Airlines jumbo making its last stop between the Far East and London, using a passport which identified him as being an air conditioning systems consultant.

As he emerged into the throng of people at London's Heathrow Airport, his eyes, behind slightly tinted lenses, worked their way in a matter of seconds over every face that was in the terminal. They relayed to the memory banks of his brain essential details of features, height and stance, information that could at any split second trigger the alarm bells. But on this hot summer morning, General Ephraim did not notice anybody whose business it might be to kill him hanging around this section of the airport. He walked smartly out,

climbed into a taxi, and ordered it to take t̶
the West Middlesex Hospital.

Twenty minutes later, he was sitting beside Baenhaker's bed in the large ward. The Mossad agent was conscious and sitting up in bed, looking sullen, and attached by a battery of wires to a large assortment of monitoring equipment.

Occupying the bed to one side of him was a 90-year-old white-haired man who was sorting out a cardboard box full of used bus tickets and muttering to himself; on the other side was an equally ancient man who appeared, to Ephraim's trained eye, to have been dead for some hours. The beds on the other side of the ward did not, in Ephraim's quick summing up, contain anyone who appeared remotely capable of carrying out even the most basic surveillance.

'How are you, Danny?' he asked.

'I don't know, you'll have to ask someone else. I've no idea how I am.' Baenhaker stared at the General for a brief moment, then turned his eyes away.

Ephraim looked him up and down carefully. Considering the distance he had come, he felt he was entitled to a slightly heartier greeting than this. It further confirmed the feelings he had about Baenhaker. He wanted him out of this hospital and out of this country. 'The Sister tells me you are making a good recovery.'

'What have you come for, General? To say goodbye?'

'What do you mean?'

'Come on, General, they don't reckon I'm going to last another week.'

Ephraim looked shocked. 'Sister said they're going to start you walking again tomorrow.'

Baenhaker gave him a pathetic look – a look that was full of defeat – and told him not to bother to lie. 'They reckon I'm crippled for life – if I don't die from my internal injuries.'

Ephraim stared at him for a long time, then shook his head. 'Is that what you're doing, Danny? Lying in bed, thinking about everything that's bad, and how it can all get worse? Is that all you're doing?'

'What else should I be doing?'

The General leaned forward. 'You should be working, Danny, that is what you should be doing. You are an agent of the finest Intelligence organization in the world; you committed yourself to working for that organization twenty-four hours a day, seven days a week. How long have you been in this hospital, Danny? Eight days is it? Do you know who else is in here? In the other wards?'

Baenhaker shook his head.

'The Parliamentary Under-Secretary for Defence; two Syrian government ministers; and an Irishman who is a key link-pin with the PLO. All scraped off the same motorway as you during the past few weeks. I've been here thirty minutes and I've found all that out. You have been here eight days, and what have you found out? Nothing.'

'You do have a slight advantage,' said Baenhaker, sullenly.

'Who knows best what's going on in a place like this? It's the nurses, they're the ones that know best. They're going to give information to anyone they feel sympathetic towards. They all feel sympathetic towards you. All you have to do is ask, and they'll tell you anything you would like to know. You've been here eight days, and you haven't asked them one solitary question, have you?' Ephraim did not wait for him to reply. He stood up. 'You want to hang onto your job, then you'd better pull your ass up off that bed, and do it fast.'

Ephraim marched out of the ward, through the swing doors and downstairs to where the cab was waiting for him. He smiled to himself as he climbed in. It had worked. Five minutes earlier, Baenhaker had been a disintegrating vegetable with nothing to drive him forward. Now Baenhaker was furious, and would be wanting to hit back at him, wanting to hit back badly; and in order to do that, he had to get himself out of that hospital. Ephraim smiled more broadly; just as soon as Baenhaker got himself out of that hospital, he would remove him from England.

Ephraim checked into the Intercontinental Hotel in Old Park Lane, put his bag in his room, then went down to the foyer and telephoned the Israeli Embassy from a pay phone and made a rendezvous with his head of United Kingdom operatives for that afternoon. Then he asked the doorman for a taxi to take him to Putney, climbed in and, as they pulled off, told the taxi he did not want to go to Putney but, instead, wanted to go to the City of London, to 88 Mincing Lane, where he had a 12.30 luncheon date with Sir Monty Elleck.

He sat back in the taxi and pulled down the window to let in some air. He felt under pressure at the moment, great pressure, and he knew he must try to relax. He thought about the nuclear mines that had been discovered in a fishing dhow in the Persian Gulf; a good job had been done by the Omanis in keeping that quiet. Rumour was circulating in United States Intelligence and in the intelligence networks of the other countries which had learned of the incident that the Israelis were, in some way, involved in it. He knew that this was rubbish, but it had not been easy to convince his superiors. The Israeli Prime Minister had given him a thoroughly unpleasant grilling, and he wasn't sure at the end of it that the Prime Minister was really convinced of his innocence or, indeed, of Israel's innocence in the whole affair. Then there had been all the extra work resulting from the second attack on Osirak, monitoring and reporting on world reaction.

Ephraim was at an age when many men had retired; but what, he wondered, did they retire to? To tend their gardens? Peaceful gardens? Not in Israel, he knew. A peaceful garden was one you could look out at and know it would be there tomorrow, and the day after, and the day after that, and in ten years' time, and in one hundred years' time. Not in Israel. You could not, he knew, look at anything in Israel and believe it was going to be there even until tomorrow.

Ephraim emerged from the elevator on the sixth floor of 88 Mincing Lane and was ushered straight into the office of the Chairman, Chief Executive and one hundred per cent owner of Globalex. The diminutive Lithuanian and the bulky Israeli hugged each other warmly. 'Issy, you look terrific, terrific!' said Elleck.

'And you look as successful as ever, Monty.'

'Come, sit.' Elleck ushered him into an ornate armchair, and then went to his drinks cabinet. 'Chivas and ice? Still your favourite?'

'Just a small one – don't go mad with the bottle.'

'It's so good to see you – how can I keep my hand steady?'

There was a bond between the two men, a bond that went back a long way, to the summer in Germany of 1944, to the concentration camp Auschwitz – to a day when a Nazi soldier had been taunting Elleck, calling him a 'fat Jewish bubble', and pricking at his stomach with a bayonet. They were in the open, digging a mass grave for several hundred of their companions and probably, within a short while, for themselves, too; there was no one else around. Elleck was yelling abuse back at the soldier, who was fast becoming increasingly violent. At any moment, Ephraim knew, the soldier was liable to pull his trigger. The Nazi never heard Ephraim, who had been a thousand times better trained than he; before the Nazi's eyes had even picked up Ephraim's advancing shadow, his windpipe had been shattered like an old china vase.

Ephraim and Elleck had fled, and made the cover of the woods. They knew they had no chance of getting any distance, and instead searched for an ideal hiding place. Under the roots of an oak tree they found a natural hollow and, by excavating it a bit more, they were both able to fit into it. They spent every day for the next five months jammed in their tiny hollow, frequently hearing soldiers walk close by or even directly overhead. At night, they foraged for anything they could eat, from berries to dead animals, although they had to eat everything raw; even if they had had matches, they would never have dared to use them. They were able to get all the water they required from a stream a short distance away. It was not until two months after Germany surrendered that they came out of hiding, and then it was only because Elleck had contracted double pneumonia, and Ephraim had gone, in the night, to a farmhouse to try to get help. It was there that he was told that the war had been over for eight weeks.

It wasn't until halfway through their grilled soles at their corner table at Le Poulbot, that their talk turned to business. Elleck swirled his glass of '71

Montrachet around in his hand, took a large sip, put a forkful of sole in his mouth, took another large sip, and allowed the king of white burgundies and the prince of fish to mingle together in the company of a motley assortment of enzymes in the dank and stagnant void between his fat and greasy cheeks. After a while, he swallowed.

'How did – er – everything work out?' asked Ephraim.

Elleck looked nervously around, and then leaned forward: 'Issy, you did wonderful. Wonderful.' He shook his head. 'The timing – the timing was so good.' He lifted his glass up to him. 'You're a good boy, Issy, one hell of a good boy.'

Ephraim grinned. 'And you're a terrible rogue, Monty. It doesn't matter which hole in the ground you are in, you'll always end up on top of the pile, won't you?'

'With a little help from my friends.' He grinned back. 'Did you do what I said, Issy? Did you make plenty?'

Ephraim shook his head. 'You know I'm not interested in that. I advised the go-ahead for Osirak because you needed a favour, and because of what you promised my country if we were successful. I did not do it to make money for myself, and I wouldn't want any of it. My country needs money badly, my people around the world need money, money for their struggle. How much money are we going to make from the raid on Osirak?'

'Who else knows about it?'

'Who else? Do you think I am crazy? If the Knesset found out my true reasons, that I advised my country to bomb Iraq's nuclear power station not because there was a danger that they were using it to manufacture plutonium for nuclear bombs, but so that our act of aggression would for a few hours send a nervous twitch around the money markets of the world, banging up the price of gold, so that you could make a killing, and bail your company out of the financial crisis you told me you had coming; if the Knesset found that out, what the hell do you think they would say? Eh? You think I'm going to go around shouting my mouth off about it? No way, Monty. I did what I did for two reasons: Firstly, when you and I were down that hole, right in those first days we were there, we made a pact; you remember? We said that if we ever got out, and survived, if either of us, at any time, ever, during the rest of our lives, was in trouble, needed help, the other would go to the ends of the earth to help him. Well, Monty, I've just done that now, and I tell you, Monty, the strain is killing me.'

Elleck nodded slowly. 'I'm sure.'

'And the second reason,' continued Ephraim, 'is the ten per cent you said you would pay to which- ever Jewish groups in the world I told you. Well – I have that list here.' Ephraim pulled an envelope from his pocket, and passed it across the table.

Elleck stared him in the face. 'There's a problem, Issy. Everything went according to plan, except for two things I had not worked out properly. Firstly, as I did not want to let anyone in on what was happening, I had to buy the gold myself. I think I must be getting rusty up in my big office – it's a long time since I have done any dealing myself. I had forgotten how difficult it can be to buy large amounts of gold quickly without attracting a great deal of attention. So I did not buy nearly as much as I had hoped. Secondly, the world is getting used to short, sharp acts of aggression. I thought gold would have jumped fifty, possibly even seventy-five – possibly more still – maybe up to $100 an ounce . . .' He shook his head, finished the last mouthful of sole and took another large sip of wine. 'But it didn't. It only went twenty-four. If I had managed to buy all the gold I wanted – which I could have done if you had held off another month, like I had asked you – I would have been okay, even on a $24 rise.'

'But—' Ephraim cut in, 'you told me how wonderful the timing was, how perfectly it all went.'

'What was wonderful was the timing of the information – the way you got the information through to me. Because of what you told me, I knew exactly when to sell. I was also able to advise my clients, and that has made them very happy. But in terms of my firm making money, Issy, we just didn't make enough.'

'But you must have made some?'

'Sure we have bailed ourselves out of a lot of problems – but I still have a long way to go.'

'So how much are you going to be able to give to the names on that list?' Ephraim was starting to sound uneasy.

Elleck stared at him for a long time, then stared down at the ground. He spoke quietly: 'Issy,' he said, 'you know me: If I possibly could, you know that I would, but . . .'

The head of the Mossad was in a fury when he arrived back at the Intercontinental Hotel. He had declined Elleck's invitation to dinner and by doing so had terminated, as far as he was concerned, the oldest and deepest friendship he would ever know in his lifetime.

He was more than a little startled when the reception clerk handed him, along with his room key, a package from the pigeon hole above it. No name was on the fat buff envelope, about ten inches long and eight across, just the room number. His mind raced for a moment; no one knew he was staying here, not even Elleck. He never stayed in the same hotel for more than one night, and he used different hotels each time he came to London.

'You sure this is for me?' he asked.

'It was delivered about half an hour ago, sir.'

'By whom?'

'Motorcycle messenger. Don't ask me which firm – there's hundreds of them.'

Ephraim nodded, took the envelope and walked to the cashier's desk. 'Please make my bill up, I have a change of schedule and I'm leaving right away.' He sent a bell-hop up for his bag. As he would not now be having dinner with Elleck, there was no reason for him to stay in London anyway. He wanted to have a brief meeting with his chief of UK operatives and then, he decided, he would fly on to Paris this evening, instead of in the morning as he had originally planned.

The envelope worried him greatly. Maybe, he thought, it was for a previous occupant of the room, but he wouldn't have put a large bet on it. It worried him because he did not know what it contained, and it worried him because someone had been able to discover his whereabouts. He climbed into a taxi, sat down, and began to examine the envelope carefully.

After some minutes he decided, with not a great deal of confidence, that the contents of the envelope were not of a nature that would liberally scatter him and the taxi around the two hundred yards or so of Knightsbridge that surrounded them, and carefully slit it open with the top of his pen. It contained an RCA videocassette. A label was stuck to it, which read: 'MEET ME AT THE MORGUE – starring I. Ephraim.'

He looked at the label, at first in disbelief, then with a grin on his face and then in terror, and he began to shake uncontrollably. There was a note also stuck to the cassette, which he tore off and opened. The note said: 'You are to be in the bar of L'Hermitage Hotel in La Baule, Brittany, at midday, Saturday. You are to come alone. If anyone accompanies you, or follows you, or if you do not turn up, then one of these will be delivered to every press agency in the world at nine o'clock on Monday morning.'

The note was typed, by an electric typewriter with a plastic ribbon. The paper was a sheet of thin white A4 that could have been bought in any stationery shop in the world. Ephraim studied everything for some clue. There was none. His shaking got worse, and he felt his head become unbearably hot. He jerked the side window down, stuck his head out of the moving taxi, and was violently sick.

CHAPTER 11

Jimmy Culundis, the Greek international arms dealer, lay back in the massive bath tub that was sunk into the floor of the huge bathroom and felt very relaxed. He was in the finest luxury money could buy, from a bath with a built-in temperature control system that maintained the bath water at whatever temperature the occupant selected, to the gold-plated taps, to the expensive soaps, to the climate-controlled room walled in marble and smoked-glass mirrors. It wasn't unlike the bathroom he had in his house in Geneva, he decided. Nor unlike his villa in Greece; nor unlike his apartment in Paris.

Culundis was in a guest suite in Prince Abr Qu'Ih Missh's private quarters, on the sixty-fifth floor of the Royal Palace in Tunquit, the capital of Umm Al Amnah. It was Friday night, and his private DC-8 had landed him at the country's airport less than one hour earlier. He ran the soap down his flabby stomach, then, for a moment tensing his muscles, he raised his pelvis up out of the water, and carefully soaped every part of his long, limp phallus, a part of his body of which he ƨ particularly fond and proud – the only part, ɪn fact. He soaped around his scrotum, the inside of his thighs and his thatch of pubic hair, and then dunked everything back into the water. Then he slid his right hand under the water, gripped his phallus, and lifted it up, so that the top of it poked out of the water like a periscope.

Then, pretending it was a periscope, he turned it, first to the right, then to the left; then he stretched it up out of the water, as far as it would go in its limp state, bent it forward like a hose-pipe, and started making the sound of machine-gun fire.

Suddenly, he became aware that he was no longer alone in the room; someone was looking at him. He lifted his eyes upwards. He saw a blonde girl, in a thin white dress that was virtually transparent and had a slit from the navel to the ground; she was smiling at him, and had an amused twinkle in her eyes.

'Abby said you might like someone to scrub your back.' She leaned forward, and the dress parted completely over her white, slightly tanned thighs. The Greek's eyes bulged, and he decided that either Prince Abr Qu'Ih Missh had curious taste in the way he liked his housemaids to dress, or else the country of Umm Al Amnah was suffering from an acute shortage of ladies' underwear. Her eyes moved from his, to a spot further down the bathwater. He looked down there too, and then went even redder. His phallus was standing bolt upright, several inches out of the water and, this time, completely unsupported by his hand.

An hour later, Culundis and Prince Missh stepped out of the express elevator onto the ninety-fifth floor of the Royal Palace, the dining quarters of Sheik Hyyad bin Bakkrah al Quozzohok, thirty-seventh Emir of Amnah, the Prince's father. Missh had changed out of the expensive T-shirt he had been wearing earlier in the day into a cobalt-blue djellabah and traditional head-dress; he was, as was customary in his father's quarters, barefoot. Culundis was in a cream silk Nina Ricci suit, a bright yellow silk shirt and a green-and orange striped satin silk tie. On Missh's tactful suggestion, he too was barefooted, and not looking totally at ease about being so, in spite of having spent his entire childhood in that state. They stepped out of the elevator into a small marble hall, in the centre of which was a huge arch, with armed guards in djellabas standing on either side. They walked through the arch into a large windowless ante-room. The room was dark, with light provided by a few open candles; the walls were hung with tapestries, which could scarcely be seen, and the marble floor was covered in a magnificent Persian rug. A servant immediately brought them a tray with two cups, each containing thick sweet coffee. Culundis frowned in disappointment at not getting an alcoholic drink, then remembered the blonde and felt better. The sweet smell of roasting meat filled the room. As they drank their coffee, Missh pointed out to Culundis the history of the family that was depicted in the tapestries; Culundis gruntcd politcly, and wondered if it would be rude for him to light a cigar. He peered through the gloom and the works of art that had taken scores of women hundreds of years to complete and decided, quietly to himself, that once you had seen one damned Arab wandering around the desert, you had seen them all.

A servant walked in from the next room, which was again connected by a huge archway, stood in the centre of the archway, and bowed slowly.

'Come,' said Missh, 'my Father is ready to receive us for dinner.' The two men walked through into a much larger, but not much brighter-lit room.

'How come there aren't any windows?' Culundis whispered.

'My father does not like anything to distract from the food and the company. Elsewhere in his quarters, there are many windows.'

The floor on one side of the room was bare marble. The floor on the other side had thick carpeting and was richly scattered with cushions; seated in the midst, on an enormous pile of cushions, Culundis could make out a frail-looking old man, very thin, with long bony arms and long bony legs that protruded from his robes.

Missh went up to his father, bowed down, and the two embraced each other; then Missh stood back and bade Culundis walk forward. 'Father, you remember Mr Culundis?'

Culundis stood awkwardly; Missh hadn't briefed him on what to do. The Emir opened his bony arms, and Culundis leaned down and received a short, cold embrace. The Emir bade Culundis sit, as with all guests, in the place of honour on his right, and his son to the left.

'It is an honour to be here once again, your Highness,' said Culundis. 'You look well.' The Emir nodded politely, and stared fixedly ahead. Culundis soon saw why. The food was arriving. Eight servants staggered in holding a massive cauldron that was about four feet wide, although only about two and a half feet high; there was a thick rim of rice, from the centre of which rose a pyramid of dissected mutton, topped with four sheep heads, from which the tongues curled outwards. Two more servants followed with a huge steaming pitcher, from which they poured a gravy sauce containing the offal over the pyramid.

The Emir leaned forward, plucked the tongue from one head, turned to Culundis on his right, and proffered it. Culundis took it, nodded graciously, looked at it, and took a small nibble. There were only two things which he absolutely loathed to eat; one was apricots, the other was tongue.

Culundis watched the Emir lean forward, cut some strips of meat off a shoulder, make a small ball with some rice, lay the strips around the outside of the ball, and place the whole assembly in his mouth. Whilst his attention was diverted, Culundis slipped the rest of his tongue into his jacket pocket with one hand whilst pretending to push it into his mouth with the other; the Emir, chewing slowly, turned to look at his son's guest. Culundis made large, slow, chewing motions with his mouth, and the Emir looked satisfied that his guest was content.

He was a strange-looking man, thought Culundis, in complete contrast to his tall and handsome son; he was no more than five-foot four, thin as a rake, with an almost bird-like face. The face was dominated by a large hooked nose, on either side of which were half-moon shaped eyes which darted nervously about every few seconds, then stopped for some moments whilst the heavy lids slowly closed together, then opened again. Those eyelids were about the only thing father and son had in common. Both had that long slow blink. It made the son look arrogant, and the father like a crow that was digesting a worm. The bird-like face of the old man was even more accentuated by his bony arms and legs, so thin they were almost scaly. Neither father nor son spoke, but concentrated on hacking bits of meat and packing their rice balls. Culundis looked around for a knife. The Emir noticed he had stopped eating, leaned forward, and pulled out another tongue, again handing it to him with a gracious nod. Once more Culundis went through the motions of eating and then slipped it into his jacket pocket. The remaining two tongues went the same way, and then Culundis relaxed a little; he hoped the stain wouldn't show too badly through his white pocket, and he looked forward to a morsel of the lamb he could enjoy. He saw the Emir looking at him patiently, waiting until he had finished chewing. Culundis completed, for the fourth time, the motions of finishing off a tongue, and licked his lips, whereupon the Emir clapped his hands together and the servants came in and removed the cauldrons. Culundis began to feel extremely glum. Finally the Emir spoke:

'I think we have met before, somewhere?'

'We have, your Highness; in 1975 I came to your country to discuss supplying you with arms for your liberation from the United Arab Emirates. I came to see your General Mamoud Hayassa, and I was introduced to you whilst I was here.'

The Emir nodded disinterestedly. The servants brought in finger bowls, dry towels, and then perfume to spray on the hands of the three diners, and then tea was brought in. The Emir seemed in no mood to talk further, and so the three men sat in a strained silence. After some minutes he turned to Culundis. 'You come from Greece, I believe?'

'Yes, your Highness.'

'I have not visited Greece.'

'You would be most welcome, should you ever wish to come,' said Culundis.

'I shall never wish to come,' said the Emir emphatically. He turned to his son and gave one

141

long positive nod. It was the signal for his son and Culundis to leave; Missh stood up, and bade Culundis to stand. The Greek couldn't get to his feet fast enough.

Neither Missh nor the Greek spoke to each other until they had stepped out of the elevator back in Missh's quarters. 'My father does not speak much these days,' said Missh.

'No,' agreed Culundis.

'He thinks all the time about modernization, about new buildings, new roads, new industry; he forgets that there are also people.' Missh pulled two huge brandy snifters out of a cupboard, handed one to Culundis, and filled it a quarter full; he then passed him an Upman's corona, and took one himself. They settled themselves into Missh's massive white velvet sofas.

'Is he not aware of the feelings that are brewing?'

'He thinks you can cure any discontent by the threat to fill in water holes, because that is the threat his father used, and his grandfather before him. He thinks that all the twentieth century has brought is an ability to utilize precast concrete and smoked glass; he isn't aware that other things have changed as well as building techniques. He saw the Saudis get rich from oil, and he thinks he can create a kingdom like theirs. But he has no idea what it means. He thinks he can build the greatest industrial nation in the Middle East – out of fifteen hundred square miles of desert and seventeen thousand tribesmen and nomads. Sure, there are a thousand of our countrymen who want it – but there are 16,000 who don't. They want their traditional ways of life, and their religion. He's built schools, brought in teachers and begun educating. But what do most of those he has educated do? Do they go into industry? No, not many – they go back out of the cities, and they start organizing their people to resist the change. There are two strong leaders, who have the support now of maybe five, maybe ten thousand people; we rule them, but we don't own them, and for the first time they are being made aware of this.'

'How big is your army?'

'Fifteen hundred.'

'And how many of those would remain loyal?'

'I do not know – it is impossible to say. Many have relatives who have died or had to resettle because of my father's punishments. I have some good friends in the army; they tell me of much discontent.'

'How long do you think you have?'

'Every day I hear talk of new plots. I have already told you of the incident with my car; I don't think we have long, not long at all. The two religious leaders, Al Hassah and Abdul bin Kakohha, both have equipped small armies. I do not know who supplies them, but I think it is the Americans.'

'And you can't turn to the Americans?'

'No. I would love to, but they would not help us – if they do, they will lose the friendship of the Emirates.'

'The Russians would help you – and the Libyans.'

'Sure they would. I don't want to be in the hands of the Russians, and I don't want to be in the hands of Gaddafi. I want one day to become friendly with the West – that is where our future lies. Perhaps one day go back into the Emirates. There is no chance of that if I get into bed with either the Russians or the Libyans.'

'But the rest of the world thinks you are supported by them anyway; that has always been the view of the press – and politicians, from what one hears and reads.'

'Of course – and the Russians and Libyans are not going to deny it. It makes them appear to have another foothold in the Gulf,' said Missh. Culundis drew heavily on his cigar, inhaled the smoke deeply, and then blew it up towards the ceiling; he swilled the brandy around the snifter, and took a large sip. 'So your only solution is a private army, one that is paid by you, and is not interested in politics, religion, ideology; only the fat wage packets?'

Missh nodded, slowly and a little sadly.

'My friend,' said Culundis, 'I can get you all the guns you could ever wish for, and more bullets than you could shoot in a million years. I could have you two hundred thousand automatic rifles delivered tomorrow. I could get you field guns, mortars, tanks, fighter aircraft. I can get you nuclear weapons – nuclear combat weapons and if you want, nuclear intercontinental missiles; give

144

me one month and I can get you enough nuclear weaponry to be able to hold the world to ransom. But none of it, none of it at all, is going to give you any future if you have thirty thousand restless people in your country. To hold them at bay, you would need a loyal army of thirty thousand men; and that it would be impossible to give you. I can put together an army for you of top-rate loyal men – but at the very most four hundred, maybe five hundred men. Although your country is small, your population is very spread out indeed. There is no way a few hundred soldiers could control your country.'

Missh nodded. 'I know. My father hoped to lure his people into the cities; he felt he could keep better control there.'

'You can coop them up, but you can't stop them from thinking, from talking. I can name you dozens of countries where the rulers thought they could; but there aren't many from those dozens where those in power today are the same people who were there ten years ago, and you're going the same way, Abby. You are right on the brink of the slippery slope.'

'So what do you suggest?'

Culundis again took another deep draw on his cigar, and a mouthful of brandy. He got up from his chair, walked over to a sidetable, took a handful of nuts and walked over to the window, eating them as he went, and looked out and down at the lights of Tunquit. He then glanced down at his jacket pocket. He had managed to flush the tongues down the lavatory, and the stain didn't show too much. He stared back out over Tunquit and could see Missh, seated, reflected in the glass of the window.

'If you want to survive, Abby, you are going to have to kill your father.'

There was a long silence. 'Impossible. I could never contemplate it. I love my father.'

Culundis spun round. 'Of course you love your father. Who doesn't love his father? But unless someone takes the reins of this country – and from the way it sounds, there may only be weeks left to do it – and gets the message across that there are going to be major changes, an end to the filling in of wells, and everything else that they want to hear, both you and your father are going to be dead. Your father has to go. You have to take the reins, supported initially by everyone upon whom you can rely in your Government, armed forces and industry, and with your rear protected by one totally dedicated group: the mercenary army that we bring in. You have to get up there and you have to say to your people: "My father is gone. I am bringing you new leadership, youth, understanding, compassion. Let us all work together!" We will see how they respond. Some troublemakers will rise up – and we will eliminate them.'

Missh stared hard at Culundis. 'Jimmy – there is something you must understand. These are my people; my family have ruled them for thirty-seven generations. Whatever has happened in the past, however cruel my family may have been, I want no more killing. I will not kill any of my people. Not one, ever. You had better understand this, and understand it well.'

'And you, Abby, had better start understanding the world, and stop spouting idealist crap at me.'

'Do you want the business or don't you?'

'I don't do any business unless I think it has a chance of succeeding. If you expect me to put five hundred men in this country with your father remaining as ruler, then I'll say goodbye now and go back home. They would have no chance. If you want a blood-bath, you can recruit your own mercenaries. I don't want to lose my lot.'

There was a long silence. Missh stood up and walked around the room for some minutes. 'I can't kill him, Jimmy; can't you understand that?'

'Then you have to persuade him to abdicate.'

'How could I do that?'

'You'll have to tell him.'

'And what chance do I have of making him agree?'

'I don't know; that's up to you.'

'And if I don't succeed?'

'Then you kill him.'

'You expect me to go to him and say "Father, either you abdicate or I kill you".'

Culundis looked at him and nodded. 'You don't have any choice, Abby.'

Missh joined Culundis at the window, and stared out. It was some minutes before he spoke.

'I think maybe I feel strong enough to ask him to abdicate – but if he refuses, then I don't know what to do. For sure I cannot harm him.'

'What you do is up to you, Abby. I'll come and do some plain talking with you, if you think it'll help. But if he stays as leader of this country, I'll give you all the hardware you want to buy, but I won't let you have one single man.'

Missh nodded, and looked at his watch. It was ten o'clock.

'My father works in his study until late every night. He will be there now, and it will be quiet. Now will be a good time for a talk. Will you wait here?'

Culundis nodded.

'Would you like some company while I am gone?'

'No,' said the Greek, with a grin. 'To show my confidence in you, I'm going to start making some plans. If we're going to move fast, I've got a lot of thinking to do.'

Missh felt far from confident as he stepped out of the elevator into the dim candlelight of his father's hallway. He had brushed his teeth and sprayed on some strong cologne, to try and mask the smell of the brandy and cigars; his father despised alcohol and smoking. He walked down the long corridor and knocked on the massive jewelled double-doors that opened onto the most bizarre room in the palace. His father called for whoever it was to enter, and Missh walked into the room.

The room occupied half of one floor of the palace. One wall, eighty feet long, was a floor-to-ceiling bookcase, packed with books. Two other walls were windows overlooking Tunquit, and the fourth wall was hung with huge blow-up photographs of oil rigs and factories in Umm Al Amnah. The floor was brown marble, strewn with crimson rugs, and the ceiling was intricately stuccoed and covered in paintings of scenes from the Koran.

Throughout the room, neatly arranged into groupings, was almost every electrical gadget that had ever been invented. There was an office section, with an IBM computer, a word processor, a telex, tele-text; a games section, with television, space invaders and a battery of other slot machines; a garden section, with a remote control lawn-mower, a computerized sprinkler system – which was plumbed in and would spray a circle of plants placed around it; there was a full-size passenger airline flight-training simulator; a robot which could walk across the floor, pick up a sheet of paper and walk back; and a device that would open and shut the window blinds depending on how it was shouted at.

The Emir was seated at his black lacquered desk in the centre of the room, and gave his son only the most cursory of nods as he entered, before inclining his head back down to the papers on his desk top. Even though, over the past ten years, Missh had become used to this spectacle, it still did not stop him from thinking about how utterly incongruous it all was: his father, in his djellaba and bare feet, spending almost all the hours of his life in this room, playing with his toys, reading glossy brochures and making multi-million dollar deals with international companies to build plants in Amnah.

The desk was the only object in the room older than the Emir. It was eight feet wide, studded with white stones and inlaid with reliefs in gold; it had been in the old palace, four miles outside Tunquit on the Suttoh road. Since moving into the new palace, the Emir had sold the old palace to the Hyatt Hotel group, who had turned it into the Amnah Hyatt.

The Emir looked up from behind the desk and bade his son sit on a bizarre chesterfield that looked like it had been found on Mars. 'You don't come to see me often, my son,' he said.

'I know, father. We are both busy with our separate lives.'

The old man shook his head. Missh felt uncomfortable. He wished he had remained standing; he didn't like sitting so low down that he could only just see over the top of the desk.

'He is a strange man, your guest you bring to eat.'

'Strange, father?'

'He says we have met before. I do not recall – I have not met him before.'

'Father, he was being polite – he did not wish to offend your memory; but you did not merely meet – you hired him to equip your entire revolutionary force, and to provide soldiers, before you declared Independence from the Emirates.'

'This man?'

'Yes, father.'

The old man shook his head. 'I hired this man? I do not believe it.'

'But you did, father.'

'I must have been an unwise man then to have hired a person such as this.'

'Mr Culundis is a good man, father. What do you have against him?'

'He has insulted us, my son, insulted us most gravely. I have never in my life been insulted in such a manner.'

'What do you mean? How has he insulted you – us?'

'You did not notice, perhaps? He was the guest of honour at our meal. I cut for him the finest meat of the animals, and I gave it to him. He did not eat this meat – he put it in his pocket.'

Prince Missh had done something his father had not: he had seen something of the world beyond Umm Al Amnah. From the age of ten, he had been sent to school in England – first to prep school, and then to Harrow; from there he went to Cambridge. Many of those things which were so sacred to his ancestors, he could see in perspective of the late twentieth century world; others, like his father, had not had this advantage. Missh personally felt only amusement at the situation;

but he could fully understand his father's anger. 'He comes from a different culture, father; perhaps, for him, tongue is like pork is to us – forbidden – and he was being too polite to tell you?'

The Emir looked at Missh. 'You are young, son. You have so much to learn, and I have such little time to teach you.' He shook his head. 'I worry, son, you have had too sheltered a life; you are so naive, so naive. Sometimes I do not even know where to begin. What will happen to this country after I am gone? You will not last five minutes, not five minutes.'

Missh stared at him for several minutes in silence. 'Father – do you not realize what is happening out there beyond the walls of this palace?'

'I realize very well, son. The revenues of oil are being used to make us into the most modern industrial nation in the world.'

'Do you really believe that?'

'What are you saying? It is true; no one has the modern equipment we have. Just take a look around you – at this office – everything in the world that is new, advanced, for industry, for agriculture, for medicine – I have either examples here, or the literature. There is nothing that is new and that is of value that we do not have either in this country, or on order.'

'But your people aren't interested – at least, most of them are not. They are plotting, father, plotting now, and any day they will rise up.'

'You talk rubbish, son. Your mind has been poisoned by your foreign education. I knew I should not have sent you – but the Sauds send their sons, Oman sends his – so I must send mine.'

Missh quietly related to his father what had happened to his car at the Quommah Beach Club.

'It serves you right,' said the Emir. 'That Beach Club is a place of decadence. The heir to the throne of this country has no business in a place like that, and your people were telling you so. It was their way of getting a message across; that is all.'

'You are crazy, father, if that is all you think it was – crazy. Unless we do something now, you and I and all your wives and all your loyal servants will be dead. The people are going to rise up like they did in Iran, like they did in so many countries. It is no different here.'

'So what do you suggest?' demanded his father, belligerently.

'I'm not suggesting. From now on, father, I am telling you what is to happen, and you are going to agree.'

The Emir stared at his son incredulously. 'I am listening, son,' he said contemptuously.

'You are to abdicate, and I am to take over as ruler. If we do this, then Mr Culundis will give us arms, and a loyal army to defend ourselves against the revolutionaries, and to rout them out.'

'You are crazy,' said the Emir.

'No, father, it is you who is crazy. I will not stand by and die because of your madness.'

'I suggest if you feel this way, then you take a plane and get out of this country, the sooner the better.'

'No, father, this is my home. I am not leaving.'

'And I am not abdicating.'

'Oh yes you are.'

'And just how do you propose to make me?'

'By asking you nicely first: and then, if you do not agree, father – by force.'

The Emir pulled open the central drawer of his desk; it took him some moments, for it was stuck, and he had to jerk it out slowly, from side to side. Then he rummaged for several moments in a tangle of papers, pens, rulers, rubbers, cellotape, before he pulled his hand back out. In it he held a Browning revolver. It was a massive heavy gun, of First World War design, and looked like something that might have been discarded as obsolete by Lawrence of Arabia. He stood to his feet, swaying, shaking with rage and brandishing the gun out in front of him. 'By force, you say, by force?'

He was pointing the gun at Missh, and shaking it about furiously. Missh put his hands up. 'Be careful, father, it may be loaded.' There was an explosion, and a bullet ripped through a window pane. The Emir's eyes bulged and he swung the gun down towards the floor in fright; somehow, he pulled the trigger again, and a bullet tore into his own foot. Howling with pain he jerked the gun up, firing into his desk top. Missh had by now flung himself to the floor; the bullet ricocheted off a metal in-tray and ripped into the Emir's stomach, flinging him backwards and onto the floor. Missh rushed over to his father and pulled the gun a safe distance away. His father lay there, ashen grey, bleeding heavily from both his stomach and his foot. Missh rushed to the telephone on his father's desk; at that moment, two guards came running in through the door. Missh rang down to the palace's residential doctor and instructed him to call an ambulance and come right away. Then he joined the guards who were kneeling by his father.

The guards looked at his father and then looked at him. Their eyes were full of suspicion. A cold wave of fear suddenly swept aside all the other emotions Missh was feeling. They suspected him of shooting his father; if his father died now, he could face a firing squad. He shook his head frantically. Ali Al Shammham, his family's short, fat doctor, hurried into the room, clutching his black briefcase.

'What happened? What happened?' he shrilled in his high-pitched voice. He knelt down beside the Emir, whose breathing was becoming slower and deeper and whose eyes now remained shut for long periods between blinks.

'My son,' said the old man. 'Bring my son.'

'I am here, father.'

'You are right,' said the old man. 'I am too old to rule – it is time I must step down. Tonight. Now. I have become a danger, a liability to you, to my country. From tonight, you are the new Emir—' He looked up and around at the peering faces. 'You here are my witnesses. From tonight, Prince Abr Qu'Ih Missh becomes Emir of Amnah.' He nodded slowly, but certainly. 'Now get me to hospital.'

Missh turned away, tears streaming down his face. The doctor gave the old man a shot of morphine, then began work to try and stem the bleeding. Missh picked up his father's head and cradled it between his thighs. As the doctor worked, he wept, loudly and uncontrollably.

CHAPTER 12

A manda sat in silence, a knot of fear gripping her stomach, her hands rigidly holding onto the front of the seat; the blurred red, white and occasional amber lights beyond the clacking wiper blades came and went like the programme of some nightmare slot machine. But she wasn't standing in front of any slot machine; she was in the passenger seat of Alex Rocq's Porsche, and she was speechless with fear.

For an hour, Rocq had cursed and sworn at the Friday night rush hour, through Battersea and then Wandsworth and then down the Kingston by-pass. They had driven down the motorway, first the M25, then the M23, at speeds ranging between 115 and 150 miles per hour; how they hadn't been stopped by the police was a miracle, and she would have much rather they had been, for at least it might have made him drive slower.

Off the end of the motorway, in the thick two-way traffic, he had forged a third lane and resolutely stayed there, lights blazing, hooting frenetically, occasionally ducking in behind a car or a lorry and shouting, 'Bastard!' at the oncoming

.ch had not given way. She looked at
.ed-up face, eyes squinting against the
.; he had been tensed up like this all week.
mething was eating him, she was sure, but he
denied anything was.

She had been to see Baenhaker again, and
hadn't bothered to tell Rocq. Baenhaker looked a lot
better, but he too was in a livid mood. He wouldn't
say why either. The doctors had told him his injuries
were not as severe as they had at first feared, and
that he could expect to make a full recovery. She
thought that news ought to have cheered him up,
but all he could do was pour out a torrent of vitriol
against everything. She had asked him about the
accident but he could remember nothing, nor even
anything he had done the day of the accident.

The Porsche braked hard, the wheels sliding over
the wet tarmac, the nose snaking viciously; a chill
went through her. 'Oh, God, we're going to crash!'
she thought, but they stopped about half an inch
short of the tailgate of the Range Rover that was
turning right. She turned to him. 'For Christ's
sake, Alex, I don't want to die, thank you very
much. We're not in any hurry – why can't you
drive a bit slower?'

'I'm not driving fast,' he said.

'You're driving like a maniac.'

'Then get out and bloody walk.'

'Right, I'll get out and bloody walk.' They started
moving forward again. 'Stop the car.'

Rocq swung the car over onto the pavement;

158

Amanda climbed out, slammed shut the door, and marched off into the teeming rain. Rocq crashed the car into gear, floored the accelerator, and, spinning the wheels right through the gears, tore off down the road.

After about two miles he began to relent, and slowed down; apart from the fact she was getting soaked to the skin, anything could happen to her on that dark road. He looked in his mirror. There was heavy traffic behind him, but nothing coming up the opposite way. He accelerated hard, spun the steering wheel hard round to the right, and then jerked on the handbrake hard for a second and a half; the car slewed around, doing a complete about-turn. He released the handbrake, dropped into second, and accelerated hard.

Just over two miles back, he saw a very bedraggled figure marching along the side of the road. He pulled over, waited until there was a gap in the traffic, then turned around and pulled up alongside her. He leaned over and opened the passenger door. Ignoring him, she carried on walking. He drove down after her and stopped in front of her, and pushed the door wide open; again, she walked past. He climbed out of the car and began to run after her.

'Amanda,' he said, 'come on, get in, this is ridiculous.'

She turned to him. 'Get lost,' she said. She carried on walking. He ran after her. 'Come on, stop, you're getting soaked to death.' She marched on, determinedly. Suddenly there was an enormously loud bang behind them, followed by the screeching of brakes, the sound of tyres sliding on the wet and an extraordinarily eerie rumbling that sounded like a thousand oil drums crashing up and down in unison. They both turned their heads; the Porsche was cartwheeling across the verge; it smashed through a hedge, rolled over three more times, and came to rest upside down in the middle of a field. An articulated lorry slithered to a halt just past the spot where the Porsche had been.

'Oh my God!' screamed Amanda. 'Oh my God, Alex!'

Rocq stared hard. He couldn't think of anything suitable to say at all.

Two hours later they sat together, facing each other in the scalding hot water in the tiny cramped bathtub in his cottage.

'They say bad luck always comes in threes,' she said.

Rocq grinned at her. 'Thanks a lot. We've had the row, right, that's one?'

She nodded.

'The car's been smashed to pieces – that's two?'

She nodded again.

'So now there's going to be something else?'

'I hope not,' she said – 'but there usually is.'

'Great.' He looked up. 'I expect the bloody roof'll fall in during the night.'

She lifted her legs out of the water, and wrapped them over his arms, squeezing him tightly. 'Then

we'd better make love tonight very, very gently,'
she said.

Rocq woke at first light, to the sound of several
noisy sparrows apparently having a fight to the
death over what he presumed was a particularly
fat worm. He had awoken full of fear, and with a
sense of dread in his stomach. The image of the
Porsche cartwheeling through the dark, bits showering off it like confetti, filled his mind. It was
difficult to see the full extent of the damage in the
dark, but the lorry had hit it at a good fifty miles
an hour and there was unlikely to be much left
intact. He now had no car, and no doubt many
months of wrangling with the insurance to get the
money for another one. He could hardly go back
to his bank manager and ask him for a loan to
buy one, having already hocked his soul. On top
of all that, he wouldn't be surprised, from what
the police had said, if he were prosecuted for
dangerous parking, having stopped on a clearway.
    Then his mind jumped to his other big worry:
coffee. He had bought at £1,042 a ton on the
Monday. It was now Saturday. The stuff had
dropped £18 this week. The *Financial Times*
yesterday predicted it would drop a bit further
during the next couple of weeks but begin rising
in early July and reach £1,200 by late summer.
Not exactly the 'going through the roof' that Theo
had predicted, but at least in the right direction.
    His mind moved next to his clients. Abr Qu'Ih

Missh had been quiet during the past fortnight; he usually had instructions from him twice or three times a day. He had only given two buy orders and one sell order in the whole fortnight; he wondered if he had upset him by taking him into gold late on the day of the Osirak raid. He hoped he would come over to England soon; he had found something that would drive Missh absolutely crazy: blonde triplets, and they were on the game, as a treble-act.

The bouncing Baron was okay, although he wasn't going to let Rocq forget Osirak for a long, long time. He was due to come over in ten days; Rocq didn't particularly look forward to it. He would have to make his usual trip to the hideous little shop in Queenstown Road to buy the Baron his rubber suit and underwear – he never travelled with his own for fear of embarrassment at the customs, and in any event preferred a new suit each time, to savour the smell of fresh latex. Rocq made a note to remind himself on Monday to telephone the shop and make sure they had the Baron's size; also to reserve the Baron's two favourite hookers.

Sa'ad Al Rahir, the Kuwaiti, had been particularly active, and Rocq had had some good commission from him during the fortnight. Louis Khylji, the immaculate Iranian, was in love and had disappeared into the bowels of France with a red-headed concert pianist and a Michelin guide. Joel Symes, the investment manager of Country and Provincial, had been busy concentrating his mind on Royal Ascot, although for two days he'd had a big thing about platinum futures and Rocq had done nicely out of the commission on that one. Dunstan Ngwan, the Nigerian drug whole-saler, hadn't been such a happy story. Rocq's handling of this account during the week had been a comedy of errors. Rocq had advised him to go big into nickel three-month futures at £2,625 a ton, so he had gone big, and twenty-four hours later nickel was down to £2,104 a ton. Rocq had pulled him out of nickel and switched him into copper. Within three hours, copper had dropped by £15. Without telling him, he liquidated that position and reinvested it in gold on the New York exchange. He liquidated it several hours later on the Hong Kong exchange, and by 8.30, when the first brokers arrived at work, he had already switched Ngwan's position back to London. But his luck remained out, and by the end of the week he had succeeded in wiping half a million off Ngwan's net worth. Ngwan wasn't amused, and Rocq knew that unless he pulled something out of the bag, and pulled it out smartly, he was going to be minus one very big and long-standing client – a client that was worth to him personally, quite apart from what the firm made out of him, about £5,500 in commission a year.

Outside in the garden, the worm decided to call it quits and allowed itself to be pulled from its burrow; the largest of the sparrows hadn't read about share-a-worm, and up-sticked and offed with its prize, leaving the remaining ones to glare and shriek a few perfunctory recriminations at each other before dispersing. It became quiet again in the small Sussex country garden beyond the window of Rocq's bedroom, and Rocq lapsed back into a troubled sleep.

The next thing that woke Rocq was a pile of newspapers – the *Financial Times*, *The Times* and the *Mail*, to be accurate, fitted one inside the other and landing near his head with a thump. The room was filled with bright sunlight, and he opened his eyes and saw Amanda fully dressed.

'Morning,' she said.

'Hi. Whassertime?'

'Quarter past ten. I've been out for a walk to get the papers. Want some breakfast?'

Rocq yawned; having felt wide awake at half past four in the morning, he now felt tired. 'A cup of coffee would be nice.'

She leaned over and kissed him. 'Who's a tired little Rocky?' she said.

'Me am.'

She went out of the room; Rocq heaved himself up a few inches against the headboard, and pulled up the pile of papers. He took the *Mail* first, for easy reading, and glanced at the front page. In his tired and fuddled state, something in the headlines rang a bell, but he had to read it a dozen more times before it fully registered. The first four were to make sure he'd read it properly; the next four to make sure he wasn't imagining it; the next four to make sure it hadn't gone away again. He started shaking, and picked up *The Times* to make sure it wasn't just some figment of a *Daily Mail* reporter's imagination. It wasn't; it was the second major headline on the front page of *The Times*. He picked up the *Financial Times;* it was there, too: 'SHOCK NEWS ROCKS COFFEE MARKET.' *The Times* headline read: 'WORLD-WIDE COFFEE BAN IMMINENT?' The *Daily Mail's* read: 'THE KILLER IN YOUR COFFEE CUP.'

Rocq ploughed straight into the editorials; the three newspapers all tallied. The World Health Organization had established definite links between coffee and several types of cancer, in particular, breast, stomach and bowel cancers. Tests and surveys proved that the risk increased in direct proportion to the amount drunk; there was little significant difference between fresh-ground and instant varieties, nor between caffeinated and decaffeinated varieties. The World Health Organization estimated that up to sixty-five per cent of these and other types of cancers would be prevented if coffee were not drunk, and was going to recommend to all governments of the world that an immediate ban be made on the growing, manufacture and sales of coffee and all coffee-based products.

Amanda appeared with the coffee.

165

'You evidently didn't read the papers yet!' he said.

'No.' She shook her head, looking a bit surprised.

'You're right,' he said, 'what you said last night. Bad news certainly does come in threes.'

CHAPTER 13

The girl took careful aim, then slowly and deliberately squeezed the two halves of the plastic gun together. Eight ping-pong balls fired out in rapid succession and bounced hard off the naked backside of Viscomte Claude Louis Santenay Jarre du Charnevrau Ducarme de Louçelle de Lasserre. Trussed up in the corner of the room like a Christmas turkey, and with a gag tightly bound over and into his mouth, there was little the Viscomte could do other than to squirm. The girl picked up another gun, and fired again. The Viscomte began shaking with excitement, and she knew now he was ready. She signalled to the second girl. Seizing him by the arms and legs, they dragged him roughly across the floor and threw him face downwards onto the bed.

'You pig bastard, you will suffer,' one spat out viciously.

'If you don't get rid of your hard, we'll break it off,' said the other.

With four ropes they lashed his arms and legs

tightly and firmly, so that he was pinned face down and quite unable to move. Both girls wore outfits that could hardly be described as conservative feminine attire. They were dressed in bras, panties and thigh-high leather boots; the centres of the bras and the panties had been cut away, and the contents beneath bulged through the holes.

One girl seized a cat-o-nine tails leather whip and cracked it down across the Viscomte's backside. He whimpered loudly enough that it could be heard through the gag. The second marched round, and slapped him hard across the face, twice. The girl cracked the cat-o-nine tails again and then again, repeatedly, and red welts began to appear. The Viscomte started to shake again, shuddering and shaking uncontrollably, whilst one girl brought the whip relentlessly down, and the second slapped him across the face.

An hour later, the Viscomte, dressed in a Prince of Wales check suit, red paisley tie and Charles Jourdan shoes paid the two girls, tipped them generously on top and walked, with some apparent discomfort, out of the apartment, down the steps, and out into the mid-afternoon Limoges heat. He checked his watch; it was ten past five. He would have to hurry. He opened the door of his red Maserati Kyalami and lowered himself gingerly into the leather-covered driving seat; his backside was in agony; the girls had become over-zealous, he decided; he must speak to them next time, it really was hurting much more than he liked. He revved the engine hard and drove off aggressively, leaving a trail of rubber and blue smoke behind him. He headed towards the N21 Perigueux road out of the town.

As was normal, the Viscomte drove fast, flashing his lights and blasting slow-moving traffic out of his path with the car's piercing air horns. As he drove, occasional important thoughts entered his mind, and he made mental notes that they must all be discussed later that evening.

He was a tall man with a handsome, if some-what weak, face. He had fair hair with some silver streaks, thick eyebrows that hooded his crystal-clear blue eyes, a long straight nose and an almost feminine rosebud mouth. His skin was of a texture and colouring that exuded health, well-being and wealth; it was a skin that seems only to be found on the faces of aristocrats – the genuine articles, not the self-made first genera-tions. He had been married three times and divorced three times, and had seven children, all living with their mothers; right now he was thoroughly enjoying his fourth bachelorhood. To those who didn't know him well, he appeared a gentle man; he was soft spoken, deliberate but delicate in his movements, and always appeared deeply and passionately interested in anyone he happened to speak to – something he had learned from carefully studying the English Royal Family. Outwardly, he was the perfect, divinely-mannered image of everything that a French Viscomte should be.

Two hours out of Limoges and one hour past Perigueux, on the N89 Bordeaux road, the Maserati slowed down and turned sharply right into a narrow, straight, tree-lined lane. The Viscomte changed down into first, and flattened the accelerator; the car raced up the lane. At fifty-two miles per hour he changed to second, still keeping his foot flat on the floor, the tyres clenched to the grey ribbon of tarmac between the trees; at eighty he changed to third, and the car leapt over the 120 miles per hour, or, as he was interested in, the 200 kilometre mark; then he began to ease off. It always gave him a kick, hitting 200 kilometres on this straight stretch.

Within a few hundred metres, the trees gave way to wall; a massive wall, over twenty feet high, with broken glass and barbed wire along the top. The wall continued for three kilometres without break, and the car continued at high speed. Then it began to slow down, the right turn indicator started blinking, the Viscomte gave two long blasts on his air horns, and stopped in front of a massive wrought-iron gateway with an elegant beige stone lodge beside it.

A curtain inside the lodge parted and a pair of eyes looked out; the curtains dropped back and, after a few moments, the electrically-powered gates began to swing open. A portly man in his late fifties hurried out of the house and stood at the side of the drive, out of the way of the gates.

The Viscomte was home. He turned in through the gateway.

'*Bonsoir, Monsieur Le Viscomte,*' said Henri Taflé, the gatekeeper.

The Viscomte nodded. '*Bonsoir, Taflé. Ça va?*'

'*Oui, Monsieur Le Viscomte, ça va bien, merci.*'

The Viscomte gave his gatekeeper an oily smile that was reserved exclusively for introductions to heads of state, conceding points when negotiating business, and for greeting his peasants on his estate, and drove off. Three hundred metres on, around the second bend in the driveway, the chateau itself came into view.

Chateau Lasserre is one of those French chateaux in which fairy tales are set. Although he had seen it come into view a million times as he had rounded this bend, it still rarely failed to fill him with a deep sense of satisfaction and, on more occasions than he could count, it had made many a girl throw aside any previous reservations she might have had about her date and decide, no matter what happened, no matter how she might feel about the Viscomte, that before she was driven back home she wanted to get laid, at least once, inside those simply stunning portals.

The chateau was awe-inspiring, and it was impossible to take it all in in one look. There were walls upon walls, turrets and towers topped with castellations, heaped one upon the other in a mixture of shimmering white stone and marble. The chateau was encircled by a deep moat; to the rear was a vast lake and, at the front, a drawbridge, complete with portcullis.

The estate was vast even by French standards, covering over seventeen thousand acres of land. Of these, a mere fifty-five were given over to the growing of grapes from which came the annual 38,000 bottles of one of France's least inspired clarets. The rest was lush parkland for hunting, the village of Lasserre, a massive pig and sheep farm, and the Lasserre racing stables and stud farm.

Two hundred metres to the far side of the lake, well clear of the chateau and of any trees, was an 800 metre grass landing strip, complete with full landing lights on both sides. On a course that would take them directly down onto the eastern-most point of this landing strip in thirty-five minutes time were, at a height of 19,000 feet, Sir Monty Elleck and his pilot, in the Globalex Mitsubishi Solitaire twin-prop plane.

Also heading for the chateau was Jimmy Culundis; he was walking down the gangway of his private DC-8 at Bordeaux airport. It had had to land there, as it was too big for private airstrips, even the mighty one in the Viscomte's back garden. Culundis walked to the terminal building to complete customs formalities before completing his journey in the chauffeur driven Citroen Pallas the Viscomte had sent.

Lasserre greeted Nicole Varasay, his current residential playmate, with a peck on both cheeks; she was wearing a slip, and seated at the dressing table in his vast bedroom, putting on her make-up. Her long dark hair tumbled around her white shoulders, and the Viscomte slid his hands inside her bra and caressed her breasts.

'Who is the Englishman who is coming tonight, *chéri*?' she asked.

'He is someone very important. I want you to be specially nice to him.' He whispered into her ear, and she giggled a long wicked giggle.

Lasserre dressed for dinner, taking care to keep his backside well out of Nicole's sight. She was still putting on her make-up as he pulled on his dark green smoking jacket. 'I have some work I must do for a few minutes in my study; I will see you when you are ready, downstairs.'

'I won't be long,' she said.

'Try not to be, it would be nice for you to be down when they arrive.'

'Two minutes,' she said, tossing her hair back away from her face.

The Viscomte walked down the carpet that ran along the centre of the stone floor of the long corridor. There were lights at intervals down the corridor, and each light that he passed threw a long shadow of himself in front of him. These weren't the only shadows, he reflected, sadly.

There was, right now, a shadow cast over the whole of Chateau Lasserre, the whole estate. The shadow was called François Mitterand. Mitterand had decided that Viscomte Lasserre had too damned much money and too damned much land, and he was going to do something about it. It was nothing personal against Lasserre; the two had never met, and it wasn't only Lasserre; it was many Frenchmen, both noble and *nouveau riche*, all with the one thing in common: wealth. Since his election to office, the French President had set about doing one of the things he had put in his election manifesto: soaking the rich. He was doing it well, too damned well, thought Lasserre, as he descended the massive staircase. Viscomte Lasserre right now was badly in need of money; the land tax Mitterand had imposed was crippling him. Before that, the estate ran at a small profit. From the wine and the farming, the costs of the racing stables, the parkland and the chateau itself were met. Sure, he owned the massive Lasserre group of companies – the munitions and aircraft industry – but now there were punitive taxes on the proceeds of sales of shares; it was not a good time to sell and, besides, how long could he keep the estate going by selling shares before the shares began to run out? Several years, without doubt, but he was a businessman. His interest was in making money, adding to his pile, not diminishing it. No; he needed additional income, a lot of it, and preferably well out of the clutches of Mitterand and his tax collectors. He was close to getting it. After tonight's meeting, he hoped he would be closer still; closer possibly to being the richest man in France.

CHAPTER 14

'That must be it down there, Sir Monty,' shouted out Elleck's private pilot, Ex-RAF Wing Commander Hopkins. Elleck looked up from his De Beers Gold Report; lounging back in the large seat in the centre of the plane, it was difficult for him to see out in any direction without stretching himself, and right now he needed all the relaxation he could get, for he had a feeling it was going to be a long and taxing night.

'Good man,' he said, trusting to his pilot's judgement to put them down on Lasserre's runway and not the middle of a housing estate.

Elleck liked his trips alone; he was fond of Laura, his wife, but her presence always seemed to restrict him, to remind him of his age, to prevent him thinking at times as lucidly as he needed to. Without her, when he travelled, he always felt a spirit of adventure. He never thought about the reasons too hard; he just supposed it was that when she wasn't there and the opportunities came up to get laid, he could take them – not that they did come up that often, and not nearly as often as he would have liked. He turned his mind to

176

Viscomte Lasserre. He was wondering why it was that the Viscomte, one of his oldest and best clients, had invited him to dinner.

As the plane began its landing descent, he started checking his clothes. His patent leather shoes still looked spotless, and his trousers looked fine. He tightened his bow tie. He had dressed for dinner before he had left the office in London. Chateau Lasserre was 400 miles from London; in this plane, with its cruising speed of 315 knots, including the stop at Le Havre to clear French customs and immigration, it had taken them less than an hour and a half to get here.

The flight was the first opportunity he had had to think clearly at all during this particular Monday, which had been the most hectic he could ever remember. The whole world was bailing out of coffee and the coffee market, at around midday, had completely collapsed. On Friday, at the close of trading for the week, three-month coffee futures stood at £1,004 a ton. By mid-afternoon today, you couldn't give it away. It was listed at a shade over £500 a ton, but there weren't many takers even at that price.

Elleck was busy doing mathematics in his head. Millions of pounds had been wiped off the net wealth of Globalex's clientele, which meant they would have less money to invest in the future and therefore there would be less trading and less commissions for Globalex. The crash of coffee had produced nervousness in other soft commodities

– sugar, cocoa and almost all the others had dropped sharply. Business in some metals had picked up a bit as a result, as some investors turned to them for security, but mostly the investors were liquidating their positions to cover their coffee margin calls.

Elleck turned his mind to the people who would be the hardest hit: the small investors, the private punters, heavily exposed on their margins. Coffee had closed on Friday night at £1,004; it had begun trading on Monday morning at £400, a drop of £604, before rising slightly and levelling out at just over £500. People who had bought on margin at around about the thousand mark – where coffee had been for some time – would have about £100 invested for every ton. With a drop of £500 in the price, it meant that when the time came for them to pay the balance of the £1,000 purchase price, they would have paid out £1,000 for coffee that they could sell for only £500 – and they would therefore have lost £500 for each ton. In common with other commodity broking firms, Elleck could not let Globalex be on the hook for this difference; so when a commodity dropped substantially in price, the investors in that commodity were required to increase their margin to cover the position. It was known as a 'margin call.'

The first job Elleck had done this morning was to check the margin positions of all Globalex's clients. He had noticed, to his surprise, that Alex Rocq held over 1,000 tons on margin. Even at ten per cent of the price, that was a lot of money he had invested – over £100,000. Elleck did not like his employees playing the markets, and particularly not through their own firm; if they wanted to invest, they were supposed to go elsewhere, although that rule was not strictly enforced. One hundred thousand pounds was a lot of money for a fellow of Rocq's age to have invested, and £1 million was an incredible amount to be on the hook for in just one commodity. Elleck had a feeling, just from looking at the figures, that Rocq was playing with fire.

Thirty seconds on the intercom to the accounts departments told Elleck the name and branch of Rocq's personal bank. Two minutes later, he was talking on the telephone to one of the directors of the bank, in his office in Cannon Street. Eight minutes later the director called him back: Rocq was hocked to the eyeballs for £102,000. Elleck thanked him, assured him he'd be the first person to receive the next hot tip he came across, and hung up. Rocq now owned only £500,000 worth of coffee, but he was contracted to buying £1,042,000 worth. Rocq would shortly be receiving a margin demand for another £400,000, and that was if coffee didn't drop any more.

Elleck pinched his nostrils together and blew hard; his ears always popped in aeroplanes. They bumped through a series of air pockets and he heard the engines change pitch a couple of times, as Hopkins lined them up for the landing approach.

He'd looked at Rocq's position at midday; by the close of play, coffee had dropped to £420 a ton; that meant Rocq's margin call by the end of the day would have stood at about £480,000. For a man hocked to the eyeballs, that was a lot of long green ones to stump up in a hurry; it was a lot of long green ones to stump up at all. Elleck smiled to himself.

The first thing that had happened this morning was that all the smart boys in coffee had tried to go short. It was the rush to sell short that had contributed to coffee's rapid decline to its £420 figure. But Elleck knew from experience that the situation would change. During the next few days the World Health Organization would clarify their views, doctors for and against would be on every news show, talk show and documentary for the next fortnight, and the newspapers would be stuffed full of arguments. Slowly, a general opinion would emerge: as bad as was feared, not so bad, or worse. Whichever way it shifted, coffee, which had overnight become the most volatile substance in the world, would shift too – in leaps and bounds. Fortunes had been lost on coffee; but Elleck knew full well that during the weeks to come, equally great, if not greater, fortunes would be made on the stuff by those that had the money to stay in the game.

As soon as Elleck had got his information on Rocq, he had summoned the Honourable James Rice up to his office.

180

'I presume Alex Rocq has spoken to you about his coffee position?' Rice hesitated, wondering whether his boss might be trying to trap him into something. 'What do you mean, Sir Monty?'

'Don't be ridiculous, James, you must know what I mean. Rocq bought £1 million worth of coffee through you last Monday. Surely it hasn't failed to escape your attention that there have been one or two adverse articles about this particular substance in the newspapers during the past twenty-four hours?'

Rice felt faintly silly; he was friendly with Rocq, but not so friendly that he was prepared to draw the wrath of his boss to defend him. 'Well, he's concerned, Sir Monty – very concerned, I'd say.'

'What's he doing about it?'

'Trying to go short.'

'Along with the rest of the world?'

Rice shook his head. 'No. Most people seem to be giving up and sitting tight; there are no buyers for the stuff at any price – haven't been any since about eleven o'clock. Hasn't been a short market at all today – those that did get out either went into cash or other commodities. A lot of people did go short very early, but they pushed the price down so rapidly that even the wide-boys got nervous.'

'Did Rocq go short?'

'No – he hasn't yet – I think he'll wait a day or two – that's what I've advised him. You know what these medical scares can be like – doctors seem to change their minds on things every few months. Cholesterol used to be bad for you; then they discovered not enough cholesterol is worse than too much. I'm not saying it'll be the same here, but who knows.'

Elleck nodded in agreement. 'I trust Rocq will get his margin call today – along with everyone else?'

'It's on the computer – along with everyone else's,' nodded Rice.

'Has he said anything about it?'

'Well – he won't receive it for probably another hour, Sir Monty.'

'No, I know he won't have received it yet – but he must know he's going to. He hasn't said anything at all?'

'Well,' again Rice hesitated, 'he wants me to have lunch with him – tomorrow.'

'And if he brings up the business of the margin then?'

'Rules are rules – I can't do anything about them, can I, Sir Monty?'

'I'm pleased with your work for this company, James. You have a good future here, a very good future indeed.'

'Thank you, Sir Monty.'

'I would offer you a cup of – er coffee – but I imagine you probably have more than you need right now anyway.'

Rice grinned and Elleck stood up. 'Thank you for coming up to see me, James – and – er, by the way – if young Alex does mention this margin business to you – I'd – er, I'd be very grateful if you would let me know.'

'Do you think he will, sir?'

'Four hundred and eighty thousand pounds is a lot of money,' said Elleck.'

'I'll let you know, Sir Monty.'

'Thank you, James.'

The wheels of the Mitsubishi bumped down onto the grass, lifted up, and then settled down; the plane roared as the pilot reversed the engines. Elleck smiled to himself. He had Rocq by the balls, and he had a feeling that to have a person of Rocq's calibre, and in Rocq's position, by the balls was, right now, not at all a bad thing.

The Citroen Pallas swept out of Bordeaux airport and onto the Libourne road. Although it was a clear summer's evening and in spite of the falling dusk it was still quite light, the chauffeur was having great difficulty in seeing, because of the incessant clouds of Upman corona smoke which blew over his head from the back seat, and cascaded down in front of his eyes.

He turned the air conditioning fan on full blast and slid the windows up and down a few times, but the plump greasy man in the back seat did not seem to get the message. Jimmy Culundis was deep in thought; he sat with his eyes closed, cigar jammed in his mouth, drawing in and belching out smoke at evenly spaced intervals of eight seconds.

Culundis was in a good mood; the few people that knew him well found it hard to tell when he was in a good mood, because he always appeared cheerful, regardless of his mood. His business with Missh in Umm Al Amnah had been concluded in much less time than he had thought, and he had been able to fly to France on the Sunday, watch his horse, Guided Missile, win the Arc de Triomphe at Longchamps by fourteen lengths, and still get back to Athens in time to spend Sunday evening with his wife and seven children.

Culundis led a dual life, which he enjoyed, and which seemed, for him, to work. He was still married to Ariane, the fisherman's daughter from the village where he was born. He had only known her as a child when he was in his teens, but he had spotted her one day when he had returned to his village to visit his elderly parents, and had married her. She was pretty and homely, and not interested in a jet-set lifestyle, although she was happy to entertain any of the friends or colleagues that Culundis brought home. She had not wanted a grand house, and so, for their home, Culundis had bought a modest house, although fitted with almost every luxury money could buy, overlooking the fishing port where they had both been born.

Whilst he did business and played in the most expensive pastures of the world, Ariane was happy to remain in Greece, with the children. Although he saw her, on average, less than one evening a week, still, after seventeen years of marriage, he looked forward to those evenings at the one residence he owned, among all the others, that he called his home.

The horn of the Citroen shrieked, and the car swerved violently to avoid a tractor that had just shot straight out into the main road from a cart track, the driver still clearly of the opinion that the motor law of *priorité à droite* continued to apply to main road intersections with cart-tracks.

'Imbecile,' said the chauffeur, from somewhere inside the cloud of smoke.

Culundis thought about the word, 'imbecile'. It was a good word, he decided, to describe Abr Qu'Ih Missh, the thirty-eighth Emir of Amnah; the word applied equally well to his father, the now-deposed thirty-seventh Emir. They were both fools, in their different ways; but the old boy had strength of character, he thought. The son was weak; very weak. Culundis smiled. He hadn't slept on the Friday night after Missh had come down and given him the news; he had spent the entire night on the telephone, giving orders. For not only did Culundis have access to any type of military equipment he might want, he also had access to the finest mercenary soldiers in the world: an almost instant army, ranging from prematurely retired English and American top-ranking officers, including generals and brigadiers, to disenchanted SAS soldiers, to freshly trained privates. And it was not only soldiers he had on his books. He had strategists, military planners, economists, politicians. In short, he had all the personnel, ready and willing at the drop of a small hat containing a large cheque, to go anywhere in the world, to any country, to soldier it, police it, and govern it, for whomsoever's benefit Jimmy Culundis instructed them.

During the long Friday night, Culundis had, on Missh's telephone bill, assembled, briefed and ordered the despatch to Umm Al Amnah of one such complete instant armed force. With the exception of himself, Umm Al Amnah had not got a friend in the world. Culundis grinned again; he reckoned Emir Abr Qu'Ih Missh would go a long, long way to keep that friendship.

CHAPTER 15

When Culundis and Elleck arrived at Chateau Lasserre, they were formally introduced, in turn, to Mademoiselle Nicole Varasay, the Viscomte's current live-in delight; to each other, since they had never met; and to an aperitif comprising a mixture of non-vintage Bollinger champagne and a framboise liqueur. By the end of their first quarter of an hour in the chateau, they had decided that Mademoiselle Varasay was gorgeous, that they did not particularly like each other, and that the drink was lethal.

There are not many people who have a portrait of an ancestor painted by either Boucher, Fragonard or Winterhalter. Viscomte Lasserre had portraits by all three. What made it all the more remarkable was that in his magnificent dining room, they looked about as insignificant as a trio of china flying ducks.

The dining room was 125 feet long; one wall was a series of arches containing leaded-light French windows, which were opened onto a balcony overlooking the seventy-two acre lake. On another wall was a marble fireplace, twelve feet high and fourteen feet wide. Although it was mid-summer, a log fire burned cheerily, fanned by a cooling breeze that came in off the lake. The room was only faintly lit, by candles burning in the massive crystal chandelier above the table.

The inlaid rosewood table at which they sat had extension leaves which would take it to ninety feet in length, enabling it to seat seventy-five people in comfort; but tonight there were no leaves in the table, only the two semicircular ends joined together, making a round table that enabled the four diners to sit cozily together, but with ample room. On either side of the Viscomte sat Culundis and Mademoiselle Varasay, and between them sat Elleck. As Elleck had become progressively more sloshed on the champagne cocktail, he had increasingly ogled Mademoiselle Varasay. She wore a shimmering ice-blue gown completely off her shoulders, and only just over the top of her nipples; her sun-tanned bare arms, chest, and almost bare breasts, her stunning face and sensuous mouth were almost more than Elleck could bear, together with the fact she seemed to be taking such an interest in him, an interest that seemed to him to go well beyond the formalities of common courtesy.

Their first course was freshwater crayfish drunk with a '69 Corton Charlemagne, followed by truffles en croute, drunk with a '62 Haut Brion, followed by rack of lamb grilled with fine herbs, drunk with a '47 Latour, followed by a raspberry pavlova, drunk with a Chateau d'Yquem 1959.

As a mouthful of the sweet rich Sauternes slipped down his throat, Elleck suddenly felt a hand feel its way over the front of his trousers, find his fly and, one at a time, undo the buttons; he gulped and looked startled at Mademoiselle Varasay. In her right hand, she was holding her glass; she raised it just a fraction at him, drank from it and put it down. The hand slipped inside his trousers, found the gap in his Marks and Spencer Y-Fronts, prised it apart and began to encircle the only three things in the world that Elleck truly cherished that weren't in a bank safety deposit box in Switzerland. Squirming with a mixture of dread, embarrassment and sensuous pleasure, he swung his eyes to the Viscomte, who was engaged in conversation with Culundis and had apparently noticed nothing, nor had Culundis. He tried desperately to think of something to say to Mademoiselle Varasay, but could think of nothing. The fingers began a short stroking action.

The Viscomte turned his head and addressed Elleck: 'I think, Monty, it is time now that we began to talk some business. Both you and Jimmy have come a long way to be here tonight – Jimmy knows why he is here, but you do not.'

The stroking action continued; Elleck shot a desperate sideways glance at Mademoiselle Varasay, but she did not bat an eyelid, and not one portion of her that was above the table was

189

visibly moving in any way that was out of the ordinary. The Viscomte turned to her. 'My darling, I do not think it would be of interest to you what we have now to discuss. Perhaps you would like to relax in the drawing room, and we will join you shortly?'

'*Oui, mon chéri*,' she replied, gracefully and pleasantly. She stood up from the table and began walking towards the door. The Viscomte did not stand up, so neither did the other two men.

It was not until she was halfway through the doorway that Elleck realized that the fingers that had been inside his Y-Fronts were still busily there.

For a moment he froze; then he tried to remember quite how much of the champagne and the dry white and the clarets and the Sauternes he had drunk, and whether it should have made him this drunk; and then he shot a glance at the Greek on his right. Without turning his head towards him, Culundis grinned and gave him a broad wink.

The butler arrived with coffee and a bottle of dust-coated Hine. While the Viscomte's attention was momentarily distracted by him, Elleck plunged his hand below the table and tried to pull Culundis's hand away. It was like trying to grip an iron rod. Culundis turned to him, leaned over, and spoke softly. 'Relax – doesn't it feel good?'

'Get it out,' hissed Elleck.

'You're gorgeous – let's get together later, eh?'

Elleck, on one of the few occasions in his life, was stumped for words. Lasserre waited while the butler set the coffee cups, poured the coffee, set the huge brandy punts that had been a wedding gift to one of Lasserre's ancestors from Louis XIV, poured the Hine and discreetly departed. Culundis continued his groping, despite the fact that since Elleck had discovered the true identity of the groper, there was considerably less inside the Y-Fronts for the fingers to grope at.

'Monty,' said Lasserre, 'for many years you have handled the commodity investments of my personal portfolio, and the portfolio of the Lasserre group of companies. On many occasions when we have met, we have joked about what we call "the big one," no?' Elleck nodded.

'Now, I am not complaining at the way you have handled my money – not at all. You have consistently beaten the market average indicators by good margins, but still "the big one" has not come.'

The butler returned with a box of Bolivars. Culundis took one, so did Elleck, and then the Viscomte selected one; while his attention was again distracted, Elleck shot Culundis a vicious look. Culundis responded by blowing him a kiss. The butler departed. The men lit their cigars in turn with a wooden taper, which was passed around.

Lasserre continued: 'I have decided not to wait any longer for "the big one." I have decided to make "the big one" happen.'

Elleck shot Culundis an exasperated look; the expression on the Greek arms dealer's face was that butter wouldn't melt in his mouth.

Elleck looked at Lasserre with as quizzical an expression as he could muster under the circumstances.

'Just over two weeks ago,' said Lasserre, 'you were convinced that "the big one" had arrived: the raid on Osirak. But the advance time you gave me was short, so very short, and you made a limit on the amount of gold you would buy for me. I had no time to go to anyone else, either. Result? We made a small profit – a nice profit indeed – about one hundred thousand dollars. Not bad for one afternoon – but hardly what I would call the "big one" that I have waited ten years for. I alone can raise from my bank, on the security of my shares in Lasserre Group, in this chateau and estate, probably £50 million; putting that into gold futures at a ten per cent margin, I could buy two and a half million ounces of gold. If some act were to happen that could push the price of gold up say fifty, or maybe one hundred – or panic it even higher – then I could make a profit worth talking about. Even a rise of $50 an ounce, that would make me £125 million profit. That's what I would call the "big one." Wouldn't you, Monty?'

Elleck nodded. He was finding it damned hard to concentrate.

'Even my disgustingly rich friend, Jimmy Culundis, would have to admit to being impressed with a profit of that size, wouldn't you, Jimmy?'

'I'd call it big, Claude.' He grinned. He plucked

his hand from Elleck's trousers and began to attack furiously an itch behind his left ear.

Elleck immediately dropped his hands under the table, and did up his flies as fast as he could before Culundis could have a chance to launch his second wave. 'And how do you propose to make this "big one" happen, Claude?'

'There are two things above all others that can make the price of gold rise,' Lasserre said: 'A shortage, or the threat of war. Correct, Monty?'

Elleck nodded. 'Basically, yes. When there is the threat of war – or actual war – paper money can become completely worthless. That has happened many times, most recently in Vietnam. When the Chinese took over there, they nationalized the banks and stated that the banks would not redeem any bank-notes. The stuff became meaningless paper literally overnight. When there is political uncertainty, people become nervous of paper; if you are fleeing and you are in the middle of the wilderness desperate for food and shelter, in a country that is being overrun by an enemy, there aren't many people who are going to be interested in your 100 franc notes. Offer them a piece of gold, and it becomes a different matter – they know that somewhere in the world – someone is always going to give them value for it – and gold is the most popular of any metal. Because of its high value, you can carry in your pocket more than enough to live comfortably on for a very long time indeed.'

Lasserre nodded; Culundis blew large smoke rings, stuck his nose inside his brandy punt, and took several large sniffs.

'It would take a great deal of gold being bought to create a shortage, would it not?'

'An average of 1,500 tons of gold is mined each year, of which an average of 1,200 tons is used for jewellery, electronics, dentistry, decorative purposes, official coins and medals, medallions and commemorative fake coins. The balance – 300 tons – ends up in banks, in the International Monetary Fund and in the hands of private speculators. Those 300 tons have a market value of approximately $4,800 million.'

'I have just calculated,' interrupted Lasserre, 'that on margin, I could buy $1,000 million worth of gold – that is one quarter of the world's annual supply. My friend, Jimmy, also has approximately £50 million he could lay his hands on – which is $100 million – as ten per cent margin that could also buy $1,000 million of gold – are you saying that between us we could buy nearly half the new speculative gold coming into the market this year?'

Elleck shook his head. 'No. You are not the only people who trade on margin in gold – many people do – so you have to multiply the value of the gold by ten – to $48,000 million. To this you must add all the rest of the year's production – because that is also traded on the open market before it is sold – worth $192,000 million – multiplied by ten, because of margin trading – to make ten billion, nine hundred and twenty thousand million dollars; to this you must add the surplus gold since time began – probably 30,000 tons – worth on margin forty billion, eight hundred thousand million dollars, much of which is traded every year; your lousy little $2,000 million wouldn't even fill the petty cash tin in those terms. No offence, you understand?'

Lasserre and Culundis both nodded. They understood; being rich was all a matter of relativity. They might be big fishes in a small pond, but out in the ocean, the whales wouldn't even contemplate putting them in the peanut bowl. 'Monty,' said Culundis, 'if the amount is so insignificant, why, when you knew about Osirak in advance, did you limit the amount the Viscomte could invest to only $1 million?'

Elleck squirmed slightly in his seat. 'There were two reasons, actually – both of them connected. You see, I had to be very careful of this inside knowledge. I didn't want to lct on to anyone that I had the knowledge that I possessed, so I did the buying myself, very quietly, through a few chums; so I had to limit it to a small amount in order to avoid looking suspicious. Of course, time played a big part – I only had the tip-off a week before; if I had known earlier, I could have bought a great deal more, spreading it further – but I have to be very careful. I don't normally do any dealing directly myself – but I didn't want my brokers getting involved and maybe getting suspicious. I, er, at the end – when I knew things were quiet-ening down – I did give some pretty clear sell instructions – but I think I managed to convey the impression that that was just the judgement of an old and wise man, rather than the result of my knowledge.'

Culundis nodded; he didn't look too impressed. Elleck looked away from him with a distasteful expression.

'So, Monty,' said Lasserre, 'if you'd had more time you could have placed much more?'

'Sure.'

Lasserre nodded thoughtfully, and re-lit his cigar. 'If we wish to make a killing on the gold market, we can forget trying to create a shortage, correct?'

'You'll have to win a lot more races with those nags of yours before you'll have the cash to create a gold shortage, Claude.'

'So the other option we have is to create the threat of war?'

Elleck's shiny forehead rose upwards to meet his shiny bald pate, which sank downwards; where the two joined became a furrowed tangle of creases. He looked at Culundis, then back at Lasserre. 'That's about it,' he said, and grinned, taking a long draw on his cigar and leaning back in his chair.

'Then that's what we shall do,' said Lasserre.

Elleck jolted upright and leaned for an instant on the arm of his chair, before discovering that his chair didn't have any arms; somehow, by clutching onto a leg, he managed to prevent himself from falling completely onto the floor, and dropped his cigar in the process. He leaned over to pick it up, and shouted out in pain; his finger and thumb had picked it up by the lighted end by mistake. He looked quizzically at his host.

'You see, Monty,' said Lasserre, 'Osirak was no good. It was all over – poof! – so quickly. They fly out of the sky, blow up the power station – and then they are gone again, and that was that. Lots of noise in the press for a few days, and then all over. The world is used to acts of terrorism, and that was just one more – although on a fairly large scale. And you know – how many people care about Iraq? Iraq doesn't mean anything to most people. No. What is needed is something that will matter to the whole world – something that will threaten the peace of the whole world – bring it right to the very brink of war. Right to the very brink. That is what is needed. That is what will push up the price of gold, but really push it up. Right, Monty?'

Elleck felt a chill listening to the Viscomte's words. There was something about this whole evening – this extraordinary chateau, the bent Greek, the sincerity with which the Viscomte was talking. All his life, Elleck had taken steps to ensure that he only played in the 'A' team. Well here he was, as usual playing in the 'A' team, and he decided that tonight he might have been distinctly more at ease had he been playing in something

197

lower down the league. 'And how do you propose going about bringing the world to the brink of war, Claude?'

Lasserre picked his brandy punt up gently in the palm of his right hand; he stared down into the gold liquid for several moments, lifted the punt to his lips, took a small sip, held the brandy in his mouth for some moments, and then swallowed. He looked across at Elleck. 'We have already started,' he said.

There was a silence that lasted for nearly a full minute. The Viscomte passed it by lowering his nose into his punt and inhaling the fumes of the elderly brandy several times, slowly and deeply. Culundis passed it by examining first the end of his cigar which had half an inch of ash on; secondly, the end of his cigar which had half an inch of damp slobber; and then the space in between. Elleck passed it without removing his eyes from a point, on one of the open French windows, that was about six inches to the left of the Viscomte's face; about halfway through the minute, he rolled his cigar over, once, in the ashtray. He had absolutely no doubt that the Viscomte meant what he said, and from what he knew of the Viscomte's attitude to life and to people, he knew that the Viscomte was cold enough and ruthless enough to carry it out. From his short acquaintance with Jimmy Culundis, and from what he had read about him on the many occasions his name had appeared in the world press in the past, he had little doubt that Culundis had come from a similar mould. He tried to consider the significance of what the Viscomte had said, but he found he was unable to concentrate his mind. 'What do you mean?' he said finally, 'you have started?'

'What do you consider to be the most important commodity that could affect world peace at the present time, Monty?' said Lasserre.

'There is only one,' said Elleck. 'Oil.'

Lasserre nodded. 'If someone were to threaten overnight to shut off half the Western World's oil supply, what do you imagine would happen?'

'I imagine the Western World would resist strenuously.'

Again Lasserre nodded. 'Right.'

'But to turn off half the world's oil supply,' said Elleck, 'you would have to attack about six different countries all at once.'

Lasserre shook his head. 'That is not correct, Monty; there is an easier way. At the present time, over half the Western World's oil supplies are shipped in tankers down the Persian Gulf. There is one particularly narrow point in the Gulf – a mere twenty-seven miles wide – called the Strait of Hormuz. Block that, and nothing can get in or out of the Gulf.'

'I'm sure you are right – in theory,' said Elleck. 'But in practice, if any one blocks the Gulf, the West will have it unblocked within hours. And how on earth could anyone block a stretch of water twenty-seven miles wide? A couple of hundred yards is one thing – but twenty-seven miles is quite another.'

Lasserre again shook his head. 'You do not listen, Monty. I said, "threaten to block," not actually "block."'

'I don't see there is much difference. If someone is going to threaten to block it, they must show they have the ability to carry out that threat.'

'Correct.'

'So how could anyone show they could block the Strait of Hormuz and keep it blocked?'

Lasserre looked at Culundis. Culundis drew hard on his cigar, puffed out his cheeks, then spat out the mouthful of smoke before speaking. 'Nuclear explosives are not limited purely to massively powerful bombs for destroying land targets; a recent development has been the nuclear mine. There is no conventional mine in existence powerful enough to sink a large oil tanker – there are plenty that could make an ugly hole in one, but none that would destroy one. One small nuclear mine – say, twenty kiloton – would turn a supertanker into a mass of metal splinters, most of them no longer than a cigarette lighter flint; in addition, it would destroy any other shipping within a three-mile radius, and send out a tidal wave that would capsize any boat, of any size, within a ten-mile radius. Four tankers an hour go out through the Strait of Hormuz and four an hour come in; that's eight tankers in an hour. The shipping channels are four miles wide each way, with a two-mile gap – that's a ten-mile area. At any given time of any day or night, there would always be at least four tankers within capsize range of a twenty-kiloton nuclear mine.' Culundis stuck his cigar back in his mouth and drew hard on it.

'So all that any one,' said Elleck, 'who wishes to block the Strait of Hormuz has to do is nip down to his local supermarket, buy a boatload of nuclear mines and announce to the world that he is going to chuck them overboard in the Strait of Hormuz?'

'No,' said the Greek, 'not anyone. Only those with access to nuclear mines.'

'And who has access to nuclear mines?'

'As far as I know, only three people can get their hands on a worthwhile quantity without any questions being asked: the Chairman of the Soviet Union, the President of the United States, and myself.'

'I'll remember to give you a call ncxt time I need some,' said Elleck.

Culundis blew him a kiss. 'It will be no problem – just let me know the quantity and send me your cheque.'

Elleck looked down at the table, then out through the French windows at the dark blue, balmy warm night. 'So how, with your unlimited supply of nuclear mines, which you will threaten to throw into the Strait of Hormuz, do you actually bring the world to the brink of war?'

'In your line of work, it must be very important you keep up with the news, eh?'

Elleck nodded.

The Greek continued. 'Some years ago, you may remember a small disturbance in the Middle East – in the United Arab Emirates? One of the Emirates, Umm Al Amnah, broke away and became once more independent. All the world said the Libyans were behind this revolution – with, of course, the Russians behind them. Well, it wasn't the Libyans. I know – because I supplied the men and the weapons to Umm Al Amnah, and the Libyans were not involved. No outsider was; this was purely an internal situation. The old Emir Quozzohok fell out with the Government of the UAE just after oil was discovered in Amnah. He and the Government had never got on too well, and he was damned if they were going to have any benefits from his oil. This coup, of course, greatly upset the UAE and alienated Quozzohok from the governments of the Western World – they didn't want to lose their valuable friendship with the UAE, so they had to spurn Amnah. The Libyans and the Russians courted Quozzohok, but he didn't want to know.

'The reason the West thought Libya was behind that revolution was very simple: I don't like to have anything traced to me. So all the contracts with the mercenaries, all the purchases of weapons and ammunition and all other related purchases were made in the name of a company, Eurocorps, the origins of which can easily be traced, first to a Liechtenstein holding company and secondly to a Panamanian Company with nominee directors, and only one share issued. That share is owned by Sahqd-As-Sah, a Libyan arms wholesaling company. Right now, to assist them with certain internal problems, soldiers, weapons and ammunition are arriving at Umm Al Amnah every day. To anyone taking the trouble to find out who is behind them, the answer is easily found: Libya.' Culundis smiled.

'Although, of course, it is actually you,' said Elleck.

'Of course,' smiled the Greek.

'So you have set up Libya, in the opinion of the world, as being Umm Al Amnah's supporter – whether Amnah likes it or not?'

'In a nutshell, yes. Libya isn't going to deny it – it's good publicity for them. Poor exploited little Amnah – it all fits into Gaddafi's Islamic revolution activities very neatly.'

Elleck slowly nodded his head. 'I'm following you. So Amnah is going to threaten to mine the Strait, with Libya as fairy godmother and Russia as the golden coach?'

'No,' said Culundis. 'We are further than that. One month ago, something happened that was kept well out of the world's press: an Oman Navy patrol boat picked up, in the Strait, a fishing dhow that was drifting with a dead crew on board. Also on board were eight twenty-kiloton nuclear mines, all with six-hour timer devices which would automatically prime themselves six hours after immersion in the water. They were utterly sophisticated devices that could not be reversed by a minesweeper. They had sonar detonators primed to go off as soon as any ship got within one hundred yards; if one of those had been dumped into the sea, the Lord only knows how it could ever have been got out again.'

'Whose mines were they and how did they come to be on the dhow?'

'The mines were Russian-made, for all intents and purposes. The dhow's registration certificate showed its home port as being Al Suttoh. Al Suttoh is the chief port of Umm Al Amnah.'

'And who was behind it?' asked Elleck.

'As far as the Western World believes, the Libyans,' Culundis smiled.

'And what does the Western World believe the Libyans have to gain by blocking the Gulf?'

'In political terms,' said Culundis, 'that's a good question. No one can be sure – but in economic terms it is very clear. Libya's chief ports are on the Mediterranean. She is the only major oil-producing Arab country that does not need the Persian Gulf. If the Gulf was blocked for a considerable period of time, Libya would be in a position to ask just whatever the hell she liked for her oil.'

'That's a pretty good reason for Libya to block the Gulf,' said Elleck.

Culundis nodded in agreement.

'But you're implying it wasn't Libya who put those mines on that dhow?'

'Correct, Monty. The mines were not, in fact, Russian-made at all – although they were made to look that way. They were actually made in France, by Lasserre Industriele. I arranged for them to be put onto the dhow.'

Elleck thought for some moments. 'How come you were careless enough to let the Royal Omani Navy capture the dhow?'

'Not careless,' said Culundis very slowly, 'careful!'

'Careful?'

'It was deliberate. Do not forget, Monty Elleck, we have been talking about a *threat* to block the Gulf – not an actual blockade. You yourself have said that a threat is useless unless you can show you have the ability to carry it out. Well, let me tell you something: Oman, because it actually occupies the land one side of the Strait of Hormuz, and because of its position at the base of the Gulf, is strategically one of the most important countries of the world. It is friendly to the West, but the Russians constantly are trying to infiltrate it, trying to erode the Government's support by propaganda to the population. Oman is one of the most heavily-surveilled countries in the world; not merely because of its position as a watch post on the Gulf, but because of its strategically important position for the Americans and for NATO. There are more intelligence agents crawling around the sand dunes and rock caves of Oman than there are almost anywhere else in the world. There is not an intelligence agency in the world who did not hear about those nuclear mines being found aboard that dhow. You might not have read one word in the newspapers – because it was deliberately kept out – but I'll tell you something: every government in the world right now knows those mines were on that dhow. They don't know for sure why they were there – they can only speculate. But they know that they exist; they know that they were there; and if someone were to tell them that there were another thirty dhows out there, carrying a further 400 mines between them, you know what they'd think, Monty Elleck?'

Elleck slowly nodded his head.

'Damned right, Monty Elleck. They'd bloody believe it.'

Elleck pulled another flat cedar taper from the silver box on the table, stuck one end of the taper in a candle flame, then held the burning taper to his cigar, puffed hard three times, then shook out the taper. 'Couldn't the mines be swept? There must be a way?'

'Impossible. You cannot get near them without them exploding.'

'Couldn't they be detonated by remote control?'

The Greek shook his head. 'Imagine 400 all within a few square miles. If one goes, there is a good chance it will set off others – perhaps even all the others; the result of nuclear mines detonating in that stretch of water is almost impossible to conceive.

It would alter the entire floor of the Gulf – the Gulf isn't that deep, and there would be a very real danger that a force of explosion of that size could raise up the entire bottom – making it impassable to all shipping for months and possibly years. It would create tidal waves up and down the Gulf that would wash away towns and villages, destroy the harbours – such a force of water that would break supertankers into little pieces.'

'There must be some way to make these mines safe,' said Elleck. 'If your bluff was called and you had to put 400 mines in the Gulf, and then your demands were met, how would you make them safe? Or would you leave them? Umm Al Amnah has a coast on the Gulf – surely it would suffer as much as anyone if these mines did go off?'

'There is a way to make them safe. These mines have been fitted with a detonating system that is primed automatically by six hours' immersion in water. They can be defused only by a coded radio signal. The eight mines we put in the dhow which was captured had no such defusing system. We did not want anyone else to learn about the detonating system – I am sure you can understand?'

'Naturally,' said Elleck. He was pushing his mind forward, trying to anticipate what was at the end of all this, and he was finding it difficult; there were too many options.

'What,' said Elleck, 'did Sheik Quozzohok, Emir of Amnah, have to say about all this?'

'He never knew about it. It was felt in the Oman

that it would be better to keep quiet – and keep watching Amnah to try and find out more about what might be going on. Amnah has no intelligence agents in Oman – nor anywhere else – for that matter,' said Lasserre. 'Now we come to the key part. Our aim is to push up the price of gold and, to do this, we need a major international conflict, preferably lasting several days, and worsening each day. You will probably not know yet, but the Sheik Quozzohok has abdicated, and the new Emir is his son, Abr Qu'Ih Missh.'

'Very interesting,' said Elleck. 'He happens to be one of my company's major private clients.'

'Indeed?' said Lasserre. 'This is a complete coincidence, I can assure you. Now this man Missh is sitting on a very rocky seat – and I understand he is totally dependent on Jimmy Culundis for his personal security, and the security of his government. He will go along with anything that Jimmy instructs him, because he has no option.' Lasserre turned to Culundis. 'I am correct?'

'We've got him by the balls.'

Elleck looked at Culundis and decided that if it had only been his balls that he had got him by, then the Sheik had got off very lightly.

'Now,' said Lasserre, 'what we are proposing to do is as follows: Amnah is being watched very closely indeed by many intelligence networks; any information that is let out will immediately be passed onto the governments of the world. We intend to let it slip out that Umm Al Amnah, supported by Libya, is planning to mine the Persian Gulf, and will not remove the mines until Israel agrees to relinquish all the territories it has gained since the Six Day War in 1967.'

Elleck frowned. Israel was an obsession with him; he had poured hundreds of thousands of pounds into charities supporting the country, although he did admit secretly, to himself, that the reason was probably as much, if not more, his desire to keep his clients happy and to cultivate new clients as any particular passionate desire to help the homeland of his race.

'Israel,' said Lasserre, 'will then, we hope, launch straight into war against Libya and Umm Al Amnah. Within a very short space of time, one half of the world will be supporting one side or the other, whilst the other half will be trying to pull them apart. Whatever the eventual outcome may be, for a period of time the price of gold must surely go through the roof?'

'Israel has suffered a lot of criticism in the past for striking too quickly. Begin only pushed Israel into the first Osirak raid because he felt it would gain him votes in the forthcoming election. The second raid was also similarly inspired – two days before an election. Without those elections immediately in front, I am not sure Israel would have attacked on either occasion. So how can you be so sure this time?' said Elleck.

Lasserre got up from his chair, left the dining room, and came back a few moments later holding an RCA videocassette in his hand. He put it on the table in front of Elleck. 'I have a little home movie; if you like, after dinner we can see it. It is a tape of an Israeli, General Isser Ephraim, who is the Head of the Mossad – the Israelis' overseas Intelligence Agency. He is one of the most powerful men in Israel, and a man whose advice, on military matters, is almost invariably acted upon. Wouldn't you agree, Jimmy?'

Culundis nodded. 'He is more powerful than the Israeli Minister of Defence. What he says, goes.'

Lasserre continued. 'This tape was made at the Tel Aviv morgue. It would seem that General Isser Ephraim has an unusual pastime: he likes making love to dead boys.'

There was a long silence, punctuated only by the sound of an English commodity broking tycoon choking on vintage brandy.

'Isser Ephraim?' said Elleck.

'Yes,' said Lasserre. 'Would you like to see the tape?'

'No,' said Elleck. 'I would not. That man is a friend of mine, a very old friend. I cannot believe this.'

'If you look at the tape, you will believe it. The keeper of the morgue said he had been coming there for ten years. Dead Arab boys. The keeper is paid a large sum to telephone him and let him know whenever they have a new one in.'

'He must be lying,' said Elleck.

'We sent Ephraim a copy of the tape, asked him

to come to a meeting at L'Hermitage Hotel in La Baule. He does not know who we are, and we intend to keep it that way. With a man like Ephraim, that is the most sensible. The Mossad is not known for its inefficiency – we do not wish to have a surprise visit from any of Ephraim's friends in the middle of the night. The report that I have had back from my courier is that Ephraim made no attempt to deny his activities. He is desperate that the news of this hideous perversion does not leak out – it would of course destroy his career, quite apart from putting him in a mental institution, at best, or a jail, at worst, for very many years.'

Elleck shook his head. 'Ephraim is a friend, a good friend of mine.'

'You seem to have a lot of friends in high places,' said Lasserre. 'You must be very selective.'

'What do you mean by that, Claude?' Elleck's face flushed.

'You know what I mean, Monty; don't get on your high horse. You and Jimmy – you both came from nothing. You have made your ways up in the world, you have succeeded; but you have not done this by cultivating the friendships of only those people that you really like. You don't have the time in life to do that when you are ambitious. No – the friends you have and the friends Jimmy has are only there because they are useful to you.'

'That is a very arrogant statement,' said Elleck, almost petulantly.

'Arrogant, Monty, yes, but true.'

'And the same doesn't apply to you?'

'Of course – if I had friends. I don't particularly like to have just "friends." I like to work always; I like to have employees and colleagues. Sure, I become friendly with colleagues – I am friendly with you and friendly with Jimmy – but if we did not do business – would we see each other? I doubt it very much. You do business with Ephraim, do you not? You must do – he must be your source of information on Osirak. If he was not helpful, would you still see him?'

'He saved my life in Auschwitz in the war.'

'The war was a long time ago, Monty. If you haven't paid him back by now, then you probably aren't going to.'

Elleck went red; he knew he had never paid Ephraim back and, equally, he knew he never would. He'd even ripped him off on the advance information he had on Osirak; he could have given him a cheque for half a million dollars and not felt the pinch, such was the profit he had made on the two Osirak attacks, but it wasn't in his nature to give a penny away that he didn't absolutely have to. He remained silent.

Lasserre helped himself to some more brandy, then passed the bottle to Culundis.

'So if I have got this correct,' said Elleck, 'you intend to leak to the world that there is a Libya-Amnah plot to fill the Persian Gulf full of nuclear mines, and leave them there until the Israelis agree to withdraw from Sinai and all other occupied territories?'

Lasserre and Culundis both nodded.

'You will then instruct General Ephraim that he is to persuade the Government of Israel to launch military offensives against both Libya and Amnah, which you expect will lead to a major international conflict, possibly bringing the world to the brink of war?'

Again the Viscomte and the Greek nodded.

'And your reason for doing all of this is so that it will push the price of gold, of which, by then, you will have plentiful amounts, up through the roof?'

Further nodding.

'And my role in this, presumably, is to arrange the buying and the selling of the gold?'

'I knew you would agree, Monty,' said Lasserre.

Later that night, Elleck took care to lock his bedroom door after he had entered it; a short while after he had climbed into bed and switched off the light, there was a soft knocking on the door. He wondered whether it was Nicole or Culundis, and debated whether to open it or not. He didn't want to miss out on a night with the gorgeous French girl, but on the other hand he didn't fancy putting up another fight against the Greek's advances. The gentle knocking came again, and Elleck decided it was definitely a female's knock. He knew also, because he was a gambling man, that he must open that door. He went over to it. 'Who is it?' he whispered loudly. The reply was further soft knocking. Terrified of being overheard by his host down the corridor, he opened up the door. Two arms hugged him around the chest, and pushed him backwards inside the door.

'Oh, you wonderful, beautiful creature, I knew you would be waiting for me.'

Elleck pushed with all his might to try and stop the slow, steady, propulsion of himself, by the Greek, towards the massive bed.

CHAPTER 16

Gyan

General Ephraim had sat at his desk for a long time on the morning of the Monday that Elleck, Lasserre and Culundis had met, staring down through the smoked glass windows at the bustle of the traffic. There were three piles on his desk: a pile of memorandums, a pile of letters and a pile of sealed despatches, and they all remained untouched. He pulled open a drawer in the desk, pulled out a piece of chewing gum, unwrapped it and put it in his mouth.

He thought over and over about the Frenchman he had met in the bar of L'Hermitage Hotel in La Baule. It was a massive hotel, fronting onto a beach which was part of a vast south west-facing bay. The tide was out, and the stranger suggested a walk along the sand. There, among the stench of putrid fish and damp seaweed, stepping across a million empty clam shells and past the occasional carcass of a crab, the Frenchman had dictated his instructions to him. He hadn't liked the Frenchman, in his fashionable pastel trousers and thin, open jacket, when they had first met, and he liked him even less during the next hour.

.ou are to return to Israel, and wait until you
.eceive your intelligence report from Amnah
concerning the arrival into the country of the
nuclear mines, and the subsequent reports you
will receive concerning the threat to use these
mines by Amnah and Libya to extort the with-
drawal from certain occupied territories by Israel.

'You will also learn that these are not the only
requests that will be made – merely the first, for
the Libyans will know that they have got you over
a barrel, and you will have no choice but to give
in to all and every demand they make. With that
information to hand,' said the Frenchman, who
had introduced himself as Arnauld Bauté, 'your
Government could not possibly treat your recommendations of immediate invasion with anything
other than full support. It would be a different
matter, indeed, if the mines were already in place,
for then there would be a danger of them being
detonated, which would cause havoc, and for
which Israel would be blamed. But the advance
intelligence you will receive will tell you that you
have probably a few days before these mines will
be despatched out in the dhows – all the more
reason to act!'

'Are the mines really going to be there?' said
Ephraim.

'But sure they are; put there by my people.'

'And who are your people?'

'We are called the "Executioners of Mohammed".
We are funded by the PLO.'

216

'I've never heard of your organization,' said Ephraim.

'You will hear of it soon. The whole world will hear of it soon. Very soon.'

It was an overcast day but although it was quite hot, and the schools were now on holiday for the summer, there were not many people on the beach. Ephraim stared ahead at the miles of wet sand, to the left at the battery of white hotels and apartment buildings, most in need of a lick of paint, which trailed off into the horizon, and then to the right, at the breaking waves and, beyond them, the calm, still sea. Somewhere, two and a half thousand miles beyond that horizon was America. It was strange, felt Ephraim, walking out here, in this vast open space, and feeling as trapped as if he had been crammed into a cupboard.

After they had parted, Ephraim had driven straight to Paris and, to his relief, Chaim Weisz, the Chief of Israeli Intelligence Operations in France, was at home. By midnight on the Saturday, he knew for sure that there was no such organization as the 'Executioners of Mohammed'. He also knew that Arnauld Bauté's real name was Jean-Luc Menton, and that he lived in an apartment overlooking the old German U-boat pens at St Nazaire. The information on Bauté he had been able to acquire through his foresight in not going to La Baule without someone to cover him.

He was so deep in thought, he did not notice his coffee being brought in, placed on his desk,

217

and his secretary leaving again. His mind was on one thing and one thing only: finding out who the hell was behind all this, and breaking them apart with his bare hands. He had filing cabinets stuffed full with dossiers on terrorist organizations, but he didn't need to open them: he could reel off pretty well every terrorist organization in the world from the top of his head by memory. He was going through them now, one by one, thinking about the way they operated, the people they used, trying to think whether the events so far matched any of their normal styles of operating. It was a difficult task; so many were unpredictable, and liable to chop and change. Menton, he knew, was his best hope. France had him under twenty-four-hour surveillance, and when offices started up for the week, at about 9.00 – an hour-and-a-half's time, Israeli time – a full search to discover everything there was to discover about Monsieur Bauté, né Menton, and his mystery employers, would be under way.

Ephraim chewed the gum thoughtfully and slowly, then removed the ball from his mouth, held it between his index finger and thumb, drank a mouthful of coffee, swallowed it, then replaced the gum in his mouth. On Friday, the nuclear mines were due to start arriving in Umm Al Amnah; by the middle of the following week the shipment would be complete. By then, he would have made his reports, and his recommendations; if he went along with what he had been instructed to do, the invasion of Umm Al Amnah and Libya should commence approximately two weeks from today.

In many ways, he would dearly have loved the opportunity to invade Libya. That country had been a thorn in Israel's side for many years. He believed that without Libya, Israel would be much nearer to a realistic, lasting peace than she ever was now, and somehow, with Libya lurking in the background of the Arab world, there was always a shadow cast on any future hopes. Umm Al Amnah until now had never bothered him much; he had always considered it a tin-pot nation, and too small to be of any consequence. It had connections, no doubt with Libya and with the Soviet Union, but it was a long way away from Israel, and he had never considered it as a likely threat. Israel had limited resources, which meant that the Mossad had limited resources; he would have loved to have had agents in every city in every country of the world, but it just was not possible on his budget, and with the manpower available.

During the past twelve hours, he had instructed twelve of his crack agents to drop everything and infiltrate Amnah; but he knew that with a tiny country it was not going to be easy. Umm Al Amnah was not as yet aware that there was such a thing as a tourist industry and as it had, in any event, at the present time, little to offer tourists other than high-rise buildings, factories, sand and camel dung, it was hardly surprising it was not to be found within the pages of Thomas Cook's glossy brochures. The chance of any agent successfully infiltrating Amnah in a pork-pie hat, flowered shirt, Bermuda shorts and an Instamatic hanging around his neck were not high. Business required visas, which were readily available, but due to a bureaucratic system established by Emir Missh's father, took nine weeks to come through. General Ephraim's team of men were faced with the options of arrival in the harbour by boat or parachute, or across the desert by foot or camel.

During the next seventy-two hours, Amnah's population of 17,328 was about to be swollen by twelve: five bedouins, two fishermen, three sailors, and a truck-driver and his mate delivering machine tool parts for a deep-freeze manufacturer.

To satisfy himself, he had already been to the electronics surveillance department and looked at the first minute of the tape. He hadn't needed to look any further; he had pressed the 'Erase' button, run the tape through forward and backwards twice, and then checked to make sure the image was completely gone. Only then did he hand the tape over, with instructions to find out everything that could be learned from a blank RCA videotape. Ephraim suspected, not incorrectly, that it wouldn't be much.

CHAPTER 17

The taxi rattled its way down the Strand; Rocq sat in the back, feeling pleased with himself and happy with life. He felt very happy indeed. The only thing that marred his happiness was the knowledge that in about half an hour the alcohol would begin wearing off and, within a couple of hours, he would have an aching head, sore eyes, and probably an overwhelming feeling of depression. But right now, he was making the most of the good feeling.

His companion in the taxi, the Honourable James Rice, was already beginning to feel quite sober, although the heat of the June afternoon was making him feel weary; he was glad he hadn't attempted to keep up with Alex Rocq's drinking today. They had started in the bar of Langan's Brasserie, where Rocq had downed four large vodka Martinis before they had ordered. They had a half bottle of white with their starters, of which Rocq had drunk two and a half glasses to his one; a bottle of red with their main course, of which again, Rocq had drunk most; and then brandy with their coffee – Rocq had had five to his one.

Lavinia okay?' asked Rocq, suddenly remem-
bering that they had talked nothing but business
throughout their luncheon.

'She's very well, thanks,' replied Rice patiently,
for the sixth time. He looked at his watch a little
anxiously. They had left Globalex at 12.30; it was
now a quarter past four.

'How're the kids?'

'They're very well. Growing up fast. When are
you going to have some?'

Rocq shrugged. 'I don't know. Don't know if I
feel like getting married again – stumping up forty
quid a week alimony to one ex-wife, bloody bitch
– don't know that I want to risk getting stuck with
paying two lots.'

Rice nodded sympathetically. 'Still seeing that
little girl you brought down that weekend – what
was her name?'

'Denise?'

Rice nodded.

Rocq thought about her with some guilt; he'd
taken her out at least once a week for over a year,
and had often taken her away at weekends. She
was easy-going and had a lovely nature, with a
pretty, homely flat just off Marylebone High Street;
after the bust-up of his marriage he had used it
almost as a second home. It was a refuge where
he had felt cosy, safe. Denise was a girl that he
enjoyed being with and she was pretty enough for
him to enjoy being seen with. And yet, after he
had met Amanda, Denise had simply gone from

his mind. He remembered, through his alcoholic haze, that it was nearly six weeks since they had last spoken. With a strong twinge of remorse, he remembered that she had telephoned the office and left messages twice – the first about ten days after he met Amanda and the second time about two weeks later. On both occasions he had been extremely busy and had told the receptionist that he would call her back. On neither occasion did he.

'No – not for a while,' he said.

'She was nice – you seemed well-suited.'

'Think that's my problem, Jimbo – I always want a challenge. The girl I'm taking out at the moment – I find her a challenge.'

'In what way? She can't stand your guts, and you're trying to convince her otherwise?'

Rocq grinned. 'You know what I mean.'

'What does she do, this one?'

'She's an architect.'

'Stick with her, Rocky. The way your career's going, you're going to need someone to support you.' The words stung Rocq, knifing through his armour of alcohol. Rice saw the expression on his face and wished he had kept his mouth shut. 'Sorry, Rocky – no offence meant.' And inhaled deeply.

The cab driver hooted angrily at a charabanc that was taking its load of tourists around the Aldwych too slowly for his liking. 'Blardy fugging tourists,' he said. 'Blardy fugging bleeding charrybanks.

223

Fuggin' bleeding taking our work, that's wot they're doing.' On another day, his efforts at engaging the two men in the back of his cab into stimulating intellectual conversation might have succeeded; today, the efforts didn't even produce a grunt.

He tried a new tack: '88 Mincing Lane, you said?'

'Yes,' said Rice, leaning forward and sliding the partition window shut.

Rocq sat back in his seat and drew on his cigarette. His lunch with Rice had not been successful, and £80 was a lot of money to have stumped up for an unsuccessful lunch. Even if he put Rice down as a client, the maximum Elleck allowed for a luncheon was £40, holding the view that £20 worth of food and booze was more than ample for anyone.

Rocq had chosen Langan's, in Mayfair, because he wanted to get Rice out of the City environment, out of the security and clannishness of the people with whom Rice was far more in harmony than himself. He had wanted to take down Rice's guard, and he felt that taking him into unfamiliar territory was the way to do this. But it had not succeeded. He sat and recalled the conversation that had taken place as they had started into their steaks.

'Jimbo – about this coffee business – you suggested waiting a couple of days to see how it stabilized – what do you think now?'

'It seems to have levelled out – it bottomed

224

yesterday at £378 a ton, climbed this morning first thing to £460 and dropped back to £421.'

'And what do you think is going to happen next? If my information is correct, and the supplies in Brazil are badly hit, do you think the price will go up, bearing in mind what has happened?'

Rice leaned forward conspiratorially. 'So far, what has brought about this crash is only theory. There is no proven fact, and everyone at the moment is waiting for a proven fact. All this news that hit the press last week and caused the collapse of coffee was hearsay and was the result of a leak. It all stemmed from a laboratory assistant working for a company that is about to launch a revolutionary new instant coffee on the market – they've produced some new method of preserving the flavour in ground coffee, and they reckon this will be the death knoll for fresh coffee. The product is coming onto the market some time next year. Well, this girl was sacked for some disagreement – she claims it was because she felt that the management were attempting to cover up this cancer discovery, and went and spilled the beans to the press. The World Health Organization claim that they were misquoted and said only that there might be a link – but nothing was positively proven. They are now conducting further tests, but they expect conclusive tests to take up to a year; however, they are expected to make an interim statement shortly, I would think certainly within the next few weeks, to try and alleviate public uncertainty.'

'Do you have any clues what this might be?'

Rice grinned and nodded smugly; then he wished he hadn't, and realized it was the alcohol that caused him to make this indiscretion.

'What are they?'

'I can't tell you yet, Jimbo, because I don't know.'

'But you must have a pretty good idea?'

Rice again couldn't resist the temptation to show how clever he was. 'I might do,' he said.

'And what's the verdict?'

Rice toyed with his rare rumpsteak, trimmed some fat off, cut a small piece of meat, put some mustard on it; slowly, debatingly, he raised it towards his mouth, then put it back down again. 'It looks very much as though the facts are correct; that there is a major cancer link.'

'And what do you reckon will happen to coffee when that little gem comes out?'

'It'll fall even further. Plummet. Depends how the public takes the news – and how the health authorities act, and how serious the link actually is – how badly the use is affected. I can't predict how far it could eventually fall – but it could be a long way further.'

'So it would be wise to go short, wouldn't it?'

'Well – nothing is definite yet. I would advise anyone to wait. By the way, Rocky – I'm sorry I had to send you a margin call.'

'Oh, don't worry,' Rocq slurred, trying to sound nonchalant. 'Win some, lose some – that's one of the hazards of punting.'

The Honourable James Rice put the forkful of steak into his mouth and pulverized it between his immaculately capped teeth, while his aristocratic saliva set to work converting it into a substance that would be acceptable to his stomach. He nodded slowly at Rocq.

'Jimbo – I think I'd better go short. Do you think you could do me – er—' Rocq paused to work it out. He was down at the present time some £480,000; he needed to make that up, and fast, and his only chance was to invest in a volatile commodity. None right now, he knew, was more volatile than coffee. He couldn't think lucidly enough to work out the sums. 'How much do you reckon I need to sell short to make £480,000?'

'A fair amount, old man. And you know I can't take any order from you until you've covered your outstanding margin.'

Rocq nodded and their eyes met, firmly, for the first time since they had sat at the table. 'I know,' he said.

Rice looked down, picked up his wine glass and drained it. Then he began sawing off another chunk of steak; he spoke without raising his eyes from the meat. 'There are a lot of people who have been caught with their trousers down, Alex, a lot.'

Rocq noticed he was now calling him by his Christian name instead of his nickname.

'A lot of people are going to go belly-up over this coffee business – and not just individuals – major companies, too. I personally would not be at all surprised if it brought a few brokerage houses down at the same time. I've been in this game for ten years and I've never seen a crash like it. All the clearing houses are going to be out to collect in every penny they possibly can – including ours. Elleck has issued instructions that all margin owed is to be paid in full – at once – no extensions, no increases, and margins must be paid up-front before any new orders are placed. He's ordered a print-out of every outstanding order of coffee on Globalex's books – it's out of my hands entirely, old man. Absolutely nothing I can do. I'd help you if I could – but just don't see how I can. Can you find the margin you need – and enough on top to go short?'

They caught each other's eye again.

'If you give me enough time,' said Rocq.

'How long do you need?'

'About forty years.'

Rice grinned. 'What are you going to do?'

'You know what I need to do? I need to go short, hope to hell coffee drops, and then I'm out of the woods.'

'And if it doesn't drop?'

'Then I hope the stuff rises high enough to get me out of schtum.'

'Right now I don't think it's safe to count on anything.'

'I can't stand still, Jimbo. I need £480,000 to stand still, and that's £480,000 more than I have. I've got to stay in the game, it's my only hope.'

'W. C. Fields was once found drunk in a hic. town, playing a rigged game of poker, and getting ripped off on every hand. Someone asked him why he kept on playing when he knew the game was rigged. He replied, "Because it's the only game in town." Four hundred and eighty thousand is a lot of money, Alex, but it's a lot less than you could lose if you stay in the game.'

'That, old wise man, is a risk I'm going to have to take.'

CHAPTER 18

Rocq got back to his office. Within seconds of sitting at his desk, the bouncing Baron was on the line from Toronto.

'What's with all this coffee business, Alex?'

'What do you mean?'

'I just lost my shirt and pants.'

'Why the hell did you go dabbling in coffee?' asked Rocq, feeling more than a trifle hypocritical.

'I got a tip-off it was going to go through the roof.'

'Sure you heard your tipster right?'

The Baron ignored the comment. 'Why the heck didn't you advise me not to go into coffee?'

'You didn't ask. Anyhow, I'm a metal broker – you want advice on coffee, ask someone that knows about coffee.'

'You're the only one who knows anything about anything,' said the Baron.

For one of the rare occasions in his life, the flattery went clean over Rocq's head. 'How much did you drop?'

'I don't know. A lot. Couple of million maybe; what you reckon it's going to do?'

'It would be unprofessional of me to give you an opinion.'

'So give me an opinion – when the hell were you professional?'

'Go short, Harry – it's going to go down some more.'

'How much?'

'I don't know. Twenty-five – fifty – maybe one hundred – maybe more.'

'Okay, Alex. If you're wrong – I'm going to get really mad.'

'Hey – now hold on – I just said I'm not an expert on coffee – if—' Rocq stopped in mid-sentence – the Baron had rung off. He put back the receiver and sat there. His headache was starting, and the depression was in full stream. Rice had annoyed him at lunch, annoyed him a lot; he had been complacent and very unhelpful. Rice could have accepted his order for the amount of coffee he wanted to sell short without the margin payment up front – he had plenty of discretionary accounts, and he wouldn't have got into a lot of trouble over it. The amount of margin that would have been required from Rocq was small beer in terms of the amounts Rice bought and sold every day. Rocq could understand Rice's position, to a point, but he didn't accept it. There were many things in life that he understood clearly, but he did not accept; often it was because he did not like what he understood. Occasionally it was because he had no choice; today was one of those occasions. He picked up his telephone and dialled Theo Barbiero-Ruche's number in Milan.

After having narrowly escaped being kidnapped on his way to the office a few years previously, Barbiero-Ruche now worked at home. 'Barbiero-Ruche,' the Italian's deep voice boomed down the phone within moments of the ringing tone starting.

'Theo – it's Rocky.'

'Ah, you bastard,' said the Italian. 'I'm not too happy with you, not too happy at all.'

'What's your problem?'

'That damn girl you fixed me up with – Dingly – Dunky – what's her name?'

'Deidre.'

'Yeah, Deidre. She gave me a present.'

'So what's the problem?'

'You know what the present was?'

'No, what?'

'The clap.' There was a long silence. 'It's not funny, Rocky.'

'I wasn't laughing.'

'You weren't laughing? You were laughing yourself stupid.'

'I wasn't, Theo – it must have been interference on the line.'

'Interference – I'll give you interference. You know how many broads I got lined up right now? I never had so many damned broads lined up – and what I got to tell them? Sorry, babies, Theo can't see you right now because he went to England and got the clap from a dog?'

232

'You don't have to screw them, Theo; girls like being taken out – you know – theatre, opera, nice dinner then drop them home. Try being romantic – you might find you enjoy it.'

'You're full of shit,' grunted the Italian. 'Anyhow – what the hell you call for? No one left to talk to in England? All your damn clients in bed with terminal venereals?'

'Superwop – just shut your face a moment and let me get a word in edgeways. I'm sorry about your problems – take the tablets and they'll get better. I've got problems of my own right now, all thanks to your damned advice.'

'What problems you got, Rocky?'

Rocq looked cautiously around him to see if anyone was listening to him. They weren't. Mozer and Slivitz were both engaged in shouting matches with clients who appeared to be on the other side of the world and stone deaf.

'Coffee.'

The Italian emitted a low moaning that sounded like a bad attack of indigestion. 'You too. How bad?'

'Bad.'

'Got to take the rough with the smooth, Rocky. I got the clap, you got the coffee.'

'Want to swap?'

'It's that bad?'

'What do you reckon it's going to do?'

'I hear the World Health Organization's got a lot of hard evidence. It's going to drop some more – whole lot more when that news breaks.'

'When is it going to break?'

'Couple of days, maybe. Week or two at the most.'

'How much is it going to drop?'

'Fifty for sure. Maybe one hundred. Could even go one hundred and fifty. It depends.'

'So you'd advise going short?'

'For sure, Rocky; you must go short.'

'What price do you have on coffee at the moment?'

'Four hundred and twenty-seven pounds sterling, September. You want the dollar price?'

'Sterling's fine. Okay, Theo, I want you to sell some coffee short for me.' Rocq paused, and did some sums on his calculator. 'Twelve thousand tons,' he said, finally.

'You've got to be kidding,' said Barbiero-Ruche. 'I'd have trouble selling 2,000, let alone 12,000.' He paused. 'I'll call you back, Rocky – after I've rung The Producers Pact. They're trying to support the market. Someone there owes me a favour.' He rung off.

Five minutes later he was on the line again. 'Okay, Rocky. 12,000 tons. It'll be crossed on the market tomorrow. I'm going to have to ask you for margin, Rocky – too much for me to carry on my own.'

'No problem, Theo,' Rocq lied.

'I'm going to need £512,000. Okay?'

'Sure – I'll tell my bank to send you a telegraphic transfer – soon as I get your confirmation.'

'You'll get that tomorrow.'

'Okay – soon as I receive it, you'll get your margin. Keep taking the tablets, fat man.'

'Ciao.'

'Ciao.' Rocq replaced the receiver and breathed a sigh. He had a chance now. Somehow, he would have to fool Barbiero-Ruche into believing that the £512,000 margin was on its way. The Italian reckoned that coffee would drop within the week. If he could spin the Italian along until then, he could be out of the woods. Communications with Italy and internally in Italy were dreadful. Cables and telexes did frequently go astray. He just hoped that Barbiero-Ruche would keep that sell order for him and not liquidate it. He was going to have to rely on a mixture of their good friendship and bad communications.

He went and got himself a coffee and returned to his desk.

'Was that your lunch hour – or did you have your dinner early?' said Mozer sarcastically, leaning over to him.

'No – I've been out trying to buy a deodorant strong enough for your breath.'

Mozer shook his head. 'I'll tell you one thing, Alex: my breath may not be so fresh, but my work record smells a damned sight better than yours.'

'Go back to your cave, Henry.'

They were interrupted by a clerk bringing a telex and placing it on Rocq's desk. He stared at it, and all his anxieties came flooding back.

It was a confirmation from Theo Barbiero-Ruche,

of his instructions to sell 12,000 tons of coffee at £427 in September. From tomorrow he would be legally bound to sell that coffee at that price. Five million and one hundred and twenty-four thousand pounds. If coffee dropped, by at least £50, he would be fine – and if it dropped even more, he stood to make a substantial profit. If it rose, however, he would be adding a mighty further amount to his slate. He would have no option but to declare himself bankrupt. He re-read the confirmation once more. It didn't make him feel any better.

CHAPTER 19

Jean-Luc Menton awoke with a start, sweating heavily, to a noise that sounded like a dog being sick – except that he didn't have a dog. As his brain focussed on reality, he knew without opening his eyes that the noise was from his girlfriend, Valerie, who always slept on her stomach, and half-suffocated against the pillow.

He slid his hand out and picked up his Casio digital watch.

'*Merde*,' he informed himself. He put the watch back, picked up a pack of Gauloises, shook a cigarette out, put it into his mouth, lit it with his Bic lighter and inhaled deeply. Then, with the cigarette still in his mouth, he jumped out of bed, and began pulling on his clothes.

The grunting gagging noises stopped and were replaced by Valerie's deep voice. '*Quelle heure est-il?*'

'*Dix heures et demi.*'

He ran into the bathroom, put the cigarette in the soap tray, chucked some cold water on his face, dried it, then replaced the cigarette. He pulled on his jacket, picked up a couple of packets chewing gum from the sidetable, mumbled '*Au .evoir, à toute à l'heure,*' and dashed out of the apartment.

Menton knew that the Viscomte did not like to be kept waiting, and he was already an hour late, with a thirty-minute drive ahead of him. As he walked down the stairs, he thought back hard on the interview he had had with the Israeli, General Ephraim, on the beach at La Baule. He had no doubt that Viscomte Lasserre would require a very detailed account of Ephraim's reaction.

He left the small modern apartment beside the old U-boat pens at St Nazaire harbour, walked over to his green Alfasud, climbed in and started the engine. He rammed the gear lever into first, and accelerated fiercely away; almost immediately, he felt a sharp stabbing pain in the base of his head.

'*Tournez à droite,*' said the man with the Walther automatic, in the back seat.

Menton arrived two hours late for his meeting with the Viscomte. He didn't mention anything about the interlude with the man with the Walther. He was too scared.

At 3.15 that Tuesday morning, the green phone on General Isser Ephraim's desk buzzed sharply. Ephraim picked up the receiver. It was Chaim Weisz, head of French operations for the Mossad. Ephraim took the piece of chewing gum from his mouth and placed it in the ashtray.

'This man,' said Weisz, 'Jean-Luc Menton. We have some information.'

Baenhaker was feeling horny. It was a feeling that had persisted continually for about a week, and almost everything he did to turn his mind away from sex invariably brought him straight back to the subject. He read the newspapers and found himself turning with avid attention to any article that hinted of rape or divorce. He tried three novels in succession, to discover limbs and organs entwined, after only a few pages, in each one. He tried the television, the radio, and then he would give up for a while and would luxuriate in ogling the nurses in the ward.

He was slightly ashamed with himself that during the course of the week his standards of who he did and did not fancy among the nurses had lowered considerably. Last Friday, he had decided that there were only two he fancied, and that the rest were extremely unattractive. By Saturday, four of them he decided were passable and by Sunday, six. It was now Tuesday morning, and he decided that even one of the elderly cleaning women didn't look too bad.

He tried to figure out exactly for how long it was that he had been in here: he knew it was about three weeks, but he wanted to be more precise. The day of the accident was still a blank. He could remember only having gone to stay with a male friend at Bristol university that weekend, and playing chess much of the time; it was a game of chess that had caused him not to leave on the Sunday and stay over until the Monday; but he could not remember actually leaving.

Something, however, nagged him. He was deeply upset still over Amanda and somehow, he was sure in his mind, there was some connection between her and his accident. He tried to go back in his mind to that Monday, but there was nothing there.

'Good morning Mr Baenhaker.'

Thoughts of Amanda's body came vividly back to him: her streaked hair cascading like a fringed curtain across her nipples as she sat on top of him in the bed.

'Good morning Mr Baenhaker.'

Her long slim legs and thighs, with the blaze of gold between them.

'Just going to take a quick look and see how we're getting on.'

The sheet and blankets were whipped back, and Baenhaker came out of his day dream to discover the surgeon, and attendant Nurse McDonald, staring down at him with faintly bemused expressions as he lay in the bed, hand firmly clenched around his poker-hard organ which protruded from the fly of his pyjama bottoms.

It was some time on Friday that Baenhaker had decided that Nurse McDonald was extremely pretty. Between then and today, he had put in a considerable amount of effort at drawing her attention and chatting her up. By the time she had gone off duty the previous night, Baenhaker was certain that he had someone who would succumb to his charms, if not in some dark corner of the hospital, then at least in the comfort of his Earls Court flat after his release. But the expression on her face as she stood now above him dispelled all of that with the tartness of a lavatory air-freshener spray. The expression on her face told him she thought he was a nasty little pervert.

The surgeon examined the stitches, then nodded. Nurse McDonald pulled back the sheet and blanket with as much grace as if she were putting the lid on a dustbin full of empty sardine cans.

'Healing very nicely,' said the surgeon. 'Should have you out of here within a few days now.' The pair of them turned to walk off, then the surgeon stopped, and leaned over to Baenhaker and whispered confidentially into his ear: 'Don't do that sort of thing in here old chap – it embarrasses everyone. If you have to, go and do it in the lavatory.' Then he strode off in Nurse McDonald's wake.

Baenhaker's face took several minutes to lose its bright red flush. He sat and glared around the ward, and then began to scrape his teeth with the nail of his little finger. An elderly orderly marched into the ward and came up to his bed. 'Mr Baenhaker?'

He nodded.

'There's a telephone call for you outside – you can take it in Sister's office.'

'Thank you.' Baenhaker followed him out through the ward to the small cubicle with a chair and a telephone from which Sister conducted her empire. He shut the door, and picked up the receiver. 'Hallo?'

The crackling and faint sound of heavy breathing told him it was an overseas call. 'Danny?' It was the voice of General Ephraim.

Baenhaker was feeling very fed up with his chief since Ephraim's visit, and in light of his present mood, he had no difficulty in adopting a sullen voice: 'Yes.'

'How are you?'

'All right.'

'I've spoken to the senior registrar of your hospital. He thinks you're pretty well okay now.'

'What the fuck does he know?'

'He's had the reports from the surgeon. I have some urgent business for you: I want you to discharge yourself, and report to the office at nine o'clock tomorrow.'

'I don't know if they'll let me.'

'In British hospitals you can discharge yourself.'

'What about my injuries?'

'I've told you – they're better.'

'How the fuck do you know? You're two thousand miles away.'

'I'll talk to you at nine.' The line went dead. The head of the Mossad had rung off.

Baenhaker put the receiver back down; as he walked back to his ward, his leg twinged like crazy right down along the scar line, and his chest still hurt like hell every time he breathed deeply. He was angry, very angry, but he knew that it didn't matter how angry he got, nor how fed up he got: he could get as angry, or fed up, or anything else that he liked. The only one thing he could not do was disobey the General's instructions.

The taxi dropped him outside the crumbling Earls Court terraced building, where he lived, shortly after 2.00. It was drizzling hard, and he pushed his way out of it through the door and into the dark corridor with its smell of musty carpets and curry. He had no idea who in the building ate curry, but from the smell that pervaded it all the days of the year, either someone was running a clandestine take-away, or else they were addicted to the stuff.

An appalling stench hit him halfway down the corridor of the top floor, the fourth, which grew stronger with every step he took nearer his own flat. He put the key in and opened the door – it was the stench of rotting meat. He went to the kitchen and pulled open the fridge door; he gagged, and nearly threw up. The fridge had packed up, and the four steaks and two pints of milk were hopping about inside it.

Baenhaker had been at a party the previous winter, and there was a woman there who claimed she had psychic powers. He had let her read his palm. She'd predicted a lot of bad news for the future; so depressed had she been by what she had seen in his hand, that she had burst into tears. That hadn't made Baenhaker feel too terrific either. When, on the New Year's Eve, he had tripped over and smashed his bedroom mirror, he had begun to feel that, possibly, the mad woman had been right; things didn't look too good.

As was his habit whenever he returned to the apartment, regardless of whether he had been out for half an hour, a weekend or, like now, several weeks, he checked each room carefully and methodically. Today, he had forgotten how gloomy the flat looked in daylight, particularly on a wet day. He'd only ever had enough money for the basics of apartment life, and several of the major items had come from second-hand shops. The exceptions were the 21" Sony colour television, his JVC video-recorder – he was addicted to movies and this was his one real luxury – and his Walther PP automatic pistol, together with some £30,000 worth of the most sophisticated electronic surveillance equipment available in the world. Both the gun and the surveillance equipment were still in their places in the hollowed-out headboard of his bed.

He picked up from the bedside table the large framed photograph of Amanda, wearing a hardhat, surrounded by rubble and smiling cheekily. He slipped the photograph out of its frame, seized it between his two hands as if to rip it in half, then relented and pushed it out of sight into a drawer.

He sat down on the bed, still unmade from the Saturday when he had set off to drive down to Bristol, and felt sad and desolate. He thought back about those months he had spent with Amanda, and then tried to stop thinking about them because they hurt too much.

They had met when a high-rise office building in Camden Town had been gutted by fire. Baenhaker's cover role in England was as an insurance loss adjuster for Eisenbar-Goldschmidt, a major Israeli reinsurance company. He had been sent ostensibly to investigate the damage and advise Eisenbar-Goldschmidt on any potential salvage items. The real reason for his presence in the gutted shell was because one floor had been occupied by a large Israeli import-export company. The Mossad wanted to know whether there was any Arab sabotage involved, as part of a plan of international sabotage against Israeli firms, and was interested in a direct report from its own personnel, whom it trusted, and not from the British Police, in whom it had doubts – the same doubts as it had about every other organization in the world that did not openly and unequivocally proclaim and prove itself to be pro-Israeli.

Amanda had been in the shell as part of the team of architects and designers which had been commissioned for the re-building. He went over to the drawer, pulled out the photograph once more, looked at it, then put it back. For eighteen months they had got on brilliantly and then, as suddenly as the flame had started, it died.

The last two occasions they had had dinner, she had lost interest in what he had to say, and no longer seemed to care about anything he had done. Then that weekend they were supposed to go away to Scotland, she had rung him on the Thursday to say she had to go to an architects' conference in Cologne. He stood up suddenly, and marched over to the window. He opened it and breathed in deep gulps of the air, then put his hands on the sill and stared down into the basement at the dustbins. He remembered now. It came flooding back: Amanda in the Porsche on the motorway: the hell she had been to an architects' conference in Cologne.

He stared out of the window for a long time, watching the drizzle. He tried to remember more about the accident, but nothing else came.

Baenhaker was conscious that he had little money. If he were paid by Eisenbar-Goldschmidt as a loss adjuster, he would have had a damned good salary and a decent car; but he wasn't. He was paid by the Mossad out of the Israeli Defence budget. The Mossad was always short of money, and those who bore the brunt of the shortage were the employees. Baenhaker had thought of quitting on a number of occasions, but a sense of duty, a deep-rooted desire to see Israel survive, and a belief that he was an indispensable part of that survival kept him in his job.

He had asked Amanda often whether it bothered her that he had little money, could not afford to have a smart car and take her to smart restaurants; she had always replied that it didn't. But he had noticed that the lifestyle of the rich seemed to lure her. Having seen her in that Porsche, he knew how she must have finally swallowed the hook deep down inside her. She had been to see him twice in hospital. The first time she had held his hand and looked tearful. The second time she had brought him chocolates, forgetting that he hated chocolates, and stayed for five minutes. A voice deep inside him said, 'Forget her.' He was trying, he knew. Damned hard.

CHAPTER 20

After the telex from Theo Barbiero-Ruche had been placed on his desk, Rocq sat and stared at it in silence for a long time. The last of the lunchtime alcohol was wearing away, and he had a strong desire to go out, buy a bottle and keep on drinking. He was emerging into full, clear reality, and he wasn't sure that was a condition he wanted to be in. Right now, he needed oblivion, and he needed it for a good long time. He tried to bury himself in work, but after two half-hearted phone calls he knew it was no good. He looked at his watch: it was five to five, and already one or two people in the office had started to pack up for the day. His intercom buzzed and he picked up the receiver.

'Mr Rocq?'

It was Sir Monty Elleck's private secretary.

'Yes.'

'Sir Monty wonders if you could spare him a moment upstairs in his office?'

Rocq thought frantically for a moment. He had a damned good idea what Elleck wanted to see him about: the small matter of a few hundred

thousand pounds of margin. He wanted to stay well out of Elleck's way until he could get hold of some money, but he realized he was going to have no chance of avoiding him unless he went sick, and he knew that he could not afford to go sick; he needed to watch the price of coffee twenty-four hours a day, until it had dropped sufficiently to see him out of trouble. He couldn't take the risk of missing the drop. He had instructed Barbiero-Ruche to buy back, if it went below £327, but if it looked like plummeting well below that, he wanted to be able to cancel that instruction and hold out for even more. Reluctantly, he got up from his desk and made his way up to Elleck's office.

He was surprised to find Elleck in an uncharacteristically jovial mood. He came out from behind his desk to greet him with a firm handshake, ushered him into a pink chair, and asked him what he would like to drink. He then went and poured two hefty Scotches, added some Malvern water, brought the glasses over, gave one to Alex, and seated himself in a lemon yellow chair next to him.

'So how are you, Alex?'

'Fine, thank you, Sir Monty.'

'Good, good. Business all right?'

'Reasonable, thank you, sir.'

'I hear you had a car accident at the weekend. No one hurt, I hope?'

'No, sir. My car was parked and a lorry hit it.'

'I am sorry to hear that. Badly damaged?'

'Smashed to pieces; a write-off.'

'Very unfortunate. A Porsche wasn't it? Expensive motor car.'

Rocq nodded.

'I presume the insurance will cover it?'

'Yes, sir. Probably take several months though, knowing them.'

'Impossible people, insurance companies. Will you get another one in the meantime?'

'I think I'll have to wait until I get the insurance money – I don't want to borrow the money at current interest rates.'

'Of course not, they are very punitive. Still, Alex, it must be very inconvenient not to have a car?'

'It is – I'm going to have to rent one at the weekends.'

Elleck took a sip of his drink, then handed Rocq a box of Romeo & Juliet coronas. Rocq took one, and Elleck helped himself. 'Not very satisfactory, renting. Very expensive. I think it would be better, Alex, if you went and bought yourself another Porsche. Put it on the Company – you can arrange it tomorrow through the accounts department. I will tell them in the morning. Then you can reimburse us with whatever you eventually get from the insurance.'

Rocq was glad his chair had arms; they prevented him from falling out of it. Less than six months before, Elleck had virtually thrown him out of this same office for asking for a financial contribution towards the last Porsche. 'Filthy Nazi toys,' Elleck had yelled. 'This firm has never bought a foreign car, and over my dead body it never will.' Rocq studied his boss carefully: he was very definitely anything but dead.

'Thank you, sir; that's extremely generous – extremely generous.' He was nearly shaking with excitement. 'They are – rather expensive, sir – you do – er – know the price?'

'I am not familiar with car prices – how much are they?'

'The one I have cost £32,000 – on the road – I might be able to save a bit by taking the radio out of the last one.'

Elleck blanched visibly at the sum of money. 'I didn't realize they cost – er – quite that much. However, no problem, Alex, no problem at all – and you needn't worry about any interest – you just go ahead and sort it out tomorrow.'

'Thank you, sir, thank you very much indeed.'

'Don't mention it; let me fill your glass up.'

Elleck walked over to the drinks cupboard, and poured Rocq nearly a half tumbler of Chivas Regal from the Steuben cut-glass decanter. 'Now, Alex – I don't like to pry into the business affairs of my employees – none of them. What you all do with your own money is your own affair. We do have a rule that you must not trade privately through any section of this company – but,' he handed the tumbler to Rocq, 'we've never enforced that rule too strictly. However, as a result of this coffee business, I have had to scrutinize our books

251

very carefully – to make sure we're not on the hook for anyone to any of the clearing houses – and during my scrutiny, I couldn't help noticing your own coffee position: you bought 1,000 tons – 200 lots – at £1,022 a ton on ten per cent margin. As you know, it has now dropped to just over £420 a ton, and under our rules you are required to cover that position – which means you're paying out, on top of your original margin of £102,000, approximately a further £400,000. I understand you have given instructions to James Rice to liquidate your position as quickly as possible – but as buyers are on the thin side, it is unlikely to rise significantly between now and then. It would seem this is more or less the amount you are going to have to pay up.' He looked quizzically at Rocq.

Rocq stared him straight in the eye, then took a large pull on his tumbler; he needed enough drink for courage, but not too much that he would lose what little concentration he had remaining. Then he carefully cut away the end of his Havana with his index finger nail. He nodded, slowly. 'Yes,' he said.

'You have this money readily available, I presume?'

Rocq pulled out his gold Dunhill and lit the cigar, slowly, deliberately, rolling the tip over and over in the flame, sucking gently, sucking deeply, caressing and nursing the end into an even bright red glow. The smoke tasted sweet, reassuring, rich and beautiful. He took one large mouthful, let the smoke curl up for a few moments from his bottom lip, then blew it hard, straight out in front of him; he swivelled his head, looked Elleck briefly in the face, then stared down at Elleck's exquisitely polished Manolo Blahnick crocodile shoes. 'No, Sir Monty, I haven't.'

'Nor the £512,000 you need to wire to your friend in Milan?'

A chill went through Rocq. Nobody had actually spelled out the enormity of the mess he was in before. The chill subsided, and he was left with a damp mixture of frustration and despair. He lifted his eyes up to meet Elleck's: 'No, I don't have that either.'

'How about forty pence for your tube fare home?' Elleck's tone had suddenly become warmer again. He grinned, and Elleck grinned back.

'I think I can just about run to that,' he said.

'Well,' said Elleck, 'that's a start!'

Rocq picked up his glass for another sip; to his slight surprise, he discovered it was empty.

'Drop more?' asked Elleck.

'Just a drop,' said Rocq, conscious that he was beginning to slur his words, and fighting hard to try and feel sober again.

Elleck marched back over to the drinks cabinet. He did not speak until he had brought Rocq's refilled glass and sat down again. 'Alex,' he said, 'I like to think of my firm as a family. All my employees are one big family. If anyone is ever in trouble, and it is within my power to help them, then I will always do so.' He paused, and lifted his tumbler: 'Your health.'

Rocq lifted his and they both drank. Then Elleck continued:

'Now, you seem to be in a lot of trouble. The sums of money you owe are fantastic – in anybody's terms – almost £1 million altogether. Everyone dreams of being a millionaire. Even today, with all the inflation we have had over the years, to be a millionaire is still to achieve a magical status. You are thirty-one and you owe a million pounds. You owe more perhaps than one man in a hundred thousand will ever make in his entire lifetime.

'You are a bright fellow. You have enthusiasm, youth, ability, no doubt. I don't know – maybe, also, you have rich relatives – but if you don't, you will need an awful lot of hard work, and luck, to ever pay even a portion of that sort of money back. It will be a millstone around your neck that you could carry for all your life. Instead of earning money to enjoy, you would be earning it to pay back the bank.'

Elleck paused; Rocq stared motionlessly at him, then slowly nodded his head.

'Of course,' continued Elleck, 'you could opt to go bankrupt. If you do that, everything that you own will be taken from you to go towards paying your debts, but beyond that you would owe not a penny more – so that would free you from one millstone. The problem with going bankrupt is your career. You have spent much time qualifying as a metal broker, learning this business. You clearly do well at it, and you know how to make a lot of money out of it. If this – er – unhappy situation were to arise, I would of course have to terminate your employment here. I am afraid, also, that as an undischarged bankrupt – perhaps even as a discharged bankrupt – you would find it very difficult ever to get employment in this field again.'

'I fully understand, Sir Monty,' said Rocq. He was thinking hard about Theo Barbiero-Ruche and his coffee. It was thanks to his advice that he was here now; he had just sold 12,000 tons short, again on his advice. If Theo was wrong again, he didn't want to think of the consequences. In spite of the warmth the alcohol gave him, he felt another chill run through his body.

There was a knock on the door and Elleck's secretary came in. 'Are you going to sign your post, Sir Monty?'

'Leave it, Jane – I don't think there's anything urgent. I'll do it tomorrow.'

'All right. Is there anything you need?'

'No thank you, Jane.'

'Thank you, Sir Monty. Good night.'

'Good night, Jane.' He waited until the door was closed and turned to Rocq. 'Alex, if this company had a million pounds spare, it would pay these debts for you gladly.'

Rocq sat up a little. For the first time since he had come into Elleck's office, the chairman had lied.

'But we do not have a million pounds spare.'

Rocq sat up a little further. Elleck had just told his second lie.

'I am, however, privy to some information that, if acted upon correctly, could enable you to earn that money, and more on top from your brokerage commissions alone.'

Rocq eased himself a little further up; he took another sip of his Scotch, and missed the table completely as he put his glass down. Elleck didn't appear to notice as it dropped and disgorged its contents into the thick pile of the carpet.

'Does such information interest you?'

'Of course it does, Sir Monty.'

'I thought it might. You are familiar with the name Umm Al Amnah?'

'Very much so.'

'You have a very good client from there – Prince Abr Qu'Ih Missh, I believe?'

'Yes.'

'His father has recently abdicated, and he has now become the ruler of Amnah.'

'Yes – that's right – he is the new Emir of Amnah. Hasn't done us a lot of good so far – I think he has become too embroiled in his ruling to think much about his metal investing. I do have a £5 million discretionary account for him, but the really large punting he does he likes to instruct directly.'

'Well – this scheme, in any event, involves not

him but his country. In a nutshell, two gentlemen, with whom I am acquainted, have secretly been providing the new Emir Missh with troops and secret police to help him against mounting opposition to his family. Unknown to Missh, at the same time, they have been building a stockpile of nuclear mines in Al Suttoh, the country's port, on the Persian Gulf. One of these gentlemen has recently added a small fleet of oil tankers to his assets. On a given day, in just over one week's time, one of these tankers, on its way up the Gulf, will be blown to smithereens by a small atomic explosive. There will be nothing left of it but matchsticks. The crew will all have been taken off earlier, secretly, by helicopter, so there will be no casualties.

'After the detonation, an announcement will be put out from the Palace of Amnah that the country has placed 400 nuclear mines in the Strait of Hormuz, at the mouth of the Gulf. Unless Israel withdraws completely from all occupied territories and frees all Arab prisoners in its jails, then they will not render the mines safe. Effectively, no shipping will be able to get in or out of the Gulf. Over half the world's oil supply will be stopped.' Elleck did a gentle karate chop with the side of his right hand, about halfway up his left arm. 'There will not have been a crisis like it since Suez,' said Elleck, almost gleefully. He stood up, and went and refilled Rocq's glass.

Rocq nodded. 'Very clever. No one would ever

have suspected that a tin-pot country like Amnah could have so much clout.'

'Precisely,' said Elleck. 'So the shock will be all the more severe. Roping Libya in adds clout to the menace, because everyone knows that right now Libya doesn't move an inch without full Russian approval.' He sat back and took a pull of his drink. 'You're an intelligent fellow, Alex – what do you think the result of all this will be?'

'I don't know politically – but the price of gold will go through the roof.'

'Good boy,' said Elleck. 'You've hit the jackpot in one.'

'Does Missh know about all this?'

'Not a thing. And he won't. Even if he were to find out, he's got no option but to keep his trap shut. Because of the delicate political situation in the United Arab Emirates, there isn't a Western country who will dare support him. Russia and Libya and the other anti-West Arab states have been courting him like mad, but both Missh and his father are fundamentally pro-West. Libya and Russia did help them originally gain independence, but since then they have been busy shaking off these countries. I think they are hoping that one day a reconciliation with the West can be made – although of course the Russian propaganda machine has always played up the original bond between Amnah and Libya, and continues to do so at every opportunity.'

Rocq nodded. 'So you want me to start buying gold for all my clients as fast as I can go?'

'No,' said Elleck, 'that is precisely what I do not want you to do. Gold is at the moment depressed – today's price is $494 an ounce. I want the price to stay as low as possible. I have a syndicate comprising the key people behind this whole business in Amnah. Between them, they have committed to the syndicate sufficient funds to buy £1,000 million worth of gold.'

Rocq whistled.

'Buying that amount of gold in one place, in any one day, would be enough to push the price up $10 to $20; but we don't want to do that. We want to keep it very, very quiet. During the next week I want you to buy that billion pounds worth, but I want you to spread your buying as much around the world as you possibly can. Don't buy more than a few bars in any one market, from any one dealer. And don't start until Monday morning of next week – between now and then I'm going to quietly buy a few ounces for myself.'

'Now in return for doing this, and for keeping your silence, the syndicate will pay you a commission rate of .05 per cent on all the gold you buy, and .05 per cent when you sell. On £1,000 million, your commission when you buy will come to £500,000. When you sell, hopefully gold will have risen from four twenty to six hundred, maybe higher. That £1,000 million will have risen about thirty per cent – to say £1,350 million; .05 per

259

cent of that will be £675,000 – giving you a total of £1,175,000 – enough to clear your debts, and give you £100,000 on top. Does that sound reasonable?' Rocq nodded his head; it sounded reasonable enough. Anything, right now, would have sounded reasonable enough.

'The name of the syndicate,' said Elleck, 'is "Goldilocks." An account has been opened for the syndicate here at Globalex, under the name "Goldilocks."'

'Someone has a sense of humour,' said Rocq.

Elleck raised his glass. 'To your good health.'

Rocq raised his. 'To Goldilocks. But not the three bears – let's hope for three bulls.'

'Goldilocks and the three bulls,' said Sir Monty Elleck.

It was 7.00 when Rocq staggered out of the elevator into the lobby of 88 Mincing Lane. He was aware that he was completely plastered; he was also aware that he had promised to collect Amanda at 6.00 sharp from her office to go to a preview at the Mayor Gallery in Cork Street. A taxi came down Mincing Lane with its 'For Hire' sign illuminated. Rocq put up his hand. The taxi slowed and stopped, and Rocq staggered towards it; he put a hand on the bonnet to steady himself, then leaned in through the front window. 'I want to – shgo – er – I shwant to shgo – er – schback of Harrods.'

'I'm not taking you in that state, mate – clear off.' The taxi accelerated down the street, leaving Rocq in a cloud of black diesel fumes.

'Fucking bastard,' he yelled, squinting hard to focus. He went and sat down on the doorstep of 88. A wave hit him, and he wasn't sure whether it was nausea or tiredness. His head was swimming and he felt he was about to pass out; he pushed his eyelids hard together, just leaving a tiny gap; in that manner, he found he could focus and see what traffic was coming down the street. Somewhere, deep inside his drink-riddled body, he felt a good feeling surging up; it had seemed a long time since he had felt good, and he was enjoying the feeling. He had sunk, and he had hit rock bottom. Now he was on the way up.

Somewhere, alongside the good feeling, something else was hatching deep inside him. He knew he wasn't in any fit state to figure out the finer details right now, but the germ of an idea was there and he knew, instinctively, that the idea was good. He looked forward to sobering up, and to thinking about it more clearly.

'Good evening, sir.'

Rocq looked up from the doorstep at the uniformed Retired Sergeant-Major 'Sarge' Bantry, Globalex's live-in security guard and night-watchman.

'Shevenig Sssharge.'

'You're going to need a banjo and collection box if you stay there much longer, sir.'

'Shink I'm going to need one anyway.'

'Think a good night's sleep will do yer no harm,' he said gently. 'I'll get you a cab.'

261

'Shank you Sarge.'

'It's a pleasure, Mr Rocq.'

'I shink I have had a bit – er – shoo mug ter drink.'

'Doesn't do any harm now and again, sir.'

'Schno – sure you're right.'

CHAPTER 21

The offices of Eisenbar-Goldschmidt were at 124 Lower Thames Street, about 400 yards from 88 Mincing Lane. Behind the brilliantly polished, but bullet-proof, windows of the Adam-designed house were the offices from which Eisenbar-Goldschmidt conducted its £400 million reinsurance business with Lloyds, reimbursing the companies within Lloyds' hallowed halls on claims on which they had to stump up, ranging from house burglaries, car crashes, skiing accidents, burned out warehouses, shipwrecks, aeroplane disasters, village fetes wiped out through rain, wrong organs removed by surgeons, and a million other items.

The offices looked much like any other city offices. Being in an old house, they were tastefully furnished with plenty of period furniture, some genuine, some reproduction; Victorian prints in simple frames adorned the walls, interspersed with photographs of Concorde, a supertanker, several factories, two high-rise buildings, and Manchester United football club. Part of the reinsurance on all of these was covered by Eisenbar-Goldschmidt.

E-G had offices in many of the world's capital cities; the controlling shareholder in the firm, although not a widely publicized fact, was the Israeli government. In London, as elsewhere, unknown to most of the staff, the building was also used by Mossad agents as a safe-house.

In a sound-proofed basement office, at nine o'clock Wednesday morning, Daniel Baenhaker picked up the receiver of the direct telephone line to the switchboard of the Mossad, at its Tel Aviv headquarters, the moment it rang.

'Good morning,' came Ephraim's voice through the earpiece.

'Good morning,' replied Baenhaker.

'Still in one piece? Nothing fallen off you since we spoke?'

'I'm in one piece.'

'Good. Have you heard of a French company called Lasserre Industriel?'

'Armaments manufacturers? Also make aircraft?'

'Correct. Their chairman is a Viscomte Lasserre.'

'I've heard of him, too.'

'Have you heard of a Greek arms dealer, name of Jimmy Culundis?'

'Didn't he supply anti-tank guns to the Egyptians during the Six-Day War?'

'And just about everything else that they couldn't get.'

'I've heard it rumoured that in the event of war between the US and Russia, they'd both be buying their spare parts and ammunition from him.'

'You have the right man,' said Ephraim.

'I was assigned once to follow him when he came to England – for a suspected meeting with Hassan of Jordan during Hassan's official visit here – but it turned out to be Jimmy Mancham, the ex-president of the Seychelles. It was shortly before that bungled coup in the Seychelles in 1981 with Mad Mike Hoare.'

'Right. Culundis and Lasserre are good friends – no doubt Culundis gets much of his hardware from Lasserre. On Monday evening they had dinner together at Lasserre's chateau in Bordeaux and were joined by a Jewish gentleman, Sir Monty Elleck. Elleck is chairman and chief executive of a company called Globalex – a very large, privately-owned City of London commodity broking firm. It has branches in several cities around the world. I need to know very badly why they had dinner together, and what their connection is.'

'Are Lasserre and Culundis clients of Globalex?'

'That's one of the things you'll have to find out. Brokerage is a very private business. But it is important to establish whether they are clients. What I am particularly interested in finding out is whether there is any current connection between these men and a country situated within the United Arab Emirates – although it is independent – called Umm Al Amnah. We know there have in the past been dealings between Jimmy Culundis and Amnah. His company is known to have supplied the armaments to Amnah in the past, and I received a report from the CIA/MI6 World Airport Surveillance that Culundis flew in his private DC-8 into Orly airport on Sunday, directly from Tunquit – Amnah's only airport.'

'The English are very private when they talk about money,' said Baenhaker. 'Getting information may be extremely difficult.'

'Globalex is a Jewish firm. The Chairman, Sir Monty Elleck, is an ardent Zionist and has given Israel many millions of pounds over the years; remember that.'

'Could be helpful. How quickly do you want this information?'

'Friday.'

'What? It's Wednesday now.'

'I know. There is very little time. You can do whatever you want to get this information – anything at all you do will have our full support. Do you understand?'

'I understand.'

'Then please telephone me on Friday evening; I shall be in my office until eight o'clock your time.'

'Yes, Sir. Goodbye.'

Baenhaker hung up. and then sat back in his chair. He looked at his watch. It was five past nine, Wednesday. He buzzed on the intercom up to Eisenbar-Goldschmidt's research department, and asked for all the information they had on Globalex to be brought down to him, then he sat back to think. Globalex was Jewish, so, as a Jew himself, people might be fairly open with him. But he knew

British financial institutions: in time, over a hundred alcoholic lunches, you could pry anything you wanted from pretty well anyone – except the Jews. Many of them did not drink, and of those who did, most drank little. They respected the privacy of their clients far more than the British did. But even if there were gentiles in Globalex, willing to drink and then confide all, it would take time, and he did not have time.

To have any chance of getting information legitimately, he needed a lure. The only lure he could think of was money. To a large brokerage house he knew it would require a lot of money to make them interested in talking to him, and an even greater amount still for them to start wooing him for it. But the promise of money could get him in through the door, into the lion's den, and with no suspicion.

When the report arrived he scanned down first to find Globalex's daily trading figures: their average weekly turnover in commodity value was a shade over £75 million. He did a quick sum in his head: their brokerage income would have been around £50,000 per week. He was going to have to talk big to impress these fellows; very big. He looked up Globalex in the phone book, lifted the receiver and dialled the telephone number.

'Good morning, Globalex', said a bright voice.

'Good morning. We are interested in opening an account with Globalex to invest funds for us.'

'Metals or soft commodities?' said the voice.

Baenhaker paused, flustered; he wasn't sure what soft commodities were. 'Er – metals,' he said, boldly.

'One moment, I'll put you through to metals reception.'

There were two sharp burrs, then another female voice: 'Globalex Metals.'

'Good morning. My company is interested in opening an account with Globalex to invest funds for us in metals.'

'Would you like to make an appointment to come and see us – or would you like someone to come and see you?'

'I'd like to come to you.'

'Certainly, sir. When would be convenient?'

'Would this morning be possible?'

'I think so, I'll just check for you.' There was a short pause. 'Would eleven o'clock be convenient?'

'Fine, thank you.'

'What name is it, please?'

'David Bernstein, of Eisenbar-Goldschmidt.'

'Very good, Mr Bernstein, we will look forward to seeing you at eleven o'clock.'

Baenhaker replaced the receiver and looked down at his battered clothes: he was wearing an open-neck shirt, slacks and cream lace-up canvas shoes. Not the stuff of which investment managers, to which status he had now elevated himself, were made.

He buzzed on the intercom to the investment manager, Gary Volendam, to ask him to come down.

One hour and a quarter later, Baenhaker was standing in Austin Reed's, in a lightweight navy double-breasted suit that could have been made to measure for him. He added a white shirt, conservative blue-and-white polka dot tie and black slip-on loafers with small gold chains across the insteps. He left, feeling decidedly New York preppie.

For some minutes, as he walked, he looked decidedly strange, for every other step, he scraped either the sole or the side of one shoe or the other along the pavement. He was in fact trying to scuff them so that by the time he arrived at Globalex they wouldn't look too new.

He arrived at the front door of 88 Mincing Lane at exactly eleven o'clock. 'Good morning, Sir, may I help you?'

The burly figure of Sergeant Major Bantry, in his full Globalex dress regalia, blocked Baenhaker's path.

'I have an appointment with the metals section of Globalex at eleven o'clock,' said Baenhaker.

Bantry ran his eyes, like stiff pointed fingers, down the full length of Baenhaker's body; they stopped on his shoes. 'Can't be much,' thought Bantry to himself, 'if he can't even afford a tin of shoe polish. 'Very good, Sir,' he said, standing aside. 'Nice day, could be rain later.'

'Yes,' said Baenhaker, 'I'm sure.'

'Reception is straight down there, Sir.'

'Thank you,' said Baenhaker, entering the building.

CHAPTER 22

'I got it, I got it, I got it!' Gary Slivitz yelled out excitedly.

'For chrissake, shut up,' said Rocq, 'I've got the most blistering hangover, and I'm fed up hearing you shout every five minutes "I've got it, I've got it, I've got it."'

'Well, I have this time – look – look!' He excitedly held the Rubik's cube under Rocq's nose. The whites were all together on one face, the greens all together on another face. He turned it over to show Rocq the oranges were all together, as were the yellows. But then Slivitz noticed there was one red cube in the blue section, and one blue one in the red section. 'Oh, shit,' he said.

'Haven't you got any work to do?' said Rocq.

'Look, Rocky – did you ever see it so close?'

'Slivitz, why don't you get yourself up to date? Rubik's cubes went out with the ark.'

'All I've got to do is this – look – like this!' Slivitz twirled the cube excitedly in his hand; there was a sudden sharp snap and the cube fell apart, showering multi-coloured blocks across his desk and onto the floor. 'Oh, shit!' he shouted, at the top of his voice, 'Oh, shit!'

Rocq's intercom buzzed. 'Yes?'

It was the receptionist: 'Your eleven o'clock appointment is here. Will you see him in an interview room?'

'Yes.'

'Room 4 is free.'

'Okay – I'll be right out.' He stood up. 'I've got another big one,' he said, rubbing it into Slivitz's misery as he scrabbled underneath his chair to pick up the pieces.

'It's probably some one-legged old bat who's just won five hundred quid on the Bingo, and wants you to make her fortune for her.'

'No, Slivitz – those are all reserved for you.'

Rocq walked out of the office. There was a rotation system among the brokers for handling new accounts: if a new client did not specify the broker he or she required, then it went around in turn. Rocq had tipped the balance more than slightly in his favour, by tipping the receptionist with some delicate trinket from Asprey's or Garrard's for each decent account he landed. If she ever passed him one-legged widows, it was only because they were very, very rich.

He walked through into the fourth-floor reception, with his standard smile firmly on his face, and marched straight up to Baenhaker, briefly studied his pock-marked face, thin dark hair, smart blue suit with dandruff on the shoulders, garish tie and scuffed shoes. He noticed a scar above Baenhaker's right eye. He summed him up right away as someone who thought he was a whizz-kid, but probably didn't have the authority in his company to go to the bathroom without permission.

'Good morning, Mr Bernstein. I'm Alex Rocq.'

'How do you do, Mr Rocq.'

'Come this way.'

Rocq led him into a small, functional office, overlooking Mincing Lane. Vertical blinds kept out the brightest of the June sun's rays, and the air-conditioning kept out the heat. In spite of his hangover, Rocq was feeling tired, but very happy. He'd called Motortune at nine that morning, and discovered they had a 911 Turbo Porsche almost identical to his previous one, in stock as a result of a cancelled order. The banker's draft from Globalex was in his wallet and he was going to collect the car at lunchtime. He had got up early, and before leaving home had put telephone calls through to Milan, to Theo Barbiero-Ruche, to Umm Al Amnah, to Sheik Missh, and to several other members of his 'A' team.

The interview room was designed to make clients feel at ease. At one end was a pair of two-seat chesterfields, facing each other, where they could sit and talk relaxedly. At the other end was a flat mahogany table, with two pairs of reproduction Queen Anne dining chairs facing each other. The idea was that business should be negotiated over the table, then sealed over a drink in the chesterfields.

They sat at the table. 'How can we be of help to you?' asked Rocq.

'We want to expand our investment portfolio in this country. So far we are only in blue chips. We feel now it is time to – er – play with a little racing money. We are looking for a firm with whom we can work, and one we can trust. We are a Jewish firm, so are you. We are interested in metals – you are among the leading metal brokers. It is natural to start here.'

Rocq nodded.

'We require, first, a great deal of information about your company. We are very choosey about whom we do business with – although we are sure your credentials will be in order.' Baenhaker managed a weak smile.

'I am sure you will find so,' said Rocq. 'May I first ask you the size of the investment you are intending?'

'We have approximately £40 million sterling allocated for this at the present time. I trust that will be sufficient to open an account?'

'Yes,' said Rocq, after a short pause for air. 'Quite sufficient.' Normally, the cash register in his brain would have begun totting up his potential earnings from commissions from an account of such a size. But there was something about this man, Bernstein, that didn't quite add up to Rocq. Rocq was no stranger to people discussing sums of money

274

the size of telephone numbers, and he had long since been able to determine when someone was genuine and when someone, as he put it, was bullshitting. He was already convinced that the man across the table was a time-wasting bullshitter; but he had no option but to hear him out.

'The first thing that I would need from you is a full client list.'

'That is quite impossible – we never divulge our clients.'

Baenhaker stared across the table at Rocq. Rocq was in a double-breasted Lanvin blazer, a blue-striped shirt with white collar, plain navy silk tie, elegant grey trousers, and polished black loafers with the much-copied green-and-red Gucci colour-band across the instep. Baenhaker wasn't an expert on Gucci shoes, but he knew these were not a copy. When he had stepped out of Austin Reed's this morning, Rocq was the sort of person he had hoped he looked like: genuine preppy. He studied Rocq's face: it was good-looking, slightly boyish, emphasized by his slightly long, schoolboy-style black hair which continually slipped down onto his forehead. He had quick blue eyes, a short, straight nose and a slightly arrogant mouth. His well-cut blazer hung from his shoulders correctly, as did his collar sit round his neck correctly, as was his tie equally correctly knotted. He looked exactly how a successful young man ought to look. He was everything Baenhaker hated, because he was everything Baenhaker wanted to be and never was. What aggravated Baenhaker further was that he knew Rocq had the measure of him. He was aware that he had an uphill struggle ahead. He paused for some moments and then spoke.

'I'm afraid, Mr Rocq, if you wish to have our business, then you will have to divulge your client list. You see, we are very particular about whom we get into bed with. If, for instance, you had any Arab clients, we would have to think very carefully, very carefully indeed.'

Rocq thought about the £40 million and the slim chance that Bernstein might be genuine: he didn't want to throw that away. On the other hand, he sensed trouble with this man. He decided it wasn't worthwhile lying; throw the cards down face up, he decided, and give everyone the chance to get out before the betting starts. 'I'm afraid, Mr Bernstein, we do have a number of Arab clients; many of them have sums invested through us that are very considerably greater than the amount you have mentioned. Perhaps it would be better if I did not waste any more of your valuable time.'

Baenhaker was beginning to feel extremely foolish, and very annoyed with himself. As far as he was concerned, he had always been a good agent, and had always taken the trouble to do his homework carefully. Today, his homework had been done in less than an hour. He had been under the impression that £40 million was enough money to have gained him, if he had wanted it, an immediate audience with the chairman of

Globalex; now he realized it didn't even rate him a cup of morning coffee with this underling. He had been rushed and he hated being rushed; he liked to work at his own pace, without pressure of time. He knew he should have surveyed all the brokers in the firm, watched them carefully, studied their habits, before picking on the one that looked the weakest, and then either softened him up with booze, or gone for blackmail. He had blown it with this one, he knew. He had put him on his guard, and it was going to be difficult to get him to drop that guard.

'The reputation of your firm is sufficient,' said Baenhaker, 'that we may be prepared to waive the fact that you have Arab clients.'

'I see.'

'I would be very interested, Mr Rocq, in a brief tour around your offices – I think it would be very helpful.'

'Certainly. It will have to be quick, as I have an urgent appointment at 12.30.'

'I understand,' said Baenhaker.

The urgent appointment was currently undergoing its final pre-delivery checks in Motortune's Service bay.

Rocq took Baenhaker around the offices, the computer room, the massive Globalex switchboard, which could plug any one of the 310 telephones in the offices directly into any of Globalex's offices anywhere else in the world. So massive was the switchboard, and so important was it to Globalex business, that it employed here in London two full-time telephone engineers.

They finally came down into the trading room and Rocq took Baenhaker over to show him his desk and chair, in between Slivitz and Mozer. He pointed out the Reuter Moniter computer terminal, on which he could receive, at the touch of a button, the price of any commodity, stock or share on any market anywhere in the world. But Baenhaker did not take that in. An object on Rocq's desk had caught his attention, and was holding him riveted: it was the framed photograph of Amanda. His face went white; he looked carefully at it, trying to see if he was mistaken – but he knew he wasn't. Proof came when he suddenly noticed, amid a pile of letters on the desk, some opened, others not, a bunch of keys attached to a Porsche keyring.

Baenhaker froze, and Rocq's words poured over the top of him. He felt as though his insides were in tatters, and he was unable to think straight.

'Would you like to see the London Metal Exchange itself? It will give you a good idea of how the metal trading business actually works, if you see the ring dealing yourself.'

'Thank you,' said Baenhaker meekly, following him out, down, across the road and into Plantation House. A few minutes later, they stood looking through the sound-proofed window, down onto the actual floor of the London Metal Exchange.

It is a circular room, around the outside of which are numbered telephone cubicles, almost all of them occupied by someone holding two receivers to his head, listening to one and talking to the other, whilst at the same time passing on an endless chain of messages which are shouted at him from one of a couple of young men. In the centre of the room is a circular red leather bench-seat, around which, on this particular day as on any other day, sat a mixture of men and women, mostly in their twenties. Suddenly, a bell rang; they got up and were replaced by a second group of people who took their seats.

'They deal in five-minute turns in each metal, in two sessions: the first is from 11.45 to 1.30, the second from 3.25 to 5.00. They've just been dealing Copper, now they're starting Tin,' explained Rocq.

The people, with few exceptions, looked young to Baenhaker. He told Rocq.

'Dealing in the ring is very high pressure,' said Rocq. 'You get burned out very quickly – and you really have to be either young, or quite exceptional, to be able to think and act quickly enough to keep pace. I did it for a while, and I occasionally do a day in there now – but if I went on doing it I would be dead by the time I reached forty.'

A clerk, nonchalantly chewing gum, carried a piece of paper from the ring to one of the kiosks; prominently displayed on his back was a notice of which he was evidently unaware, in spite of the entire rest of the London Metal Exchange's sniggers. The message read, 'I'm a burk.'

'What happens in the evening?' said Baenhaker. 'Do your offices close?'

'They do in London – but we have offices in cities covering all the world's time zones. So we keep buying and selling for our clients twenty-four hours a day. One of our rivals has the slogan: "Twenty-four carats, twenty-four hours." We go one better. Our slogan is: "At Globalex, we make you richer while you're just dreaming about it!"'

'I prefer 24 carats 24 hours,' said Baenhaker.

'Yes – maybe it is better,' said Rocq, defensively. 'But we've just taken on a new ad agency, so maybe they'll come up with something better.'

'I'm sure they will, Mr Rocq.'

When they parted company, at 12.15, Rocq went straight back to his office and telephoned Eisenbar-Goldschmidt.

'Good morning,' he said to the switchboard operator. 'Can you tell me – do you have an Investment Manager by the name of David Bernstein? You do? Is he about six foot two, with blonde hair? No? About five foot eight with dark hair. I see. No, thank you very much – I'm thinking of the wrong person.'

Rocq was not to know that the switchboard operators at Eisenbar-Goldschmidt were every bit as trained in the art of lying as many of the others who worked there.

Rocq replaced the receiver. So Bernstein was genuine, he thought. He shook his head. Something was bothering him about Bernstein. Bothering him a lot. All the same, he decided, now that he had discovered he was genuine, he could turn out to be a useful client. He buzzed down to Sergeant Major Bantry and asked him to hail a cab; then he dashed for the stairs, not bothering to wait for the lift.

He settled back in the seat of the cab, forgot about Bernstein, and thought about his new Porsche. He would take Amanda out in it tonight. Thinking about her made him feel horny. He reflected; hot summer days always made him feel horny, he decided. He looked forward to seeing her tonight even more than usual.

After Baenhaker parted company with Rocq, he walked back to Lower Thames Street feeling as if he had been hit with a sledge-hammer. He was surprised at the intensity of the hatred he felt for Rocq; it was stronger even than he could ever remember feeling against the Arabs, after his mother and two sisters had been blown to pieces by a terrorist bomb in a Jerusalem vegetable market. He found he could not prevent himself from shaking with rage. He was filled with a desire to go home, get his Walther and go back and blow Rocq's brains out. All his training in the control of emotions, never to let personal feelings intervene, was of no use. He could not get it out of his mind: he wanted to smash Amanda to pulp and blow Rocq's brains out.

He reached his office, and began to stab out her home phone number on his push-button phone. Then he stopped. He realized she would be at work; he began to stab out her work number.

'Garbutt and Garbutt,' said the receptionist of the Knightsbridge architects.

'I'd like to speak to—' he paused, then hung up; he shook his head. There was no point, he knew. He began to attack an unpleasant spot that was festering just above his shirt collar. Then he sat back and thought about his meeting with Rocq. Other than discovering who it was that had pinched Amanda from him, he had achieved very little. He had blown any chances of a quick answer to anything from Rocq. However angry he might have felt with Ephraim, first after his visit to the hospital and then after his phone call, he wanted to stay on the right side of the chief of the Mossad. Ephraim could, he knew, make life very unpleasant indeed for him; equally, he could make it very much better. The information Ephraim had asked for really should not be that difficult, he reasoned; after all, it was a private company, not the vaults of MI5, which held the information.

The offices of Globalex did not operate around the clock, Rocq had told him. All the office staff would have left by eight thirty, and the cleaning staff by nine thirty. He wondered if the doorman he had seen lived on the premises, not that that particularly bothered him.

He forgot about the aches and pains in his body from the accident, and started to think hard:

It was Wednesday today: he had tonight and Thursday night; there was no time to lose. He would go straight in tonight. He began to draw up in his mind the list of things he would need. For the first time in a long time he felt excitement, felt his adrenalin begin to flow. 'You can do whatever you want to get this information,' Ephraim had said. 'Anything at all that you do will have our full support.' The words were like a drug to him, like a deep snort of cocaine. He began to feel good, very good and very protected; it had been a long time, he reflected, since his Control had given him carte blanche. Far too long.

CHAPTER 23

Amanda, standing above Rocq, carefully unscrewed the top of the can of Mazola corn oil, then tipped the tin upside down. The cooking oil gushed out all over him. She poured it over his chest, down his body, down each leg, then back up again; the oil gushed over his body and onto the polythene sheet on which he lay, and which stretched out not only across the bed, but across several feet of the thick pile carpet all around the bed.

'Enough – I'm drowning!'

She dropped a small studded leather ring, about one inch in diameter, onto his stomach; 'Put that on,' she said.

'What the hell is that supposed to be? A lifejacket?'

'No silly, it's the very latest thing.'

'Latest what? If it's meant to be a condom, it's not much use – it's got a bloody great hole in it.'

'It's from the States – a girlfriend of mine just sent it to me. Haven't you seen one before?'

'What is it?' Rocq inspected the object carefully:

it looked like a miniature dog collar. 'A Hoopla for mice?'

'No,' she said, 'it's an extra special small size for you.'

'Small size what?'

'You're really thick at times, aren't you. Where the hell do you think it goes?'

'I'm meant to put that on?' he said, astounded.

'Sure you are.'

'What does it do?'

'It's meant to keep a certain part of you interested in me – regardless of how the rest of you feels.'

'Is that meant to be a hint? I didn't know I was such a crummy lover I needed propping up.'

She kissed him deeply. 'You're a wonderful lover.' She rubbed some oil slowly across him. 'Simply wonderful. I thought it might be fun to try one of these out, that's all.'

Reluctantly, Rocq tried it out. Two hours later, when he was finally allowed to remove it, he collapsed into a coma.

The alarm went off at 6.30 and Rocq snapped out of the dream he was having that he was drowning in a butter dish. He lay back and began to focus his mind; it was his normal practice, before he got out of bed, to recall the events of the day before, and plan the day ahead. It was something he'd done ever since he was a child.

He remembered the row he and Amanda had had the night before last. After the taxi had dropped him outside the Mayor Gallery in Cork Street, and in full view of 120 guests at the Andy Warhol preview, he had fallen flat on his face, and proceeded to be sick onto the pavement. Maybe it wouldn't have been so bad, he reflected, if he hadn't then proceeded to enter the gallery, collar Warhol, spend five minutes explaining to him in a slurred voice, while Warhol helped to prop him up, why, in his view, the pile of vomit on the paving stones was a more important personal statement than Warhol's life work. For a further half hour, he had staggered about among the guests, avidly lecturing anyone he could collar on the poetic beauty of tomato skins and diced carrots, before eventually falling asleep for half an hour in the ladies' lavatory.

Sometime around midnight that night he had finally shaken off the worst effects of Elleck's Chivas Regal, and by dawn he was beginning to feel sober. Before leaving for work, he had made a number of telephone calls, first to Milan and then to Tunquit, in Umm Al Amnah, then to Toronto, then Lagos, then Kuwait. When he had arrived in the office, shortly before 9.00, yawning and with a splitting headache, the first thing he had done was check the gold price. The London Exchange hadn't yet opened, but gold, which had closed on the London Exchange the previous night at $494 an ounce had risen during the night, and had closed on the Hong Kong exchange at $521, which would be the opening price in London. Rocq had smiled to himself. By the close of the London exchange on Wednesday afternoon, gold had risen again, another $8, closing at $529.

He stretched a hand out of the bed, found his handkerchief, wiped off as much of the Mazola as he could, picked up the telephone receiver, and dialled Globalex's closing prices. The recorded voice informed him that gold was currently at $538. Rocq slid out of the bed and waded his way over the polythene, and through the broadloom, to the shower.

The traffic was thicker than usual as he pulled his new Porsche into his parking bay, in the multi-storey NCP car park behind Lower Thames Street, at five past nine, twenty-minutes later than usual. He switched off the engine, and sat back for a few moments, savouring the smell of the new car: the fresh leather and hot oil. He climbed out; the door shut with the neat clunk that he liked; he reflected that there was no other car he knew of where one could get pleasure out of merely shutting a door.

He crossed Lower Thames Street, and walked up towards Mincing Lane. His feeling of well-being suddenly disappeared and was replaced with one of disquiet; up ahead was a cluster of police cars, with blue lights flashing, as well as an ambulance. Part of the pavement appeared to be cordoned off. As he got closer, he saw that the area around the entrance to Globalex was cordoned off with white tape.

He walked straight up to a police constable who was standing behind the tape.

'What's happened, officer?'

The policeman looked at him, suspicious of anyone that tried to suck up to him by calling him 'officer' when it was clear as a bell to anyone that had a pair of eyes, or even one, come to that, that he was not an officer, but a plain constable.

'Do you work in here?'

'Yes.'

The constable lifted the tape and jerked his thumb towards the doorway. 'Okay.'

Rocq ducked under the tape. 'What's happened?'

'Someone's been murdered.'

'Murdered?' He dashed inside the entrance. He had heard of the expression 'crawling with policemen,' but he'd never actually seen a place that fitted the description – until now. They were everywhere, dusting, scraping, examining, interviewing. As he waited by the lift, the manager of the metals section, Tony Zuckerman, came down the stairs with a man he presumed to be a detective. 'What's happened, Tony?' said Rocq.

'Sergeant-Major Bantry's been murdered. Burglars – whole place been turned upside down during the night – he must have heard them and gone to have a go – poor sod.'

'What – how?'

'Bust his neck,' said the detective. 'Professionals, whoever did that; vicious bastards.'

Rocq got out of the elevator on the fourth floor; the receptionist, Miss Heyman, was looking ashen faced. 'Good morning,' said Rocq.

'Good morning, Alex.'

'Nice start to the day,' he said.

She burst into tears. 'Poor old man – why did they have to kill him? Surely they could have just tied him up and gagged him?'

Rocq nodded silently. 'Sickening, isn't it. What did they take? Ten quid petty cash and Sarge's wallet?'

'I should think that's about all there was of any value in this place.'

'What the hell do these bastard burglars think?' ex-ploded Rocq, angrily. 'That we've got bloody gold bars lying all over the place?'

'Probably,' she said.

He shook his head exasperatedly, and walked through to his office. He recoiled when he saw it: the drawers of all the filing cabinets were pulled out, and papers were strewn everywhere. Slivitz, Mozer, Prest, Boadicea and the rest of his colleagues had already begun the clearing-up. For a change, nobody got at anyone, and nobody felt like cracking any gags.

At eleven o'clock, Elleck called Rocq up to his office. As he walked down the corridor, he saw Elleck's secretary checking through a filing cabinet. She stood up and announced him to Elleck.

'Good morning, Sir Monty,' said Rocq.

'Morning, Alex.'

'I'm sorry about Sarge,' said Rocq.

'Yes, yes,' said Elleck, 'everyone is. Now, I wanted to see you about the gold situation. As of this moment, gold is $549 – that's a rise of $51 in a day and a half. This is an unbelievable rise – it seems there is some very heavy buying going on, and it isn't in this country. But no one seems to be able to pinpoint the source. It's having a strong impact on the world market – people are starting to panic buy.'

Rocq was taken aback for a moment that Elleck didn't seem to be affected by what had happened to Sarge Bantry. 'This is nothing to do with your syndicate?' asked Rocq.

'No – well – unless they're playing some game they haven't told me about, it isn't. I just don't understand it – I don't understand it at all.'

'Do you think I ought to start buying for the syndicate now – and not wait until Monday, sir?'

Elleck shook his head. 'I don't think so; this buying must subside during the next day or so. There's nothing to sustain it. Have you heard anything at all? You boys down there often hear far more than I ever do.'

'Nothing at all.'

'I don't know what to make of it; 549 is too high – we must wait for it to go down before we start. It should be at 500 to 510 – that's the right price – no more. Don't buy any until it has dropped back to at least 510.'

'Even if it is higher still on Monday.'

'Even if it is higher still – unless I tell you. Is that clear?'

'Yes, Sir Monty.'

'Good.'

Rocq went back to his office. In the five minutes it had taken him to go and see the Chairman, gold had risen a further $4; by the time he went to lunch, gold had topped 560, and at the second fixing of the gold price that day at Rothschild's at three that afternoon, the price of gold was fixed at $568 an ounce.

Whatever the power, authority and influence of the men from the largest bullion dealers in the world, within an hour of their fixing, people were eagerly stumping up $5 above it. In Rocq's office, the death of Sarge and the burglary of the building had already become a thing of the past. There was a gold rush on, and nothing mattered any more except the price people were prepared to pay for those long, thin, dull-yellow metal slabs, over which a thousand wars have been fought, and a million fortunes made and lost, and with which a trillion teeth have been filled.

By nine o'clock Friday morning, the price of gold had soared over the 590 mark, and was soon nudging 600.

In the first hour's trading in London, the price rocketed to 604 before dropping back to 598. At lunchtime Friday, it stood at 609, and at two o'clock in the afternoon it hit 612. At the Friday afternoon fixing, at 3.00 p.m., the price was fixed at 616; by the close of the London market, gold was at 621, and strongly tipped to go over the $650 mark on Monday morning.

Mozer and Slivitz engaged in a heated argument about the continuation of the boom, and Rocq listened.

'As long as people keep buying, it will keep rising. I reckon it can stand another hundred, maybe hundred and fifty dollars.'

'You're full of shit, Mozer; everyone got caught with their pants down last year when it was up in the early 700s. There were billions bought in the early 700s; the moment the price gets back up there, it's going to pop like a balloon: bang! There's going to be so many people bailing out of gold they won't be able to give the stuff away by the end of next week – just like coffee.'

'Don't talk rubbish, Gary – what do you think they're going to discover – that gold fillings make people's tongues drop off?'

'I'm not letting any chick with gold fillings give me a blow job if that's the case.'

'You're disgusting, Slivitz.'

'At least I know it, Mozer; you're disgusting and you don't know it. You've got B.O., bad breath, and every orifice in your body is plugged with something nasty.'

Rocq got up from his desk, and closed his briefcase. 'Night girls, have a sweet weekend.'

'What's your hurry?' said Slivitz. 'Got to get the

suit back to Moss Bros, or the Porsche back to Avis?'

'No – I just want to go to the lavatory before you two block it for the weekend.'

CHAPTER 24

Shortly before 5.00 p.m. Friday, French time, Viscomte Claude Lasserre's secretary was put through, by Globalex's switchboard operator, to Sir Monty Elleck's secretary. As usual, Lasserre's secretary spoke in English, and Elleck's secretary spoke in French; in spite of this, the two men were promptly connected.

'Good afternoon, Monty, how are you?'

'Well, thanks, Claude. Very enjoyable dinner on Monday.'

'Thank you. You had a good flight home?'

'No problems – the airways still aren't as congested as the roads. To what do I owe the honour of this call?'

'I was talking with Jimmy and he asked me to call you. We must be making out pretty good with the gold already, no?'

There was a pause. Elleck scrabbled in the box of Havanas for a cigar: 'Well – er – sure – I – er – can you hang on?'

'Yes.'

Elleck put the receiver down, cut the end of the cigar, and put the cigar in his mouth; he pulled out his gold Dupont and lit it slowly; all the time he was thinking hard. 'Hallo, Claude?'

'Yes, I am here.'

'I'll have to check how much we have actually bought so far.'

'You haven't bought it yet?' he sounded incredulous.

'Oh, no – sure, we must have bought some – as you know – I'm not doing it directly myself. We didn't want to draw attention, right?'

'That's what we agreed.'

'But I just don't know how much we have – got to be careful buying in a bull market – I think this is only a temporary bull—'

'Bull?'

'Oh – it's a – er – trade expression – a rising market.'

'Okay.'

'My personal view is that the gold price could drop as quickly as it has risen – and we don't want to get stuck having paid top dollar.'

'I see.' The Viscomte didn't sound at all convinced. 'Then it is not our purchasing which is causing this rise?'

'Good lord no, Claude; if we'd banged ours in all at once, it might have pushed the price up ten dollars or so – but our sort of money could never create a bull like this.'

'Now if the price – does not – er drop – you are going to have to pay this new price for our gold?'

'If it steadies out at this new level, then yes, we

will have to; but if it steadies, then it will not affect our plan – because our plan will still push it up. But first we must see if it steadies. I am certain it won't. It must drop. A lot of punters are going to start selling. You'll see, Claude, it all will start changing at the beginning of the week.'

'We only have until next Friday – is that going to be time enough?'

'I'm not a clairvoyant, Claude – we'll just have to wait and see what happens and play it by ear.'

'Why didn't you buy the moment you saw it rising?'

'Firstly, we agreed we had to keep this whole thing quiet. We didn't want anyone tumbling what we were doing – and that means buying in small amounts here, there, a bit in Tokyo, a bit in Toronto, a bit in Amsterdam; buying through different dealers, some Kruger-rands from here, bars from there. A bit of this and a bit of that. Opening bank accounts in Switzerland, Liechtenstein, and perhaps elsewhere. A thousand million isn't much in gold terms, Claude, but it's one heck of a lot of money to have to spend in a hurry without anybody noticing.'

'I understand.'

'Secondly, there isn't anyone in the world who could have predicted this price rise. It's unbelievable, illogical.'

'A word of warning, Monty,' said the Viscomte. 'My friend Jimmy thinks you may be behind this, and he does not like to be double-crossed.'

'What are you saying?' Elleck's voice rose several octaves.

'Jimmy Culundis thinks you may have something to do with this rise; he is not going to be pleased to find our syndicate has missed out on it.'

'I can't help what your nasty little Greek poofter thinks – he'll have to sit on his little greased bottom and wait for the results.'

'I'm just warning you, as a friend,' said Lasserre.

Elleck suddenly realized that the tone of Lasserre's voice had become chilling. 'What exactly are you warning me?'

'I am warning you as a friend,' said Lasserre, 'that is all. I understand the world of money, of commodities. Jimmy Culundis has a more – how do you say – simple outlook on business. He provides a service and he gets paid for it. He does understand that you cannot buy gold today because it may go down tomorrow. He is a man with much power and he is a very ruthless man indeed. I am warning you my friend, that if he feels – how you say – that he is going to get screwed – in a way that he does not consider pleasant – he is a man who will get revenge.'

'Do I understand exactly what you are saying, Claude?'

'I think so, my friend. Have a good weekend.' Lasserre hung up.

Elleck sat and stared at the humming receiver, then he replaced it on the hook. He tapped a button on his Reuter terminal. Gold had risen yet another $4. Thank God, he thought, that it was the weekend. Perhaps the investment world would come to its senses over the next couple of days. He sincerely hoped so. For the first time since his days in Auschwitz he felt scared – very scared.

CHAPTER 25

Baenhaker looked at his watch: it was two minutes to five, Friday afternoon. He rubbed his eyes, and stacked up the last of the pile of micro-fiches that had been developed and printed from the hundreds of photographs he had taken on Wednesday night, in the Globalex offices.

He wasn't pleased that he'd killed the security guard, but it didn't bother him; as far as he was concerned, he had had no option. The man had crept up on him while he was working on the computer, trying to get an account list printout, and in their ensuing struggle, had made it clear that he recognized him: ' 'Ere,' he had said, 'you were 'ere this morning – came to see Mr Rocq.'

He dialled Ephraim's number in Tel Aviv. It was answered after less than half a ring. 'Hallo.'

'This is Marvin here.' Marvin was the code Baenhaker was assigned to identify himself by.

'Hallo Marvin.'

'I have some information, but not everything. Lasserre is a client of Globalex – both a personal client and corporate. The total account is some

£25 million sterling; it is fairly widely spread over a range of commodities mainly soft, but some metals.' Baenhaker was pleased he had now grasped the difference, and hoped Ephraim was impressed. He paused and then went on. 'I don't know why Elleck went to dinner, but it may have something to do with a syndicate that has been formed between Lasserre, Jimmy Culundis and Sir Monty Elleck, which is called, as far as I can ascertain, Goldilocks.'

'Goldilocks? Isn't that a children's story?'

'Yes – the name is obviously supposed to be humorous. This syndicate is buying £1,000 million worth of gold. They are doing it very discreetly, and are using a broker within Globalex to buy the gold in small quantities – a few bars at a time in a large number of different markets, and through a variety of dealers, banks and brokerage houses.' Baenhaker stopped for a moment. 'That's about all I know, sir.'

There was a long silence down the phone. Then Ephraim spoke: 'You have done well, Marvin, very well. Do you know the identity of the broker?'

'Yes, I do. Alex Rocq.'

There was another long silence. 'I'd like you to keep a close eye on Rocq and Elleck – understand?' said Ephraim.

'Yes, Sir,' he said.

'Good,' said Ephraim. 'Then I'll wait to hear from you. Time is of the essence.'

'I understand, Sir. Goodbye.'

Baenhaker hung up the phone, and then sat back in his seat. He rubbed his eyes again, stretched his arms, then laid his head right back. Ephraim had, by the words 'close eye' instructed him to put Rocq and Elleck under 24-hour surveillance. There were three surveillance teams available to him. He would put them all onto Elleck. Rocq, he decided, he would watch himself.

When he came up from the basement, the building was empty, apart from the Italian cleaning woman hoovering an office. He walked out of the front door, into the balmy evening heat. The Friday evening exodus out of the City had begun, and he watched the cars in the jam down Lower Thames Street with envy. They were going to their summer weekends, to their cottages and mansions, to their wives, girlfriends, lovers, boyfriends – companionship. Tonight was an evening for Pimms in the countryside, for sitting at a table with a beautiful girl and a bottle of wine, and a candle flickering.

He thought about evenings in Israel when he was a child, hot balmy evenings like this, and he felt nostalgic. London was a grand city, a great city; in spite of the bad that was happening in England, London still retained its dignity. But to Baenhaker, after five years here, the doors were still as closed as the day he had first stepped off the aeroplane at Heathrow. Twenty months ago, those doors had opened for the first time, in the form of Amanda. He had someone to share the city with, to share all the experiences of his life, at least the ones that he could talk about. Now he was back in the loneliness, hoping that maybe, one day, a single unmarried secretary that he fancied might join Eisenbar-Goldschmidt or, alternatively, that somewhere, as in that gutted building where he had first met Amanda, there might be someone else that he could find to love, who would also love him. But so far, no one.

As he walked down the street, he decided to do something he rarely did; he went into a pub, and had a pint of bitter. He stood at the counter, looking around. The barmaid was about forty, not bad-looking, but not the girl he dreamed of. The rest of the bar was full of men, mostly in suits that were too thick for the heat.

He downed the pint slowly and then left, feeling a little drunk. He went down the steps of Cannon Street tube station, bought his ticket and stood on the platform; opposite him, a long slender leg, wrapped in a sensuous Pretty Polly stocking, slunk out from a poster. She was the girl for the discriminating man, the poster told him. He was discriminating, but evidently someone must have got to her first.

He put his hands in his pockets and stared at the dark tunnel; there was no sign of a train. A young plump negress stood near him, clutching a carrier bag; two men, extremely drunk, in short-sleeve shirts, were having an argument about football players. Suddenly, he didn't want to be here any more; he wanted to be back in Israel, on a kibbutz, in a large family of his own people. He was tired of this existence, tired of the sacrifice. Someone had to do it, he knew, but he didn't feel any longer that it should be himself. He wanted the lushness, the dryness, the heat, the wind, the smell of fruit; he wanted to go out and dig up fields under a blazing sun, not to be standing here on this platform which smelt of damp sacks and old socks.

The train arrived, the doors opened, and he sat down. They slid shut again, and he looked around the carriage, looked at ten faces numbed into silence by something – perhaps the same shyness, perhaps the same apathy, perhaps the same boredom. He looked at them aloof, for he was a big person, an important person, and they were nothing. He had been instructed to kill men for his country; what had they been instructed? To bring home chicken dinners from Colonel Sanders?

Then he felt afraid, and a wave of guilt hit him. Two nights ago he had killed, and thought no more about it. It had even made him feel good. He wondered what had happened to him, that he could kill as easily as this and then think no more of it. He wondered if it was normal or if, somewhere, in the last five years, he had lost a vital part of himself. He cast an eye around to ensure no one was looking at him; then he closed his eyes and began, without moving his lips, to say a prayer. 'Please God, guide me to do what is right, amen,' were the words with which he finished the prayer. He opened his eyes and felt better again, warmer, more courageous; he had succeeded in passing the buck to his Creator. It was up to God now to decide what Baenhaker did, and it would be God who would have to carry any blame.

The doors slid open at Earls Court, and Baenhaker got out; he had a lot of work ahead of him, and he wanted a clear head. He wanted to relax tonight, and thought about whether he wanted to read a book or see a movie. He felt that he didn't want to be alone tonight, didn't want to go back to his flat. He decided that what he really fancied was getting laid, but he had no idea where he could get a whore in Earls Court. The only whores he knew were the two at the Israeli Embassy who were occasionally wheeled out for blackmail purposes, but they were going to have to be replaced soon; at thirty-six and thirty-nine, with three and five children respectively, they were getting beyond the point where they could successfully pass as innocent young chambermaids.

Then he decided, to hell with it, he would get straight on with his work. He left Earls Court tube station and walked in the direction of Redcliffe Square. When he had returned to E-G, he had changed back into his casual clothes, and he felt inconspicuous as he walked along.

He had found Rocq's address while going through Globalex's offices, had photographed it along with everyone else's – but Rocq's he had taken special note of. He thought it mildly curious that in addition to working less than 400 yards from where Rocq worked, he should also live less than 400 yards from where Rocq lived.

He scanned the square for any signs of a Porsche, and saw none; then he walked down past number 34, where Rocq lived, without stopping; he carried on to the end of the terrace, then walked around the side, to check the terrace from the rear. It was eight o'clock, but still fairly light; certainly light enough for people to be clearly identifiable. He figured that on a Friday evening, Rocq would either be out or have gone away for the weekend; he was pretty sure he would be safe for the few minutes he needed in Rocq's flat.

He rang the bell and waited; after a few minutes, he rang again. Either no one was in the flat, or the bell wasn't working. He slipped the latch on the front door of the building, with a small piece of plastic in his pocket, and walked in. It was a typical communal entrance; cream plastic lino, a few circulars lying on the floor, a take-away pizza menu, an invitation to join a new religious sect, and a scattering of letters. One for Miss A. Moussabakias, two for F. A. Watling FCA, and one for Lady Rowena Melchenth-Henty. That last name added a certain class to the place, he decided – not that he'd ever heard of her, but there was no one titled living anywhere in his tip, unless it was the phantom curry-freak, which he doubted.

If Rocq had any great valuables in his apartment,

he wasn't giving any hints away with the lock he had on his door – a child of three could have picked it with a piece of wet string. Baenhaker closed it quietly behind him, and took a careful look around. The door opened into a huge open-plan drawing room and dining room. A white wall-to-wall shag carpet filled the floor area; there were two white velour sofas facing each other across a massive marble coffee table. By a window was a white marble topped table, with black lacquered legs, and a black lacquered chair; the dining table was smoked glass and had eight white velour-upholstered carver chairs around it. The colour in the room came from several vivid geometric original paintings. He walked down a corridor and came to a large bedroom. The bed was low and massively wide; built into the head-board, and matching bedside-tables were stereo speakers, lights, and a complete control panel on each side, which Baenhaker presumed was for the television at the foot of the bed. The bed was unmade and well tousled; a large fur rug hung off the side of it. It looked like a good romp had taken place in it. Baenhaker noticed the photograph of Amanda beside the bed, and emotion began to well up inside him again; he looked at and puzzled over the large roll of polythene on the floor by the wall. He walked over to the bedside telephone, and pulled a tiny microphone from his pocket, when suddenly there was the sound of a key in a door – then voices:

'Amanda, you have the most filthy mind!'

'And you love it, don't you.'

'I feel so horny I don't know if I can wait to get to the bedroom.'

Baenhaker froze, and cursed himself for not having jammed the door lock. He looked frantically around for an escape. He rushed over to the window; it was double glazed, and only a small portion at the top would open. They were coming towards the room. He did something he had never done before in his life: he dived into a cupboard.

He heard them come through the door, and then there was a crash of bed springs.

'Alex! Let me get my shoes off.'

'Keep them on!'

'Well, at least let me get my jacket off – ow – now I'm stuck – oooh, your hands are cold – ooh Alex – oh – oh – oh that's good.'

Baenhaker listened in silence, quaking with a strange mixture of fear and fury. There was a creaking sound; it got louder and louder. With a panic, he realized it was the cupboard door swinging open. He put out a hand and slowly pulled it to. There was a loud 'clunk' as its magnet locking mechanism connected.

He began to feel baking hot in the cupboard; he was sitting uncomfortably on some very hard shoes, and was surrounded by suits and ties which draped themselves around his head. The bed began to creak consistently, faster and faster, and Amanda began to groan and shout. So many emotions rushed through Baenhaker that he was paralysed. For a moment he wanted to burst out of the cupboard, grab Rocq in one hand and Amanda in the other, and smash their skulls together. For another moment, he wanted to curl up in the cupboard, and just give up and die. He just hoped that after they finished what they were doing, neither of them was going to feel much like hanging any clothes up.

An hour passed; for the last quarter of it, there had been silence in the bedroom. Amanda's voice broke the silence: 'Do you really have to go to Switzerland tomorrow?'

'I don't want to Amanda, but I have to.'

'It's going to be such a gorgeous weekend – it'll be rotten without you.'

'It's not going to be much fun for me – the last thing I want to do is spend half my weekend in an aeroplane.'

'It's only an hour's flight.'

'By the time I get to the airport, hang around – then Verbier is an hour and a half from the airport. And there's fuck all to do in Verbier this time of year – I'm not exactly into mountain hiking.'

'You say it's business – why can't you go during the week?'

'I would, normally – but we have a panic on at the moment, and I cannot afford to be away from the office for even a few hours. Look – I tell you what – I'm catching the first flight out in the morning – it leaves nine o'clock. I'll be in Geneva at 10.15 – with luck I'll be in Verbier lunch time, sign everything I have to sign – and I may be able to make a late afternoon flight back here – be back in time to go out for dinner? How does that sound?'

'Okay,' she said dubiously. 'That sounds fine – in theory.'

They talked for another hour, then made love again for another hour. Baenhaker continued to crouch in his stifling cupboard, half his body seized with cramp, the other half raging silently.

Finally, at a quarter to three, Baenhaker had heard no sound from either Amanda or Rocq for what he guessed had been an hour. He pushed the wardrobe door open gently. There was a report like a starting pistol as the metal catch on the inside of the door separated from the magnet, and Baenhaker froze. He listened carefully for several minutes, but there was no sound.

He climbed out of the cupboard, debated whether to risk trying to place the bug in the telephone, decided better of it, and quietly let himself out.

CHAPTER 26

After General Ephraim had spoken to Baenhaker on the Friday evening, he had stood up and paced around his office without stopping, for half an hour; then he sat down, opened a drawer in his desk, and pulled out a computerized chess set. He played against the machine, set to its toughest level, and beat it in seven minutes; then he snapped off the switch and put the machine back in the drawer. He wished the current real-life game, in which he was an unwilling player, was as simple to win.

This week he had to send 100 Israeli sailors into Umm Al Amnah, quietly, without publicity. They were to be smuggled in, in a container in a cargo plane. It just didn't make sense. Why sailors? Soldiers he could understand, that would be easy – a *coup d'état*. But sailors? He thought about the man Bauté, who had spoken to him on the beach at La Baule; and then about Elleck flying in to have dinner with Lasserre, and joined by Culundis, who had already supplied arms and, Ephraim was pretty certain, soldiers, to Umm Al Amnah.

He still smarted over the way Elleck had treated

him after the Osirak raid. He had completely ripped him off. He was sure that a second rip-off was under way. Somewhere, at the end of the bizarre line, there had to be a massive profit in all of this for Elleck. But how? What was there with a tiny country like Umm Al Amnah? It did have a coastline on the Persian Gulf, but not much of one. There was the Libya connection, but there was nothing particularly unusual in that; Libya meddled in the affairs of a lot of countries, with and without their leaders' approval. He remembered the report about the Umm Al Amnah's registered fishing dhow drifting loose in the Persian Gulf with a cargo of nuclear mines, and a chill went through his body. Was that the connection? Was he going to be forced to order the sailors to commit some act of aggression – some massive terrorist act of sabotage?

He went to the window and looked out; it was dark, with the lights of the traffic moving down below him. He should call the Prime Minister and level with him, he knew, that was his best bet. He had a repugnant obsession, and it had finally caught up with him. It was not right that he should put his country at risk to protect himself. His time was nearly over in any event; a year or two more, and he would be expected to retire. He had no further ambitions for himself. He was tired; he wouldn't mind stepping down now. He needed a rest. A long, long rest.

He tried to think how the Prime Minister might

react, and each time he drew a blank. He had no idea. A fear suddenly struck him that the Prime Minister would go for the complete hard line, call his blackmailer's bluff, and he shuddered. He thought about his wife and children, going through the rest of their lives, his children with their brilliant careers ahead of them, tarnished forever with the fact that they came from a man who liked to make love to dead boys. Necrophiliac. He shuddered. They would be destroyed; there was no doubt. Ami, his eldest son, already a captain in the army: Nathan, who had passed through law school with a first and had joined the top law firm in Israel; Helene, his daughter, engaged to the son of the Chief Rabbi.

While parents around the world despaired so often of their children, he and his wife Moya could sit in the evenings, when they were alone together, and reflect on their fortune that their children not only were healthy but were intelligent and successful. It was the careers of his children and, one day, the arrival of grandchildren, that he and Moya had to look forward to. He turned away from the window; not for his country, not for anything, did he want to give that up; not for anything would he destroy their lives. Ephraim clenched his fists in anger. It was the greed of Elleck, the man whose life he had saved in Auschwitz, that had put him in this position, he was certain of that. This was Elleck's way, forty years later, of showing his gratitude.

Ephraim marched back over to his desk, stood beside it, and dialled the number of Eisenbar-Goldschmidt in London. Being a major control centre, the switchboard was manned through the night. The girl who answered informed him that Baenhaker had left over an hour ago. He tried Baenhaker's home number: it rang several times, without answer; he hung up. He then dialled Chaim Weisz's number in Paris; to his mixed relief, his chief of French operatives answered.

'Good evening, Montclair!' said Ephraim, using Weisz's identifying code.

'Good evening,' said Weisz.

'I have a job for you. Viscomte Claude Lasserre – can you buy him out?'

Weisz paused, surprised, the other end. 'When?'

'As soon as you can?'

'I'll do my best for you.'

'Good. Let me have a progress report.' Ephraim hung up the receiver. He had just instructed the chief of the Mossad's French operations to kill Viscomte Lasserre.

Ephraim next dialled Athens, and had a similar conversation with the chief of Athens operations regarding Jimmy Culundis. Then he tried Baenhaker's number again; still no answer. He telephoned Moya to say he would not be home until very late, then pulled out his chess set again; he would try Baenhaker at half hour intervals, right through the night, if necessary, until he got hold of him.

At half past three he succeeded.

'Hallo?' Baenhaker's voice sounded breathless.

'Have you been running?'

'I just got in – heard the phone ringing, so I had to run up the stairs.'

'Your friends, Elleck and Rocq. I don't think you should associate with them any more; they are not good company for you.'

'No, Sir,' said Baenhaker, 'I understand.'

'Good. Give me a call and let me know how things are going.'

Again, Ephraim replaced the receiver; this time, he slid the chess back in the drawer, put on his jacket, and went home to sleep.

It was some time before Baenhaker slept. He sat reflecting on General Ephraim's words, which had instructed him to kill Rocq and Elleck. If he carried out the General's orders, London was going to get a bit too hot for his liking. It wouldn't take the police too long to connect Rocq and Elleck's deaths with the murder of the security man, and the break-in; multiple murders tended to interest policemen more than almost anything. He would almost certainly be pulled from London, and probably from England. He would have loved to be pulled from London, except for one thing: with Rocq out of the way, he wondered if he might have another chance with Amanda. She was still under his skin, as deep as ever, probably even more so after his night in the cupboard. Then he smiled to himself. There was a way he could keep a low profile on one of the murders. He picked up the telephone, and dialled a number in Geneva. There were occasions, he reflected, when he could pass the buck along with the best of them.

CHAPTER 27

Rocq drove out of the Avis compound at Geneva in a Volkswagen Golf, following the signs for Montreux and the St Bernard Tunnel. It was a stunning summer's day, and a slight heat-mist hung over the lake; he looked across, through the front passenger window, down at the lake and at Geneva, which was fast disappearing over his right shoulder.

Although there was little breeze, the air that buffeted in through his window was just cool enough to lift the edge off the heat. Rocq felt good; he felt free and relaxed, momentarily unshackled from the chains of London and, although he was extremely fond of Amanda, it felt good to be completely on his own, even though it was just for a few hours.

He checked his speedometer: he was doing 120 kilometres per hour. Some way back, there was a beige Range Rover; he had noticed it in his wing mirror for several kilometres. It almost seemed to be pacing him. He thought it might be a police car, but doubted the Swiss Police would use Range Rovers; then it seemed to be dropping back and he forgot about it. He passed Lausanne, then Montreux, where the road cut through the mountains, then the motorway descended down into the Rhone valley and became a three lane road. At Martigny, he turned right, and began the climb up towards Verbier.

The air ticket and the car were on the Globalex account at Thomas Cook, although it wasn't purely for Globalex that Rocq was making this journey. He was, indeed, going on behalf of Elleck's syndicate, to open an account at the Verbier branch of the Credit Suisse bank and to sign the papers authorizing the formation of a Swiss Company by the name of Three Bears Ag. Among the nominee directors of this company would be a lawyer friend of Theo Barbiero-Ruche, who had very kindly agreed to relinquish a part of his precious weekend in order to see Rocq. But Rocq's private reason for the trip was to sign the papers for the formation of another company, Rocksolid Investments Ag, which would also be banking at the Credit Suisse.

He drove into the centre of Verbier, thinking how strange the famous ski resort looked in the middle of summer, with no snow except for the Montfort Glacier and the peak of Mont Gelé. The town was very busy, with a stream of cars and hordes of people, many carrying rucksacks, and wearing stout walking shoes and long socks. To Rocq, it lacked the elegance of the winter months, when the snow came down and brought the rich people

317

with it. The town gave the appearance of tolerating these hordes, but all the while waiting patiently for the winter, the first blanket of snow, and a pace and calibre of life to which it was altogether more accustomed.

M. Jean-Luis Vençeon, *avocat*, lived in a chalet just below the Savoleyeres lift, according to Rocq's instructions. The signpost to the Savoleyeres pointed up to the left, and he drove the car around the tiny traffic island and up the hill, past a short parade of smart shops on the right, then a modern Catholic church on the left, with a spire that looked like a sawn-off boomerang. He read the names on the chalets and then saw the one he was looking for, Rossignol.

Rocq's image of a Swiss lawyer had not been a six-foot-three-inch-tall man in a pink Lacoste tee-shirt, white running shorts and Adidas tennis shoes. Jean-Luis Vençeon was polite, precise and formal. He spent one minute on introductions, five minutes explaining the documents, seven minutes pointing out to Rocq the places where he needed his signature, one minute explaining where and how Rocq should get in touch with him if he needed to, and a further thirty seconds gathering up his tennis racquet and balls and saying goodbye to Rocq. No drink, no food; no small talk.

As Rocq walked down the steps towards his car, the Swiss *avocat*, jogging at full tilt, was already halfway to the village. Where else, reflected Rocq, could one form two companies, open two bank accounts and be finished inside fourteen minutes? It seemed a hell of a long way to have had to come for so little, but then, he knew, the Swiss didn't hang about when it came to business.

He stepped out into the road, walked around, and opened the door of his car. A roaring made him look up, and he saw a beige Range Rover bearing down on him, coming straight at the door. Instinct made him leap clear, and a fraction of a second later, the door was torn off its hinges. Rocq stood looking, in shock. 'Fucking maniac!' he shouted, as it screeched to a halt. Oddly, he thought, instead of reversing, the Range Rover began to turn around; there were two men in it. Rocq stood by the Golf and waited. The driver put the Range Rover into first gear, and began to drive back up the hill. Rocq continued to stand by the Golf. Suddenly, to his horror, it dawned on him that the Range Rover was accelerating fiercely and had no intention of stopping. He did not know how he managed to do so but he vaulted up onto the bonnet of the Golf, just at the moment the Range Rover hit it with full force.

Rocq was catapulted backwards into the long grass at the side of the road. Fear ripped through the shock: one of the men was getting out of the Range Rover. Rocq scrambled to his feet and began to sprint back down the hill, for all he was worth. He looked over his shoulder; the man had stopped after a few yards and the Range Rover was turning again, to come after him. Rocq saw a grey Renault 30 pull up outside a supermarket. The driver, leaving the engine running, dashed into the supermarket. The Range Rover had stopped to pick up the second man. Rocq jumped into the driver's seat of the Renault, slammed the automatic gear into drive, and floored the accelerator. The bonnet rose up and snaked about for a moment, the tyres fired off gravel from the road in all directions, then the wheels gripped, and the Renault accelerated fiercely up the road. The driver of the Range Rover swung his steering wheel, slewing the car over to try and block Rocq's path, but Rocq swung over onto the grass verge and just passed the nose of the Range Rover. In his mirror, he saw the reversing lights come on and the vehicle began, once more, to turn around.

After a quarter of a mile, he came to a junction. To the left, which Rocq guessed led back down into the town centre, the road was blocked by a massive road surfacing machine and a large yellow diversion sign pointing traffic back down the road he had just come up. Right, he guessed, would lead further up the mountain-side. He tried desperately to think what the men in the Range Rover were up to, who they were, and whether they had mistaken him for someone else. He remembered, suddenly, having noticed the Range Rover behind him on the road out of Geneva, and on the way to Montreux; but surely that one, he thought, had dropped way back? He realized now that they must have followed him all the way from the airport. But who knew he was going to Geneva? He racked his brains. Elleck and Theo were the only ones. He was convinced Theo was straight. It had to be Elleck. Elleck wanted him to get the account opened and the company formed, then he was going to get him out of the way. But Rocq hadn't done any of the buying yet. Surely, he reasoned, if Elleck had been planning to kill him so that he could not talk, he would have waited until Rocq had finished the job? In the mirror he could see the menacing nose of the Range Rover coming up the hill.

He accelerated hard again, turning right, and drove past a cafe with a sunny terrace, full of men and women with their shirts off, the men with bare chests, the women in their bras and occasional bikini tops, sitting out, roasting in their sun tan lotions, as they sucked up the early afternoon sun. Rocq came to another intersection, with a choice of straight on, which appeared to go into woods, or a sharp left. Either way, the metalled road ended and it was cart-track. He didn't want to get trapped in the woods, so he turned hard left, the tyres spraying out dust and pebbles.

The road was only fractionally wider than the car, and climbed steeply up above the cafe, before hairpinning round sharply to the right and traversing the side of the mountain. He slammed the gear shift into low and the car surged upwards, the rev counter racing around towards the red mark, the nose occasionally snaking as the ground beneath the tyres gave out, the engine howling. He took his eyes off the narrow road for a fraction of a second to look at the fuel gauge, and noticed with horror that it was on the empty mark. In his mirror he could see the Range Rover starting to turn up past the cafe. He wasn't at all happy about this terrain; he had no idea where the track went nor when it might become unpassable in this car. Right now, the Range Rover had every conceivable advantage over him, including, he had no doubt, a full tank of petrol.

He came around the next corner, in a rallying power-slide with his nose dug in and tail hanging so far out he was concerned he was going to put a wheel over the edge, and found himself heading straight into the midst of a family of six in hiking gear, spread across the road walking downwards. He stamped on the brakes and they jumped angrily out of the way, shouting and gesticulating: he accelerated off, and immediately came across another family around the next corner. He climbed up through some trees, and then the road turned back on itself in the sharpest hairpin he had yet come across. As he climbed the next stretch, the road dropped almost vertically away to his right; if he drove off the road now, he knew the car would drop several thousand feet and land right among the rooftops of Verbier. He concentrated fiercely on the road, half wondering whether he should stop at the next group of hikers he came to, but fearful that they would be powerless to do anything against the men in the Range Rover, particularly if, as he suspected, they were armed.

The road began getting worse, and the car pitched violently through two potholes; he prayed the suspension would hold. Luckily, the car he was in was strongly built and, being French, had a suspension system that could cope with these types of road; even so, he had to hold on with all his strength to the four-pronged steering wheel as it bucked and tried to tear itself out of his hands. There was a long straight incline now, and as the rev counter surged over the red line, he pushed the gear shift into second, and kept the accelerator hard on the floor. The speedometer raced up to the 100 kilometre mark. There was a fearsome bang and the car bounced violently up in the air, over the root of a tree and snaked wildly to the edge of the road; one wheel went over the edge, and Rocq was certain, as he held the accelerator resolutely to the floorboard and the steering wheel on full left lock, that the car was going over the edge. But somehow, the wheel came back onto the top, and he managed to steer the Renault back into the centre of the track.

There were two loud blasts, and around the corner ahead came a truck, travelling fairly fast for its size and the incline. Miraculously the road widened for a few yards and, so close to the edge that it was a matter of luck whether or not the offside wheels left the road or stayed on, he managed to scrape through; then he smiled. The truck must surely, he thought, block the Range Rover's path. The hard angry blasts of hooting behind, the sound of grinding metal, then to his horror, only a hundred yards back, he could see in his mirror, the Range Rover surging down the road after him. It was catching him now. The track had become so rough his speed had dropped to 40 kilometres, and even so he was hard pushed to tell when it was the wheels or when it was the sump that was hitting the ground. The Renault bucked and crashed, and he knew something must break very soon.

He flung the Renault into the next bend: there was a hair-pin turn on a steep incline. The front wheels refused to grip and he began sliding backwards. He stamped on the foot-brake, shoved the gear into reverse, reversed the car a few yards down; then he slammed the gear lever into low and tried again, as gently as he could with his whole body trembling in fear. The Range Rover was almost on top of him. The tyres gripped this time, and he began to accelerate again. There was thick woodland on either side now, and the track was not improving. He had to slow down to take the next bend, and again the Range Rover loomed menacingly in his rear mirrors. There was a bang, and the Renault lurched forward, followed by another bang, which broke Rocq's grip on the steering wheel, and flung him upwards, cracking his head on the roof, then forward so that he cracked it again on the windscreen.

Somehow, Rocq managed to round the corner. The track suddenly improved, and the Renault was able to out-accelerate the Range Rover up it. They approached another hairpin: he changed down into second, then, at the last moment, stamped hard on the brakes, pulled the gear lever back to low, wound the steering wheel tightly over and yanked the handbrake on as hard as he could. The back of the car slid round and, accelerating fiercely again, he released the brake. The car came out of the bend accelerating hard, and the Range Rover dropped even further back; then the road deteriorated back into rutted cart-track, and he had to slow right down.

There was another jarring crash, and the Renault started snaking, right, then left, then right; the steering wheel did not respond and he realized to his horror that he was being pushed. There was another hairpin coming up ahead, and he could see the end of the tree line just beyond it; down to the left was an awesome drop. He had less than a hundred yards to get the car steering again, or he was going to be pushed over for sure. He accelerated furiously, and suddenly the Renault started to pull away. Bouncing and lurching ferociously, he somehow got around the corner.

There was a closed gate ahead of him; he aimed at the centre and carried on accelerating hard. There was a loud cracking, barbed wire whipped at the windscreen and then he was through and as he rounded a gentle curve, he saw they were at the top of the mountain and in what was clearly a local beauty spot, judging by the fifteen or so cars that were parked there. One couple stuffing their faces with sandwiches, in a Mercedes saloon, waved brightly at him; he wondered whether to stop and scream for help, but the menacing nose of the Range Rover on his tail decided him against that. He began the descent down the other side of the mountain. He accelerated hard, then slammed on the brakes; the terrain was now loose gravel, and the car slid wildly down it; for a moment he was terrified they were going to slide straight over the side, but then they slowed down. At that moment, the Renault was hurled forward several feet by the Range Rover, which then rammed it again; somehow, he managed to accelerate away from it again.

He knew it could not be long before he ran out of petrol. They came to another closed gate, and again smashed through it. He slid the Renault sideways around another hairpin, to discover a massive lorry crawling up less than 200 yards below him. Right now he no longer cared about anything, nothing except getting away from the Range Rover. He was not going to stop, he did not dare to stop; he knew he was going to have to fit past that truck, and if he didn't and died, then so be it. The driver flashed his lights and hooted angrily, but Rocq carried on racing down towards it, trying to size up in his mind on which side he had the best chance: to the right was a sheer drop; to the left, shrubbery and the hill slope. He picked the left. For a brief moment, he thought there was going to be enough room, and the side of the lorry began flashing past, inches to the right; then the Renault slipped down the bank and the offside of the car came into contact with the lorry. The noise was fearsome: the windows smashed out, there was a rending, renting, grinding, then suddenly the lorry was past, and there was empty road ahead of him.

He heard, over the noise of the truck's exhaust, the sound of locked rubber sliding across cart-track, then a tremendous bang followed by a clattering sound, followed by a hollow clanging interspersed with the splintering of wood. He stopped. Through what had been his offside window, he saw a streak of beige drop past. He jumped out of the Renault, and ran to the side of the road. Two thousand feet below him, the Range Rover was rolling and bouncing, pirouetting like a tiny ballet dancer on a trampoline. He saw it hit a rock ledge and bounce upwards; its two doors, bonnet and tailgate flew open together, then it carried on plunging down, and disappeared from his view.

Rocq got back into the Renault. He wasn't enjoying his day out in Switzerland any more. He wanted to go home, and quickly. He carried on down, and eventually came out into the small village of Riddes. He wondered where he could find a policeman, then decided that, with his limited grasp of the French language, he was not quite sure how he would be able to explain why it was that he had found it necessary to steal a car and race a Range Rover up and down a mountainside. He looked at his Piaget watch; there was a plane back to London at 3.30. If he hurried he might just make it.

He passed a garage, but decided not to risk stopping; with all its dents, the car looked much too conspicuous.

He drove out of Riddes; a number of people, mainly children, shouted to each other and pointed at the smashed-in side of the car. He decided it would not be wise to stay in the car longer than was absolutely necessary and, when he came down into Martigny, he abandoned it in the first empty parking bay he saw, and took a taxi to Geneva Airport.

It was not until the Caravelle was airborne that Rocq began to unwind a little. He was still trembling, and wasn't sure whether it was fear or rage. He ordered a Bloody Mary from the stewardess and then sat back to try and think clearly.

It was possible that it had been mistaken identity, but he discounted that. Four people knew he was going to Verbier: Elleck, Theo, Amanda and the *avocat*. Amanda he could discount. Which left three. Had he perhaps been conned into signing his life away to Theo and the *avocat*? Possibly, but he couldn't believe his Italian friend was ruthless enough to have anyone murdered. There was only one person that he knew who he believed could be capable of murdering, or of having people murdered: Elleck. And yet, that didn't make sense. He hadn't even begun the buying yet for Elleck's syndicate, and Elleck could hardly think it worthwhile having him bumped off just for his signatures – unless there was some immensely clever stunt Elleck had pulled; but he doubted it. He thought about the syndicate. Elleck had said little to him about his partners, but in Rocq's view, any syndicate that was capable of setting off a chain of events that could, as Elleck had said, bring the world to the brink of war, was more than capable of ordering the bumping off of one solitary metal broker.

Rocq's drink arrived; he put it down on the table and stirred it slowly, then took a large sip. There was something going on with this syndicate, he decided, that Elleck hadn't mentioned. There were three reasons, he decided, why he might not have mentioned it: because he didn't want Rocq to know; because he had forgotten; or because he himself did not know.

No one had ever tried to kill Rocq before, and he didn't like the feeling one bit. Warning bells were ringing inside him, based on a cross between a hunch and the influence of many books he had read and films he had seen, that, having tried once and failed, whoever it was would almost certainly be going to try again. The two men in the Range

Rover were almost certainly dead. News of their deaths would not filter back to whoever had given them their instructions for several hours, at the very earliest. During that time, it would be presumed that they had succeeded and that Rocq was dead. He decided it would be tomorrow, at the earliest, before they came looking for him again. By then, he intended to have wrung the truth out of Monty Elleck's fat little neck.

CHAPTER 28

The Monday following Rocq's trip to Geneva was a blazing hot summer's day, without exception right across Europe. There was plenty to do for the estate workers at Chateau Lasserre and it was this, coupled with the general feeling of lethargy that the heat brought about, combined with the thick summer foliage, that enabled the two men at the edge of the dense L-shaped forest, to work quietly and unspotted.

The men had in the woods two large reels, around which were wound lengths of wire flex and to which were attached, at twenty-foot intervals, light bulb sockets. Alongside the edge of the trees, so close that many of the sockets almost nestled against the roots, they laid one wire, 600 metres long and coming to a halt just in front of the L-part of the forest. As they unwound the wire, they placed a 150-watt light bulb into each socket.

When they had laid the full length, they repeated the process with the second wire, laying the trail of lights parallel, twenty feet apart. Then they connected the ends of the two wires into a junction box and connected that into the mains

331

ectricity supply of Chateau Lasserre, via a power cable that traversed the estate. When they had finished, it was seven o'clock in the evening.

Eight hundred kilometres away, in Switzerland, Viscomte Lasserre and Jimmy Culundis waited their turn on the Eighteenth green at Crans Montana Golf Club. The Viscomte was looking grim. He had lost the game at the Eleventh, and he was now one down on the bye; the best he could hope for was to halve it. The foursome in front of them appeared to be inspecting the borrow of every blade of grass. Lasserre was anxious to finish as he had a long flight back home, and unlike the Greek, he did not have the luxury of a personal private pilot.

'Tell me, Claude,' said Culundis, 'you are really sure you trust that man Elleck?'

'Jimmy – I am not going to risk 500 million francs of my own money on someone I don't trust. He knows best – because he is the best.' He leaned over towards Culundis conspiratorially. 'I am reliably informed that he has investment portfolios for many of the English Royal Family.'

'So what does that signify?'

'It signifies, Jimmy, that he is a man who can be trusted.'

Culundis grunted. 'I wonder what's happened to the gold price this afternoon? He told you it was going down today; well, by lunch time it was up to $650 – it closed Friday at $625. In my language that's up, not down.'

Lasserre nodded. 'Look at those people,' he said, almost exasperated. The four players had placed ball-markers down, and were now cleaning their balls and arguing about something at the same time. He turned to Culundis. 'He assured me he would buy today – regardless of what happened.'

'If he had bought last week, at four hundred and ninety-four, do you realize how much we would have made? We wouldn't have needed this whole damned business with Amnah.'

'If we could foretell what was going to happen in the markets, we'd be playing with gold golf balls, Jimmy.'

'It doesn't look good, Claude; I don't like it. I think it's Elleck who has caused this price rise. Look, it's just too much coincidence: except in the Osirak crisis, the gold price does not move for eighteen months; then, the week we talk with him about doing something about it – bang – it goes through the roof. Surely to God, that is a little strange?'

'What are you suggesting, Jimmy – you want to pull out?'

'I think we're crazy to stay in – we're being taken for the biggest ride of our lives.'

'Look at him,' shouted Lasserre in frustration. 'A ten-centimetre putt – how can anyone miss a ten-centimetrc putt? I shall have him thrown out of this club!'

'Did you hear what I said, Claude?'

'Sure, I heard. What are you going to do with

your 100 Israeli sailors that are sitting this moment in the docks at Al Suttoh?'

'Who gives a shit about them? Take them out and drown them – or give them back. What does it matter?'

'It matters a lot, Jimmy. I need that money; we have planned this carefully, it is all going according to plan. Why the hell should we pull out now?'

'The plan was to force up the price of gold and make a killing. Someone – or something – has already forced the price up, and you and I are not on that boat – although I'll bet your friend, Mr Elleck, is.'

'I think you have something personal against Monty.'

Culundis glared at him.

'So gold has risen $156. When Israel announces she is going to block the Persian Gulf, you think it's not going to rise any more? The world has gone gold-mad this week – *Mon Dieu*, Jimmy, are you going senile? When Israel announces her intentions, you know what is going to happen? I'll tell you: Gold is going to go not to one thousand, but to two thousand!'

The foursome finally plopped their last ball into the hole and moved off the green. Culundis took his nine-iron and bent over his ball. 'I hope you're right,' he said. He swung at the ball and it dropped to a halt less than six inches from the hole. 'Hey!' he said. 'How about that?'

'Shot,' said Lasserre, grudgingly.

Lasserre took his own nine-iron, and swung;

the ball dropped short of the green into a bunker. Culundis looked at him quizzically: 'Want to bother to putt out?'

Lasserre shook his head. 'I concede – well played.'

They walked to the green and collected their balls and then walked towards the Clubhouse. 'You played very well today – better than ever.'

The Greek shrugged his shoulders, and spat out a mouthful of phlegm in full view of the Club Secretariat and about ten other members. Lasserre winced as a battery of dubious frowns greeted them at the Nineteenth hole.

'I'll buy you a drink,' said the Greek.

Lasserre looked at his Tissot watch. 'Just a Perrier and a coffee.'

'You really have to get back tonight? Why don't we have dinner and both leave in the morning?'

'I have to be in Limoges tomorrow at nine – and I don't want to have to get up at five. You're okay, you have your own pilot. You can go to sleep in your plane – I have to fly myself.'

'Claude,' said Culundis, 'you know – you are so poor, I feel so sorry for you. Seventeen generations of Lasserres, and what you got to show for it? A few acres of piss and a lousy golf swing.'

Lasserre grinned. 'Just you better watch out next month when we play – you'd better bring plenty of moncy.'

'Why – you going to have golf lessons?'

'No – I'm going to give you one.'

★   ★   ★

At ten o'clock, Viscomte Lasserre looked down from the cockpit of his Piper Navajo at the lights of Bergerac, cut back the throttle and began his descent. It was a crystal clear night, and he had navigated visually the whole way from Sion Airport – it was a route he knew almost with his eyes shut. He stared at a point in the darkness about ten miles beyond Bergerac, leaned forward and pushed a button at the top of the instrument panel; within a fraction of a second, the lights of a runway appeared in the darkness. He smiled to himself; his new radio-controlled switch system worked well.

There was no wind tonight, so he could go straight down from this direction. Ahead of him, he could make out some of the rooms of the chateau. His height dropped to 1,000 feet, then 900; he checked the airspeed, lowered a little more flap, corrected a yaw. Funny, he thought, the runway seemed a fraction further from the house than usual. He decided he must be more tired than he realized. He pressed the undercarriage button and felt the clunk of the three wheels locking; the three green lights on the instrument panel showed him they had locked safely into place.

He lined the aircraft up exactly on the centre of the runway and pushed the throttle lever further in; he gave a little more flap and eased the throttle a fraction further, until he was happy with his approach.

The altimeter read 200, 150, 100; he was almost onto the runway, still perhaps a fraction high. He pulled the nose up and gave still more flap, and they began to drop a fraction faster. Now he was completely satisfied. The altimeter read fifty, then something, something he knew was not right: the huge shadows to his right. 'It couldn't be! – impossible—' Before he had time to think further, the right-hand wing of the Piper ripped into the pine trees, and snapped off halfway down. The plane dropped onto its starboard side, hit the grass with the stump of the wing tip from which petrol was gushing, and cartwheeled at eighty miles an hour towards the trees. It slammed into a clump of six trees close together and exploded on impact, setting the whole forest on fire. Somewhere, still strapped in his seat in the midst of the blazing mess, remained the seventeenth Viscomte Lasserre.

CHAPTER 29

At about the same time as the forest on the Chateau Lasserre estate began to burn, Jimmy Culundis's DC-8 touched down at Athens Airport. Thirty minutes later, his helicopter landed on the lawn of his house, in the hills, overlooking the fishing village where he was born.

The children had gone to bed, but his wife, Ariane, was up and had dinner prepared for him. She poured him a glass of wine and sat down at the table with him, but he wasn't talkative.

'How was your game?' she asked.

'It was good – I won – how about that, hey?'

She smiled. She had met Lasserre when he had been to her house. Such an impressive man. She still could not get used to the fact that her husband lived all his working life, and much of his private life, in the company of the rich and, frequently, the famous. Lasserre was a Viscomte: she wasn't clear what a Viscomte was, but she was profoundly impressed that a Viscomte had deigned to visit her home. Now she was even more impressed that her husband, a simple Greek fisherman, had managed to beat a Viscomte at golf.

Culundis lapsed into silence and munched his way through his salad, occasionally stopping to swill down a mouthful of the cold wine.

'You must be tired,' she said.

'No – not really – I have some problems on my mind. I'm okay.' He smiled reassuringly and she sat for the rest of the time in silence, while he ate.

Culundis churned over in his mind the events of the past few weeks. Something was worrying him a lot, and he wasn't sure what it was. He was certain they were being screwed by Elleck and if he found that was the case, then Elleck would be a sorry man, a very sorry man indeed.

He went through the operation in his mind: everything was in place. The 100 Israeli sailors there, in secret. They were happy. They had been briefed by Ephraim that they were on a top-secret mission and had to follow orders either from him or from Hamid Assan, Culundis's chief of staff in Amnah. Culundis had picked an Arab as his chief of staff for many reasons, the most important of which was in order to be sure of a rapport with the Emir's own armed forces. The nuclear mines were all in place too, in the warehouse, ready to be loaded. Steaming towards the Gulf, under remote control, at this very moment, was the SS Arctic Sundance, with a twenty-kiloton nuclear explosive charge taped to the inside of her oil-storage tank. On Thursday night, as she started the run up towards the Strait of Hormuz, her crew would leave by helicopter; Friday morning, as she entered the Strait, in full view of the Omani coastguard, and programmed by her computerized auto-pilot not to be within ten miles of any other ship, the charge would detonate, reducing the SS Arctic Sundance into tiny slivers of metal and glass.

Within ten minutes of the detonation, a message would be sent, direct from the Knesset, to every Head of State in the world. The message would state that Israel had taken command of Umm Al Amnah, and from Amnah it had organized the mining, with nuclear mines, of the Strait of Hormuz. The mines would be difficult to locate, and impossible to defuse if found. No mention of the quantity of mines would be given. The message would continue that only Israel knew the position of the mines and the signal that could defuse them; it would not make the Strait of Hormuz safe for shipping until new borders for Israel were agreed between Syria, Jordan and Egypt. These would be ratified by the signatures of the Governments of every major power in the world and, as security against a future break, all export oil revenues to every Arab country must be paid for a period of ten years, through the Israeli government. Culundis twiddled with his ear. After that, there would be no further demands by the syndicate on General Ephraim. Culundis wondered what kind of rumpus there would be in the Knesset when the Prime Minister learned of what had happened – that, unbeknown to him, the head of the Mossad had invaded and conquered another country and had blockaded the Persian Gulf. Israel would have egg on her face for months while the Prime Minister issued denials – which would not be believed, because of the actual presence of the Israeli sailors in Amnah. Maybe Lasserre was right, he thought. Regardless of what it was now, gold would go straight up through the heavens.

Culundis smiled to himself at the thought of Emir Missh – that he had conquered the man's country without his even knowing it. He would be mad, mad as hell, for no one would ever believe that he was not in complicity with the Israelis. All the Arab countries would turn against him, as would all the Western World. He was a weak man, thought Culundis, a feeble and weak man; his father, old Quozzohok, was better, he reflected – a tyrant, yes, but at least he had gumption. Culundis knew he could never have walked all over Umm Al Amnah if the old man had still been at the helm. He downed his wine glass, smiled at his wife, and rose from the table.

At four o'clock in the morning, the telephone by the bed rang; Culundis was awake in a second, apprehensive.

'Culundis,' he said.

'It's Hamid. I'm sorry to call you at this hour.'

'Don't worry,' said Culundis to Hamid Assan, his Chief of Staff in Amnah. 'What's up?'

'We've been flung out of Amnah.'

'What?' Culundis sat bolt upright in bed. 'What did you say?'

'Every one of your soldiers has been rounded up, their weapons removed, and they have been put on a plane out of the country. I have to leave in one hour's time myself.'

'This is an outrage. What is Missh playing at?'

'He has instructed me to telephone you to say that the services of you and your men are no longer required, and where would you like them delivered to?'

Culundis sat in the bed, speechless, for nearly a minute. When he next spoke, he was nearly shouting: 'Is Missh there? I must speak to him myself, at once.'

'I don't know where he is; I'm in Tunquit prison.'

'Give me the number. I'm going to call you right back.'

'Hold on – I will ask for it.'

There was a pause and then Assan's voice came back: 'It's Tunquit 448 – the Tunquit code is 62 – and the international code for Amnah is 010971.'

'I must speak to Missh – then I will call you right back.' Culundis hung up. Throughout the conversation, his wife hardly stirred. She was used to his telephone calls at strange hours of the night.

He began to dial Missh's private number at the Royal Palace in Tunquit, when the doorbell rang. Puzzled, he put the receiver down. After a few minutes, it rang again, a long positive ring. He wondered who on earth it could be, and looked at his gold Cartier: it was five past four. There was a night security guard on the gate – he would never let anyone past at this hour, and if he needed to speak to Culundis, there was an intercom system by which he could buzz the house. But this was the doorbell. Culundis was baffled; the telephone call from Hamid, followed by the doorbell ringing, was too much for him at this hour. Maybe the security guard needed to speak to him and the intercom was broken, he wondered.

He slipped out of bed, put on his paisley silk dressing gown, which he had bought at Harrods, and walked over to the bedroom window. The view was as always, stunning. It was a view he could never tire of, the little fishing port where he had been born and lived as a child, the tiny white houses. He could see the one where he had lived. The sun was a red ball on the horizon, and the sky was cloudless; it was going to be a beautiful day. There was the steady staccato diesel phut-silence-phut-silence-phut-silence of a deep-sea trawler coming back in after its night's work; several other smaller boats were also heading in towards the stone mole of the port. There was the smell of sweet wet dew in the air.

Culundis padded downstairs in his bare feet as the bell rang a third time. 'All right, all right,' he said. 'I'm coming!' He opened the door, just a fraction, and peered round. He saw a short man in a thin, dark raincoat; the man smiled pleasantly. 'Good morning, Mr Culundis,' said the stranger, politely.

'Er – good morning,' said Culundis baffled.

The stranger forced the door wide open; for a second, Culundis could not quite understand the man's behaviour, and then he saw for the first time, that the stranger held in his hand a Walther automatic pistol with a silencer fitted to the end. For the first time in his life he felt real fear, an icy chill wind that swept through his veins, pumped into his stomach, down through his bile duct and into his rectum. He shat onto his feet. It probably would not have cheered him to know that this actual gun, silencer, and the bullets inside it had all been supplied by him, as part of a large order, to General Isser Ephraim's team of Mossad agents.

The man fired four bullets into Culundis's chest, two of which completely removed his heart. As with all products supplied by Jimmy Culundis, the silencer worked perfectly.

The man from the Mossad closed the front door, walked back to the gate, past the security guard with the broken neck, and drove off into the night. Culundis's family continued to sleep for three more hours.

CHAPTER 30

A t 5.15 on Tuesday evening, Rocq drove the Porsche down the ramp of the multi-storey car park behind Lower Thames Street, nodded to the attendant, and stopped, waiting for a gap in the traffic to pull out into the street. Even if he were looking closely, he would have been unlikely to have noticed the figure in the shadows on the second floor of the concrete buildings who watched the appearance of the car with interest, stop-watch in his hand.

The gap came, Rocq gave a light tap on the Porsche's accelerator, and the car surged out into the traffic stream. Rocq was feeling extremely vulnerable; he had barely slept the last three nights, and Amanda told him she thought that he was cracking up. He wanted desperately to tell her what had happened in Switzerland, but he didn't want to frighten her.

He had thought about the incident a million times, and each time he was no nearer a firm opinion. When gold had gone through the $700 mark, Elleck had called him up. He had watched Elleck's face closely, and thought that Elleck

345

..ed strained, under pressure – but there was nothing Elleck did or said that gave him any possible cause to think Elleck might have been involved in an attempt to murder him.

Maybe, he wondered, the Range Rover driver had just been a nutter? Maybe he had accidentally carved him up somewhere around Geneva Airport and the guy had a screw loose and had come after him. He had heard of incidents like that occurring. But it had lasted for several hours – surely the driver's companion would have calmed him down. It was a possibility and he felt a little comforted by the thought, but not much.

For two days, he had racked his brains backwards and forwards to think of any enemies he might have made. He knew there were people jealous of him, people in the office, but none he believed could be so jealous as to try to kill him. No, he knew each time, it came back to Elleck's syndicate. It had to be them; and if they had tried once, he had little reason to doubt that they would try again. He thought about going to the police, but he dismissed that idea; he decided they would think he was nuts and, in any event, the British police would hardly be interested in something that happened in Switzerland.

He looked constantly in his mirrors, noting any car that appeared to be staying close behind him. He was paranoid, he realized; but he equally well realized he would have to be a fool not to be. He decided not to stay in his own flat tonight, but to

346

stay at Amanda's. He couldn't relax in his own flat, and he knew he was going to end up as a basket case if he had to endure another night without sleep, listening to, and thinking about, every single noise.

It had altogether been one hell of a day, he reflected: gold had continued to rise all through the morning, hitting $700 just before noon. Elleck had called him up to his office and told him he was still convinced it must start dropping, and to hold on until two o'clock in the afternoon. At two o'clock, gold was at $712 and Elleck was a very agitated man. Between two and five o'clock, on Elleck's instructions, through Johnson Matthey of London, Mocatta, Rothschild, and a number of commission houses throughout Europe, Globalex, Goldilocks Ltd and four other companies that Rocq had established on behalf of the syndicate bought 2,500,000 ounces of gold. The world gold market was not aware of the single buying entity and, by the close of the London market, the price of gold had dropped off to $707.

Elleck had buzzed him every half hour throughout the afternoon to ask him how he was getting on, and the only thing that gave Rocq any satisfaction at all was listening to the squirming nervousness of his chairman's voice. He remembered a couple of weeks ago how he had ventured an opinion to Elleck about the price of gold, and had been shot down in flames. If Elleck wanted to hang himself on gold right now, Rocq was more than prepared to give him all the rope he asked for. The thought cheered him up considerably: maybe, he thought, just maybe, no one was going to kill him after all.

Sir Monty Elleck had spent the most twitchy day of his life. The threatening words of Viscomte Lasserre had hung over him like a funeral shroud. It had never occurred to him that by mixing with those in the killing business he could ever be in a position where he could become a victim himself, and he didn't like the feeling. He was annoyed with himself, too, for he had missed out on the chance to make a personal fortune on the rise in gold over the past few days. He had deliberately held back on buying for the syndicate because he had wanted to buy a few million pounds' worth for himself first, to cash in on the rise he knew the syndicate's buying and subsequent activities ought to have produced: but then, when gold had begun to rise on its own accord, on the strength of a whole mixed bag of rumours, he had held back, waiting for a drop. No drop had come, not until 4.15 that Tuesday afternoon; not until the full £1000 million committed by the syndicate had been spent.

Elleck had decided not to put money in himself after all. The rise was too high, far too high, for his liking. Even though he felt it probably would go higher still on the news that was to come from Israel and from Umm Al Amnah in the morning, he had been at the game long enough to know when to keep his chips off the table. He was going to make a handsome enough profit out of commissions from just handling the deal: he didn't need to take any risks himself. He smiled. Let Lasserre and Culundis be on the hook; they could afford it.

When Rocq had buzzed him to tell him the final amount of the thousand million had been spent, at 4.45, Elleck buzzed his secretary and asked her to get him Viscomte Lasserre.

Two minutes later she buzzed him back. 'I can't get through, Sir Monty,' she said. 'All the lines are engaged.'

'Keep trying, will you, Jane?'

'Yes, Sir Monty.'

The anger he had felt at the time the Viscomte had passed the thinly veiled threat to him welled up in him again, only much stronger now. He thought of the elegant but weak French aristocrat, and the greasy fat Greek pervert, and he was amused that his delaying had lost them so much money. He wasn't going to be threatened by anyone. He was the king sitting on his throne at 88 Mincing Lane. When it came to money, God help anyone who tried to get one over him; when battles involved money, he won every time. He knew how to fight with money the way field marshals know how to fight with soldiers. His company client list didn't read like an elongated version of *Who's Who* for nothing: he was the best in the Commodity Market, not only in this country, but anywhere in the world. He wasn't scared of anyone – he would take on all the best fighters in the world – as long as they fought with money.

His chain of thought was interrupted by his secretary bringing him in the evening paper, the *New Standard*, as she always did at five o'clock. He glanced at the headlines: 'BLOODY END FOR THE MERCHANT OF DEATH.' The photograph beneath it struck him like a fist between his legs: it was the contorted face of Jimmy Culundis.

> Constantinou 'Jimmy' Culundis, billionaire international arms dealer, was found shot dead in his Athens home early this morning. A personal security guard was also found dead nearby. An Athens police detective said Culundis had many underworld connections as well as many international political connections; it was known that he supplied armaments to a wide variety of organizations ranging from right-wing governments to left-wing terrorist organizations.

The journalist who wrote the ten-column article concluded with the words:

> It is inevitable for a man who profits by violence, in the way Culundis has throughout his career, that one day, one of his dealings must come home to roost: For Jimmy

Culundis, under a blazing dawn sky on a perfect Greek morning, that day was today. Culundis leaves a wife and three children.

Elleck sat back in his chair, and began to think hard. A moment later, his intercom buzzed. It was his secretary, and she sounded strange.

'Sir Monty – I have Viscomte Lasserre's personal secretary on the line now – would you like to speak to her?'

'Er – isn't he there?'

'I think you'd better speak to her.'

'Put her on.'

There was a click, and then a voice in broken English: 'Allo? Sir Montay Hellix?'

'Yes, speaking.'

'I 'ave to tell you bad news. The Viscomte Lasserre was killed in an aeroplane accident last night.'

'Viscomte Lasserre?'

'I am afraid so – yes, sir – he—' she broke down and began sobbing. After a few moments she stopped. 'I can't talk more now. I am sorry; I am so sorry.' The line went dead.

Elleck stared blankly into the receiver for a few moments, then replaced it. He began to pick his fingernails, violently. He felt numb. For ten minutes he sat, staring blankly across his office, trying to focus his mind on what had happened.

The £1,000 million of gold that Rocq had bought on the syndicate's behalf today – Globalex had guaranteed the payment of the entire amount.

His arrangement with Lasserre and Culundis was that they would transfer the funds to his bank each day, as the gold was bought. As he hadn't bought until today, he had not required the funds. The purpose of his telephone call to Lasserre had been to ask Lasserre for immediate payment of the £100 million of margin. There was nothing in writing, nothing at all; he had never had anything in writing with Lasserre – everything was always done verbally. Globalex was now on the hook for £1,000 million worth of gold, which it had bought at the top of the market. With the drop of $5 an ounce at the close of play it meant, on the 840,000 ounces they had bought today, they were down over £2 million already.

His brain raced; he had a chill fear run through him as he wondered if the two deaths were connected. The coincidence was too great, he decided, for them not to be. Was it the syndicate someone was wiping out, or were they killed because of some other business dealing? He thought with an even deeper chill about the break-in, the murder of Sarge, and suddenly he did not want to be alone in the building; he pressed the intercom. 'Jane – would you mind staying on for a bit longer? I – er – I may have a few urgent letters to give you.'

'Well – I can stay another half hour, Sir Monty – we have to go to a dinner tonight, and the 6.10 is really the latest train I can catch.'

'Okay, fine. Can you get Rocq, please. I need him up here immediately.' With Lasserre and

Culundis dead, he had no idea whether the plan would still go ahead or not. Perhaps they had set it into irreversible motion? Perhaps their deaths were intended to stop it?

He couldn't risk it: £1,000 million of gold was a lot of money to be on the hook for, a damned lot, by anyone's standards.

Elleck did some calculations in his head: he had cash reserves on short-term deposits of £40 million, specifically for covering particularly good clients whom the company did not want to bother with small margin calls. He had another fifty million on one-year term deposits, and a further forty million in stocks, shares and commodities. The Globalex building was worth about three million. At a pinch, he could rustle up £140 million. If gold dropped twenty per cent, he would have to fork out £200 million; he didn't have £200 million. His legs began to tremble. It was impossible he thought, impossible; he could never have allowed such a thing to happen. But he had allowed it. He had actually allowed himself to get into a position whereby he could go to the wall.

The intercom buzzed and he pushed the button: 'Yes?'

'I'm afraid Mr Rocq left about twenty-five minutes ago, Sir Monty.'

'Damn. Try his home.'

'I just did, Sir Monty – no answer.'

'Keep trying it every five minutes. Do you have any idea where he might have been going?'

'No, Sir Monty, and there's no one to ask in his office – they have all left for the day.'

'Okay – well, keep trying his home.' He let go of the switch. He wanted to sell the entire thousand million pounds-worth of gold now. Take the two million loss, that was okay. He could not take the risk of the plan not coming off and, with the two principals dead, it seemed to him pretty unlikely that the plan could come off. He had to get hold of Rocq, because he had no idea where Rocq had done the buying. He had bought in bits and pieces all over the world, including the Swiss company and numbered accounts. 'What a mess,' he said to himself. 'What a bloody mess.'

CHAPTER 31

It had been a long time since Baenhaker could remember a bollocking as severe as the one he had received from General Ephraim on the Monday afternoon, when Ephraim had telephoned him at Eisenbar-Goldschmidt. It was Wednesday morning, and he was still smarting under the General's torrent of abuse.

Switzerland had never been particularly helpful towards the Mossad at the best of times: Israel had been doing its best for some years to woo the Swiss, and their efforts had been beginning to pay off. 'What the hell do you think you're up to, trying to get your killing done for you, and in Switzerland of all places?' Ephraim had shouted.

Baenhaker knew what he'd done, and he tried to explain it to Ephraim: that he hadn't wanted to bring the full weight of Scotland Yard crashing down upon them by having killed three people from the same company within a week. Ephraim's anger was all the more fuelled by the fact that he had given his instructions on Friday, expressed the urgency of the situation, and it was now Monday. Apart from losing two of his top Swiss agents and

355

_aving the wrath of the Swiss government brought down upon his head, nothing had been achieved. The threat to relieve Baenhaker from the assignment and instruct another agent to do the job had hit Baenhaker hardest of anything.

'It's Monday afternoon, General,' Baenhaker had said. 'By Wednesday night, they will both be dead, I promise you.'

'They had better be,' replied Ephraim.

Baenhaker had not had an altogether happy weekend. He had planned to kill Elleck while Rocq was in Switzerland, only to discover that Elleck had gone sailing with friends and would not be back until Monday morning – and he had no idea where Elleck had gone sailing.

He had spent Sunday evening surveilling Elleck's London home in Bishop's Avenue, Hampstead, but Elleck had in fact remained on the boat Sunday night, and had driven straight to the office on Monday morning. It was now Wednesday morning; he hadn't yet killed Elleck because he wanted to plan the killing of Rocq and leave as short as possible a time gap between the two killings. This evening, at about five o'clock, Rocq would be killed. Elleck was going to a City Livery dinner at Cutlers' Hall; his chauffeur would be driving him home afterwards. Baenhaker knew the exact spot in the rhododendron bush opposite Elleck's front door where he would be waiting, with the silenced Walther in his hand.

At exactly five to nine, he watched from the

street corner where he was standing as Rocq's metallic dark-grey Porsche turned into the entrance to the Lower Thames Street multi-storey car park. He smiled to himself. A few minutes later he saw Rocq emerge, holding his neat briefcase in one hand, and with a mackintosh slung over his other arm. Baenhaker looked up at the sky; there were quite a few clouds. Maybe Rocq was right, he thought, maybe it would rain today.

He waited a full ten minutes, just to make sure Rocq had not left anything behind in the car, and then he slipped up the fire escape staircase of the concrete building. The Porsche was in the same bay as the previous evening, and he was pleased to notice all the other bays around it were also taken, which meant it was unlikely he would be interrupted with his work.

He slid, with his large briefcase, down between the Porsche and the car next to it, a blue Ford Cortina. He opened the briefcase, and pulled out a slim metal cylinder with a fixing plate at either end, a small drill, a screwdriver and two screws; then he eased himself under the bottom of the Porsche, directly below the driver's seat.

Half an hour later, the explosive charge was firmly in position, Baenhaker slid further back underneath the car and then proceeded to wire the time-fuse into the car's electrical circuit, so that when the ignition was switched on, the countdown on the fuse would start. Eisenbar-Goldschmidt used this same car park for many of their vehicles;

357

he would not have been popular if the Porsche had blown up in here and damaged any of their cars. Yesterday, it had taken Rocq forty-five seconds from the time of starting his engine to the time he left the car-park entrance; he did not want Rocq to get too far away, because he wanted to be able to witness the explosion with his own eyes, make sure that Rocq was dead, so that he could report positively himself to Ephraim. There had been no other cars leaving at the same time yesterday. He decided he should make a contingency allowance for a delay in case there were some today. He set the dial to two minutes, ran a final check over the fixings and the wirings, and then eased himself out from under the car. It was 9.45 a.m. He didn't want to take his eyes off the car today – just in case the extraordinary should happen and someone should steal it, or in case Rocq left early. He did not want to miss the fireworks for anything. He found himself a safe position on the stairwell, from where he could clearly see the Porsche and could hear anyone coming either up or down, and then settled down to pass the day in his lonely, dreary watch-post.

Elleck, who had not slept a wink, had left a message summoning Rocq, who had also not slept a wink, up to his office the moment he arrived.

'Where the hell were you last night?' said Elleck, half shouting. 'I tried to get you all through the night! Don't you ever go to bed?'

'I didn't know it was a Globalex rule that I have to sleep in my own bed.'

'You were with a girl?'

'Might have been; might have been with a boy.' Rocq felt belligerent. It was none of Elleck's damned business, he felt.

'In future, if you're sleeping around, you bloody well leave me the number you're going to be at. This company operates around the clock; if you want to work for it, you have got to be on call round the clock also. Understand?'

Rocq didn't answer; he didn't agree, and he was too tired for a fight; he stared at Elleck in silence for some moments, and then spoke. 'That arms dealer who was shot yesterday – Culundis – is that the Culundis of your syndicate?'

'Yes – and not just him: Viscomte Lasserre, the other partner in it has been killed in a bloody aircrash – yesterday – no – the night before. Both of them dead – and not one damned piece of paper signed. We're on the hook – that is, Globalex is on the hook for £1,000 million. Did you see what happened to gold during the night?' Elleck was shrieking, almost hysterical.

'I saw this morning. It's dropped $30.'

'That is a £25 million loss to this company,' said Elleck. 'Twenty-five million!'

'Do you want me to unload everything?'

'I wanted you to last night – when it had only dropped $5 – we could have got out with a two million loss – that would have been tolerable. But

359

25 million – I don't know about that. Has that $30 come off as a reaction to the sharp rise – or is there some heavy selling going on? That's what I have to find out. I don't know if this coup is going to go ahead or not – if the coup goes ahead, then gold's going to go back up, for sure. But if it doesn't come off, gold is going to go down – it's way higher than it should be right now. I'm going to make some telephone calls – you better go back to your office – and be ready to unload any moment I tell you – don't leave the office without telling me.'

'I presume, Sir Monty – that the same commission arrangement stands?'

'What?' said Elleck, looking apoplectic. 'That commission rate I agreed on was based on our making a massive profit out of this deal – that has changed now – we're trying to save our necks – how do you have the nerve to come in here and talk about commissions?'

'It's not my neck that's on the hook on this gold, Sir Monty, it's Globalex – which means yours. My neck is on the hook on this coffee – I've got the best part of a million pounds to find: 480,000 for you, and 512,000 for Barbiero-Ruche.'

'So – you should have paid us last Monday. But we haven't pressed you for the money.'

'I know; but we did make a deal.'

'You want your commission, or you want to see Globalex go down the toilet?'

'I want my commission and I don't want Globalex to go down the toilet.'

'Well I'm afraid, Alex, the situation has changed; you are not getting any damned commission.'

'In that case, Sir Monty, you'd better book a course of guitar lessons while you've still got the cash.'

'Guitar lessons? Are you cracking up?'

'No, Sir Monty; if gold drops any further, either you pay me the commission in full, today, for the buying and the selling, or else you are going to have to take up busking. I'm not selling one bar for you until that commission is in my bank; and if gold keeps dropping at the rate it is, by the time you manage to find out the thirty-seven different companies, banks and brokers where I've bought all that gold from, you're going to discover it's far too damned late.'

'Get out of my office,' bellowed Elleck.

Rocq got out, and went back downstairs. He was seething with fury, but he knew he had no option in what he had said. If Globalex did go bust and he was shown as owing the company money, the creditors would come after him for every penny. He had lost everything once before, when the stockbroking firm he worked for had gone to the wall. He wasn't going to lose everything again: this time he was looking after Number One first.

By midday, gold had dropped to $635; over $70 had been wiped off its price since yesterday evening; there was an international panic on to get out of the stuff. By half past twelve, a further $30 had been wiped off the value. Rocq's intercom buzzed: it was Elleck. 'The £992,000 has just been transferred into your bank account; you can call the bank yourself and check. Now please unload our position,' he said, meekly as a lamb.

'Thank you,' said Rocq. He rang his bank. The money was there. He smiled to himself, a smile of relief. Then he stopped smiling: he didn't have much to smile about yet. Not unless he thought it would be amusing to be the richest man in the graveyard.

Twenty minutes later, Rocq buzzed Elleck: 'No one wants to buy gold right now, Sir Monty; the best price I can get anywhere on a five-bar lot is—' he paused, 'five hundred and ninety-four dollars.'

There was a long silence. 'That would cost more money than I have,' said Elleck curtly. 'Don't do anything; we'll have to wait for an upturn.'

It was strange, Rocq reflected, but he almost felt sorry for the bastard.

At half-past four, gold had dipped to $578; $129 had been wiped off its value. It was the largest single drop in the price in one day in the history of the metal. The atmosphere in Globalex was funereal. The brokers around Alex were frantically trying to bail their clients out of the gold they had so eagerly urged them into during the boom of the previous days. Rocq was the only one in the room who appeared to be unflustered in his actions.

At a quarter past five, the receptionist rang Rocq

to say that Amanda was outside, waiting for him. He cursed. He had forgotten they were driving to a dinner party near Sevenoaks tonight. He buzzed on the intercom up to Elleck's office. Elleck's secretary answered; 'He's left for the day, Mr Rocq; he wasn't feeling too well.'

'Oh, I'm sorry,' said Rocq.

He shut his briefcase, picked up his mackintosh, and went out to greet Amanda.

It had rained heavily during the day, and now the late afternoon sun was drying the streets, sending little wisps of steam up. Suddenly, Baenhaker saw Rocq appear; in the same instant, he saw to his horror that Amanda was with him. The two of them stopped at the pavement, then crossed the road and disappeared out of his sight into the ground floor of the car park; Baenhaker heard their footsteps as they began climbing the stairs.

For a moment, he froze, then retreated further up the staircase, in case they missed the floor, which was all too easy, judging by the twenty or so people who had done so during the day. He heard them stop at the second floor; Rocq said something, and Amanda laughed. Baenhaker was seized with more emotions than he knew how to cope with; it had never occurred to him that Amanda might be accompanying Rocq.

'Let me drive,' he heard her say.

'Okay – I'll get it out the parking lot for you.'

'Alex Rocq, I am quite capable of reversing a motor car,' she said indignantly.

'Okay, okay – I'll see you out.'

'Okay – thanks.'

Baenhaker heard the sound of the door open, then shut, then the engine turned over by the starter motor; the fuse would now have been triggered off and in less than two minutes, the car would explode. He heard her second attempt at starting, still to no avail.

'Pump the accelerator, twice!' he heard Rocq's voice, shouting through the window.

Then he heard the engine fire, and the sound of a gear being engaged.

Baenhaker was shaking and sweating; his head was swimming; he couldn't, not her. Something! He had to do something! Frantically, he pulled the Walther out from inside his jacket, sprinted down the steps; Amanda was in the middle of backing out, and Rocq was anxiously signalling with his hands.

'Right hand down,' he coughed, as the exhaust smoke enveloped him. Out of the corner of his eye he saw a man sprinting full pelt at him, gun outstretched. He flung himself onto the floor. Baenhaker ignored Rocq, grabbed open the driver's door. 'Get out, get out!' he screamed, hysterically.

'Danny!' she screamed in fear, staring frozen at the gun.

Baenhaker grabbed her under the arm, yanked her out of the car and flung her onto the floor; Rocq started to get up.

'Stay down Alex, he's got a gun!' she screamed.

Baenhaker flung himself into the driving seat of the car, crashed the gear into first, and flattened the accelerator. He did not know where he was going, he just knew he had to get the car away from Amanda. He had never driven a Porsche before, let alone a turbo-powered one, and the acceleration took him by surprise. The tail snaked viciously across the concrete floor and he swiped the front of two parked cars, then smashed into the side wall of the exit ramp; he pulled desperately at the steering wheel, but the turbo had now cut fully in, the rear wheels gripped, and the car began to ride up the side of the wall; it crashed down onto its side, rolled onto its roof, and slid crazily down the ramp onto the next floor, slamming into a parked Rolls Royce. Baenhaker tried frantically to orient himself and disentangle himself. He scrambled for the door handle, couldn't find it, scrabbled more desperately, found a handle, wrenched at it, and heard a smooth whirring sound as the electric motor adjusted the door mirror. Cursing wildly, he moved his hand first up, then downwards, then he found it and pulled; nothing happened. He shoved against the door, desperately; it wouldn't move; he gave another shove.

Rocq scrambled to his feet. 'Stay down,' he shouted at Amanda. He ran after the Porsche then froze in his tracks as he saw it turn on its side and slide down the ramp; it crashed into the Rolls and then rocked to and fro. The figure inside was scrabbling desperately to get out. Suddenly the Porsche leapt several feet into the air; as it fell back down, a sheet of white flame engulfed it. The driver's door tore off and smashed into the side of a car parked to the left; then the whole Porsche turned into a ball of flame. Rocq heard screams of terror from Amanda; he knelt over the edge of the parapet, and threw up into Lower Thames Street.

CHAPTER 32

E phraim felt relaxed; it was the first time in many days that he had done so. Lasserre was dead and Culundis was dead. He hadn't yet had the report from Baenhaker about the two in England, but he was no longer concerned about them. He unlocked the bottom drawer of his desk and took out a white envelope, and removed the sheet of paper containing his instructions from his blackmailers. He had already sent a coded message to Joseph Brilej, commander of the 100 sailors he had despatched to Umm Al Amnah, ordering their immediate return. He took out the message he was supposed to have telexed to the leaders of the world's nations this morning and lit it with the cigarette lighter on his desk. He then carefully mushed to pieces the charred remains. At that moment, the yellow telephone on his desk rang.

The yellow phone linked him directly to certain key members of the Knesset, together with key members of the armed forces. Very few people called him on this phone, as it was kept clear only for use in crises.

'Ephraim,' he said.

'Good morning, General,' said the unusually grim voice of Commander Yitzak Mehne, Chief of Naval Security.

'Morning, Yitzi,' said Ephraim, bullishly. 'How are you keeping?'

'Could be better,' he replied, tersely.

'What's your problem?'

'I don't know that I have a problem – yet – but there's something I think you ought to know about just happened in the Persian Gulf – Strait of Hormuz.'

Ephraim's good cheer drained out of him, like air from a burst tyre. 'Go on,' he said.

'An oil tanker – the Arctic Sundance, on its way up to pick up a cargo – four miles off Goat Island, just blew to smithereens. An incredible explosion – no one ever saw anything like it.'

'Empty oil tankers often blow up, Yitzi – they get a build-up of gas – they don't pump it out enough, get an electrical short or something – and bang. I wouldn't worry about it.' Ephraim was sweating profusely; he could hardly hold the telephone, his hand was so wet.

'I agree with you about tankers, Isser, but apparently this explosion was just unbelievable.'

'I'm not with you.'

'No one ever saw an explosion like it.'

'How many of them ever saw a tanker blow up before?'

'None of them, I shouldn't think.'

368

'So what are they getting so excited about?'

'There's a bit of speculation it might have hit a mine, Isser – that's what they're getting excited about.'

'Ridiculous.'

'That dhow with the four Israeli sailors on it a few weeks ago – the four Israeli sailors and the eight nuclear mines? Remember? Now a tanker suddenly blows up. A lot of people are trying to put two and two together. What are those sailors you got in Amnah up to, Isser?'

'Nothing – they're on their way home – now come on, Yitzi, you don't think they've been out laying mines?'

'Look you old devil, knowing the way you operate, nothing would surprise me – okay?'

'Well I can assure you that whatever blew that tanker up is not my doing. Okay?'

'Sure okay – just thought you'd better know about it. Talk to you soon.'

'Sure. 'Bye.' Ephraim replaced the receiver; he was drenched in sweat. He telephoned Haifa; the sailors had not arrived back yet. No sooner had he hung up, than his green international secure telephone rang: it was Ellie Katz, chief of London operations, calling to inform him that Baenhaker was currently being scraped off the walls of the Lower Thames Street multi-storey car park. The loss of Baenhaker did not please him at all. He thought hard about Elleck, whom he knew, and the man Rocq, whom he didn't;

there was still a fury deep inside him over Elleck, but professionally, he knew his death would be too late now, as would Rocq's. He could still order Elleck's death, but now it would be personal, not in the cause of business. One day, he vowed, he would get even with Elleck, face to face: that was how he would like it, but now was not the time. He thanked Katz, weakly, for the call, and hung up. He had a distinct feeling this was not going to be his morning.

Half an hour later, the feeling was proved right. The yellow telephone rang again; it was the Prime Minister and he wanted to see him – in Jerusalem – immediately.

When Isser Ephraim left the Prime Minister's office, the security guard on the front door of the Knesset building was remarkably well informed. 'Good morning, Mr Ephraim,' he said. For the first time in all the years he could remember, Ephraim left the Knesset building unsaluted. It was also the first time that there had not been a chauffeur-driven car waiting for him. There was, in fact, no car waiting at all: the car and driver that had been at his disposal for the past fifteen years, that had become as natural a mode of transport to him as putting on his shoes in the morning, had quietly and discreetly vanished.

Humiliated, he turned right and walked along the road, in search of a taxi to take him the twenty miles back to Tel Aviv. The Prime Minister had, in the last hour, stripped him of his rank and his job, effective immediately. His passport was cancelled, and he was to face an in-camera court martial for, in the words of the Prime Minister, 'Performing traitorous acts calculated to bring the state of Israel into international disrepute.'

Ephraim reflected on the last hour and a half, which was the most unpleasant hour and a half he had ever spent in his life, concentration camps included. The United States Armed Forces in Oman had detected a concentrated mass of radioactive fallout, compatible with the fallout resulting from the exploding of a nuclear weapon, spreading downwind from where the Arctic Sundance had exploded. Their only possible conclusions were that either the Arctic Sundance was carrying in its cargo a nuclear explosive, which was detonated when the oil tank exploded, or that the ship was blown up by a nuclear device either placed in it or in the water, such as a mine.

The mine theory was lent not a little weight when an American frigate went to the rescue of a coaster which had run out of fuel, to discover it was carrying 100 sailors from the Israeli Navy, with its decks and cargo hold piled high with nuclear mines.

There was, as Ephraim had said to the Prime Minister, and thought, puzzled, to himself now, no immediate answer he could give to that.

CHAPTER 33

There were two men who knew the answer to the riddle the ex-head of the Mossad could not solve, and both of them were happy men. One of them was Sheik Abr Qu'Ih Missh; the other was Alex Rocq. Three and a half thousand miles apart, they replaced their telephone receivers and calculated their respective gains.

Sheik Missh stared out of his sixty-sixth floor window in the Palace of Tunquit and smiled again: during the past week he had bought a fraction less than $2 billion worth of gold, all on margin, and all of it below $550 an ounce. Indeed, some of it he had bought below $500 an ounce. Fuelled by this buying, which had been spread into small parcels throughout the world by Theo Barbiero-Ruche and masterminded by Rocq, and fuelled equally by the rumours the influential Barbiero-Ruche had spread that there was to be a major Israeli-Arab conflict, Missh had used his nation's entire reserves to buy in at the very bottom of one of the greatest rises in gold the world had ever seen. At $710, on Rocq's advice, he had started to sell, using a different broker Rocq had arranged for him in Dubai. He had made a profit on the deal, he estimated, of some $6 billion, quite satisfactory enough for one week's work, he decided.

But there was more than just the money, something which to him was far more important: he had managed to avoid what could have been a devastating blow to the international standing of his country. If Jimmy Culundis had had his way, the Persian Gulf would have been knee-deep in fishing dhows, all clearly registered in Umm Al Amnah and all carrying crews of Israeli sailors and cargoes of nuclear mines. Amnah would have been inextricably entwined and implicated in the conflict that would ensue between Israel and the rest of the world. It would have destroyed, for years, any chance of friendship with almost any country in the world, and friendships with other nations were something his tiny nation needed badly. Rocq's warning had enabled him to sabotage Culundis's plans extremely effectively: he had flung Culundis's entire army out, arrested the entire force of 100 Israeli sailors, and set them adrift into the Gulf with a cargo of the mines and no identification other than their Israeli passports. Someone, somewhere, was going to be taught one hell of a lesson. He smiled.

Rocq sat at his desk, finding it hard to contain his excitement, harder still to keep his activities out of range of the telephoto ears of Mozer, Slivitz, and the rest of his office.

On a split commission with Theo Barbiero-Ruche, he calculated he had earned £380,000; he was out of the hole and into big money. The Toronto light on his switchboard lit up; Rocq picked up his phone, and pushed the button: the voice of the bouncing Baron Mellic boomed down the receiver.

'Hey, Rocky – what did you do wrong?'

'What do you mean?' Rocq became worried.

'You got something right for a change.'

'And what a fucking waste to go and give it to you.' A wave of relief swept Rocq. 'You did it properly?'

'You ever know me not to do anything properly?'

'Only when you have a puncture.'

On Rocq's advice, Missh had gone along with every penny he had, when gold was at its lowest. Knowing that when Missh sold, coupled with the no-show of the Lasserre-Culundis plot, the price of gold would cascade downwards, Rocq had advised the Baron to go short, with every penny he had, at the exact moment Missh issued his sell instructions. The Baron had gone short when gold was at $712 an ounce. The price was now $558. The Baron was not quite in the money league of the Emir of Amnah, but he had still netted some $120 million on the deal. Rocq's half share of the commission, which he had split with a tame broker in Zurich, came to £500,000 – tax free, paid into the numbered Swiss account Monsieur Jean-Luis Vençeon, the Swiss *avocat* in Verbier, had kindly opened for him.

'Up yours, Rocky – I'm off to go and spend some of my loot.'

'Does that mean I ought to go long on rubber?'

'Yeah – and you'd better hurry.' The Baron hung up.

'You talking to your bicycle repair man?' said Slivitz.

'If you want to stick your ears over here, for God's sake clean them first, Slivitz – I've got wax all over my desk.' Rocq dialled Amanda's office. 'Hallo, sweetheart,' he said. 'I'm going to give you a special treat tonight: I'll buy you dinner in any restaurant you like anywhere in the world. Pardon? What do you mean you had a big lunch? Yes, I'm sorry about Baenhaker too – you know I am: I thought it might cheer you up. Of course it would. Okay – right, leave it to me – what do you feel like most, Italian or French? Okay!' Rocq hung up, then dialled International Directory Enquiries. 'Hallo,' he said, 'I'd like the number of a restaurant in Paris – it's called the Tour d'Agent.' Thirty seconds later, he had the number. He thanked the operator and hung up. He pressed the button on the Reuter monitor: gold was at 553; Elleck still had not given him any sell order, which meant he was now in the hole for a cab fare's change from a £500 million note.

'That's life, Monty,' he said, to himself, smugly; you're five hundred million down. I'm five hundred thousand up. Never forget, Monty, the old legend: "Be careful how you treat people when you're on the way up – you never know who you're going to need when you're on the way down."'

'Talking to yourself?' interrupted Slivitz.

'It's the only way to get any straight answers in this business, Slivitz.'

'That's about the only intelligent thing you ever said, Rocq.'

'Tell you what, Slivitz, you know what I'm going to do today?'

'No Rocq, what are you going to do today?'

'I'm going to take you out and buy you one slap-up lunch.'

'I don't know what's come over you Rocq! Two intelligent statements in one day.'

'Keep pushing your luck, Slivitz, I've got a third on the way.'

By half past three, two extremely drunk metal brokers staggered out of the elevator at the fourth floor of 88, Mincing Lane. One was still ecstatic with joy; the other, inside his shell of alcohol, was trembling with fear from what he had learned over lunch.

Slivitz had a wife, three children and a large mortgage; it wasn't cheerful news to discover that the firm into which he had put eleven years of his life, and ten per cent of his annual salary for a pension, was days away from going belly-up to the tune of half a billion pounds.

Rocq left the office early that day; by the time he returned, at eleven o'clock next morning, having been delayed on the shuttle from Paris, there wasn't anyone in Globalex who didn't know the news. As Globalex telephone operators spent most of their time chatting to different telephone exchanges around the world, by close of play on Friday, anyone who was anyone in commodities, throughout eight-tenths of the world, knew of Globalex's problems.

When Sir Monty Elleck received a phone call from Chicago to ask if it was true, followed by calls from Tokyo, Sydney, Zurich, Panama, Liechtenstein, Guernsey, Vienna, Berne, Rome and fourteen other of his international business chums, he knew it was time to have a chat with his local friendly bank manager. His only problem was that he was not quite sure what to say. He needn't have bothered trying to say anything; as far as his bank manager was concerned, Sir Monty Elleck had contracted a bad case of leprosy.

Rocq breezed into his office, tired and hung over after having eaten much too rich a meal. He had been sick three times in the marble-floored bathroom of his suite at the Crillon in Paris. Lester Barrow did not chirp out his usual 'Morning, early bird.' There was no snide remark from Mozer or Slivitz; the whole place had all the cheer of the foyer of a crematorium. Rocq's intercom buzzed: it was the switchboard.

'Mr Rocq – a Mr Barbiero-Ruche has called you four times this morning.'

'Thank you – I'll call him now.'

'Oh, wait a second – yes – he's calling again now. Shall I put him through?'

'Thank you.'

The Italian's voice came on the line. He did not sound his normal ebullient self either. 'Okay, Rocky – very clever, hey where's this goddam Middle East War then?'

'What war, fat man?'

'Yeah – that's right – what war?'

'You can't win them all, fat man. It didn't happen.'

'How you mean, it didn't happen? You know how much money I put on that war happening?'

'Nope.'

'A lot, Rocky, one hell of a lot.'

'So – how much commission did I make you on buying for Missh?'

'Half a million bucks. You know how much you lost me on that war?'

'No idea, fat man.'

'Millions, that's how much, millions.' The Italian, thought Rocq, sounded sore. Really sore.

'Let's just call ourselves quits, fat man, hey? You tucked me up good and proper on that coffee – I just got a little revenge on you on the gold, okay? Now we're even.'

'You crazy bastard – you nearly put me to the wall just to get even?'

'I don't like wrong advice, fat man. I don't know what the fuck you were up to, but boy, you got me in a mess.'

'Are you blind and deaf?'

'What do you mean?'

'Didn't you read any newspapers today?'

'No.'

'Don't you know what happened to coffee?'

'No, what happened to coffee?'

'The World Health Organization? You didn't hear? The whole business with the cancer – it was all a hoax. Three of the directors have been arrested – it was all a huge conspiracy to force down the price of coffee – they all went short for billions, then put out the rumour. It's going up again, Rocky, going through the roof. There's a bad coffee rust, early frost, just like I said; you put me to the wall on your goddam war, and now I'm making you millions on coffee.'

Rocq went white. 'Theo, you fat jerk; I closed out my long coffee. I went short with you, remember?'

'You what?'

'I went short with you! Remember? Paid your goddam invoice. Twelve thousand fucking tons. What the hell's the price now?'

'Four hundred and forty-eight pounds and rising fast; what you sell short at?'

'Four hundred and twenty-seven pounds.'

'Holy shit, Rocky.' There was a silence. Rocq could hear the sound of a calculator the other end. Rocq didn't need a calculator; he knew how much he was down – almost to a penny, exactly half of the half a million he had just made.

'Get me out of it, fat man. Get me long again, fast.'

'It's limit up, Rocky, and the sellers are running away. No chance of getting you out yet. Won't be for several days; it's going to go limit up each day for the next five days. I may be able to get you out at about 470 I reckon – somebody owes me a favour – and you'd better count yourself lucky if I do.'

Rocq did one more quick calculation: if the Italian could bail him out when it hit £540, he would have lost, to the penny, the entire profit he had made on the gold dealings.

'Oh, shit!' said Rocq, smashing his desk with his fist. 'Oh shit!'

'Is that a buy instruction?' said Theo.

'Yes it fucking is,' said Rocq, hanging up with a force that nearly broke the telephone. He sat at his desk and stared at his blinking switchboard; although Milan was a thousand miles away, he swore he could hear the Italian laughing. And yet, he smiled to himself, there had been times in his life when he might have been a whole lot more upset than he was now. He had to admit that on the whole, he had not come out of it too damned badly.

CHAPTER 34

It was Thursday, six days after Rocq's telephone conversation with Theo Barbiero-Ruche, and England was in the grip of a sweltering heat-wave. It was just after eight in the morning when the Chairman of Globalex arrived at the front entrance of 88, Mincing Lane.

As yet the morning was deliciously cool; although the sky was clear blue, the heat of the sun had not begun to penetrate; it was the kind of early morning that would make anyone feel good. The Chairman of Globalex felt very good, very good indeed.

He took the elevator up to the sixth floor, stepped out and walked to his office. The morning cleaning staff were already busy and he smiled at them. Although the air conditioning was already on, he opened a window and breathed in some of the air that, for a change in the City of London, was almost fresh and heady, or at least certainly felt so to him.

He took off his Louis Feraud jacket and slung it on the back of his imposing leather chair, and leaned forward onto his massive dark brown smoked-glass desk. He liked the new colours in the room, the pale mushroom walls and the white woodwork and the thick David Hicks geometric brown and beige carpet, and he stared admiringly around at the new furniture: at the two huge white velour chesterfields, at the smoked-glass coffee table, the Pioneer hi-fi system, and the JVC video-recorder.

A couple of Roy Lichtensteins hung on the wall, depicting Superman travelling through the air and, next to them, standing quietly, were a pair of Stubbs horses. He smiled, loosened his Ted Lapidus tie, and began to pore through the massive print-out of accounts, studying carefully the names of every client, the amounts they had invested, and exactly where every penny was invested.

He had a lot of work ahead of him and eight o'clock starts were, he knew, going to be a part of his life for some time to come. He did not mind. Right now, for the first time in his life, he was so idyllically happy that nothing could bother him.

At a quarter to nine, his secretary came in. 'Good morning,' she said.

'Good morning,' said the Chairman. 'Were there any messages after I left yesterday afternoon?'

'Yes: Sir Monty Elleck telephoned. He wondered if he could come and collect a couple of files – he wanted to come up last night, but I said he had better obtain your permission first.'

'Do you know what they are?'

'Personal matters – he told me he is leaving

England permanently and retiring to France – I believe he wants to tie up various loose odds and ends.'

'Tell him he can come any time,' said the Chairman, graciously.

'Yes, I will. Would you care for some coffee?'

'I think I'd like a glass of Perrier.'

'Right. Are there any tapes?'

'Yes – two.' The Chairman handed her them from the top of his Grundig dictaphone, and then turned back to his list of accounts.

At ten o'clock his secretary buzzed him. 'Sheik Abr Qu'Ih Missh is on the line, Sir.'

'Thank you,' said the Chairman. 'Put him through.'

A moment later, the Emir of Amnah was on the line.

The Chairman of Globalex treated the Emir with the greatest of respect. There was, the Chairman knew, as he twiddled with the Porsche key-ring in his jacket pocket, no other way to treat the owner of one's company.